COLUMBO

COLU

William

A TOM DOHERTY ASSOCIATES BOOK
NEW YORK
Based on the Universal Television Series COLUMBO
Created by Richard Levinson & William Link

MBO

THE GRASSY KNOLL

Harrington

FORGE

c.1

This is a work of fiction. All the characters and events portrayed in this book are fictitious, and any resemblance to real people or events is purely coincidental.

COLUMBO: THE GRASSY KNOLL

COLUMBO: THE GRASSY KNOLL
a novel by William Harrington
Based on the Universal Television Series COLUMBO
Created by Richard Levinson & William Link

This book is printed on acid-free paper.

A Forge Book
Published by Tom Doherty Associates, Inc.
175 Fifth Avenue
New York, N.Y. 10010

Design: *Diane Stevenson / SNAP • HAUS GRAPHICS*

Library of Congress Cataloging-in-Publication Data

Harrington, William G.
    Columbo : the grassy knoll / William Harrington.
    p.   cm.
    "A Tom Doherty Associates book."
    ISBN 0-312-85536-2
    1. Columbo, Lieutenant (Fictitious character)—Fiction.
    2. Kennedy, John F. (John Fitzgerald). 1917-1963—Assassination-Fiction.
    3. Police—United States—Fiction.   I. Title.
    PS3558.A632C65   1993
    813'.54—dc20   93-26555
                                                                         CIP

First Edition: November 1993

Printed in the United States of America

0   9   8   7   6   5   4   3   2   1

COLUMBO

ONE

In spite of every effort to clean up the air in Los
Angeles, Wednesday, June 2, was a smoggy day. No clouds
diminished the force of the fierce bright sunlight on the
smog layer. Down inside the smog, the white light was
oppressive; dispersed by the smog it came from all directions; there was no shade and no turning away from glaring
white light. Sepulchral voices on every television channel
warned of the health hazard and repeated endlessly what
Angelenos should do: stay inside as much as possible, avoid
exertion, leave cars at home, and so forth and so forth and
so forth. All day people were irritated and irritable. Only in
late afternoon did a wind off the Pacific rush in and
dissipate the layer. By four o'clock or a little after, the sun
became a point of fire in a blue sky, and Angelenos began to
breathe.

The irritation remained. People whose eyes,
noses, and throats have burned all day do not become
abruptly cheerful when the air clears. There was a
statistical increase in automobile accidents that day—
not because drivers could not see but because they were
aggravated and aggressive. The number of street
crimes increased also, as did the number of murders,

---

beyond what was statistically likely to occur on any day.

But the murder that would occur on Hollyridge Road that night was neither due to smog nor statistically predictable.

At 6:30 the producer, assistant producer, and director of *The Paul Drury Show* were sitting around a table in a conference room at television station KWLF Los Angeles, themselves struggling to overcome a persistent peevishness. They had turned down the volume on the monitor hanging from the wall at one end of the long room, but the smog and street crime and accidents dominated the station's evening news being fed live to the monitor.

"Kennedy, Kennedy, Kennedy . . ." sighed Alicia Graham Drury.

"Nobody asked me," said Tim Edmonds.

Tim Edmonds was the producer of *The Paul Drury Show*. Alicia Graham Drury was assistant producer. She had been assistant producer when she was Alicia Graham, continued during the two years of her marriage to Paul Drury, and remained assistant producer after the divorce. Tim Edmonds was the show's second producer and had been with it three years.

"I counted it up," said Marvin Goldschmidt, the newly hired director. "This is the forty-eighth show Paul has done on the Kennedy assassination. I went through the book and counted. The forty-goddamn-eighth!"

"Argue with Paul," said Edmonds. "Argue with the ratings."

"All right," said Goldschmidt, surrendering. "Who's Blake Emory?"

"He is an assassination researcher," said Alicia.

"What the hell is an assassination researcher?" asked Goldschmidt. This was his first month as director of *The Paul Drury Show,* and he had not yet picked up a full working knowledge of the vocabulary.

"An assassination researcher," said Tim, "can be anyone from a dogged detective who's never given up the idea that he can solve the mystery of the Kennedy assassination and has spent years working on it—to some asshole who's read three books about it."

"Which kind is Emory?"

"I don't know," said Tim. "You can bet Paul knows."

"He'll have Emory's name in the computer," said Alicia dryly.

"Paul's computer," said Tim, "is the world's largest collection of assassination minutiae."

"Of minutiae of every kind," said Goldschmidt. "I couldn't believe him last night, contradicting Tommy Lasorda on how many baseball players have ever hit .400—and then naming them."

"That's not exactly an accident, Marv," said Alicia. "It's part of Paul's technique to chase down a fact or statistic, then turn the conversation on the show toward an opportunity to use it."

"The form-u-la, the form-u-la," sang Tim. "We must *never* tinker with the form-u-la."

"I know *I* wouldn't dare," said Goldschmidt.

Marvin Goldschmidt was thirty-four years old. He had been hired by Paul Drury to replace a director who had been with the show eighteen months, because Drury had grown tired of the old director. "Got stale," he'd said. Goldschmidt had impressed him by his work on a Los

Angeles morning game show, and Drury had surprised everyone by calling in the director of a local game show to be director of a syndicated news-interview show.

Goldschmidt was a balding, diminutive young man, awed by Drury and deferential to him. He wore dark-framed spectacles. At first he had worn suits on the set. Then, seeing how everyone else dressed, he had begun to come to work in blue jeans and sweatshirts. Drury had given him a gray sweatshirt with bold black lettering—DIRECTOR—and usually he wore that, as he did today.

Alicia Graham Drury was a handsome woman, six feet tall or maybe a little more. Her dark brows arched over arresting brown eyes that were her most striking feature— she could fix them on another person's eyes with the cold concentration of a snake. Forty-three years old, she had been married twice, once to Paul Drury, and had never borne a child. She was known in the television industry as capable and dedicated: a weather girl at first, then a street corre- spondent, briefly a Los Angeles news anchor, finally an assistant producer. She had moved around, from one station to another, one show to another, as was routine in the industry. For six years she had worked at KABC, and so had network affiliation. She had come to *The Paul Drury Show* at its inception, and had been with it longer than anyone but the star himself.

Tim Edmonds was forty-five years old. His blond hair was slowly turning white. He had played football for UCLA in the sixties and still had the muscular, broad-shouldered body of a defensive back. He had not been drafted by a professional team, so had gone on to a graduate degree in television production. He inherited a small fortune shortly after he gained his master's degree and used it to establish Tim Edmonds Productions.

TEP, as it was called, had produced several successful shows, especially sports shows concentrating on sports like soccer, softball, volleyball, and billiards, which were not dominated by the networks. *The Paul Drury Show* was not a TEP show but a Wulf Network show. Tim was producer by virtue of a contract between TEP and Wulf.

"Who besides this Blake Emory?" asked Goldschmidt.

"There's a man who will defend the Warren Commission Report," said Alicia, "Professor John Trabue of the University of Texas. He takes the position that Oswald was the sole assassin and that's that. Then there's Jackson McGinnis, who claims he witnessed the assassination and saw a man on the Grassy Knoll shoot Kennedy."

"Any deviation from the formula?" asked the director.

"No," said Tim. "Paul will do the show. Paul *is* the show. See that the cameras catch *his* reactions. No matter what a guest is saying, it is not as important to the viewer as seeing Paul's eyebrows go up or the corners of his mouth turn down. Watch him for the signal."

Everyone who worked on the show knew the signal. When Paul Drury was offscreen and touched his left earlobe with his left index finger, the director was to cut to the camera focused on him, immediately. Seeing himself on the monitor, Drury would then lift his eyebrows, turn down the corners of his mouth, nod or shake his head skeptically, and so on.

He had another signal. When he touched his chin with his right index finger, the volume on a guest's microphone was to be turned down, because Drury was about to override him. The guest's microphone was never cut off, but his volume was turned so low that anything Drury wanted to say would be heard over him.

The same was true of the volume on incoming telephone calls.

The Paul Drury Show was meant to suggest a free exchange of ideas, but there was never an instant when Paul Drury was not in total control of what was said—even though the show was seen live in the East. He was a master at concealing his control. He appeared to allow others to talk and to respect their ideas. Actually, his entire attention was fixed on what *he* would say next and how he would interject it.

Goldschmidt looked up at the monitor. The evening news was over. The cameras in the newsroom remained live, and in the conference room the screen showed workmen dismantling the news set and bringing in the set for *The Paul Drury Show*.

They had an hour and a half before they went on the air, but Goldschmidt said, "Well, I suppose I better get out there and start kicking butt." He was a meticulous director and would find plenty to occupy him until airtime.

When the door closed and Alicia was alone with Tim, she shook her head. "Forty-eight. Forty-nine. Fifty. Sooner or later—"

"Not tonight," said Tim. "This isn't the night."

She got up and went to the window, looking out on La Cienega Boulevard. "Or maybe it is," she said. "Actually, this *is* the night."

"Yes . . ."

He stood and came up behind her. He was shorter than

she was, but he put his hands on her shoulders and turned her around to face him. She put her arms around him and welcomed his kiss.

The last hour and a half before airtime was Paul Drury's private time, spent in his locked office, where he would not take telephone calls. Most of his staff thought he took naps. Alicia knew better. Having been his wife, she knew he spent that time reviewing material from his files, phrasing and rephrasing questions and comments he would make on the air, and psyching himself up. He used the time to prepare himself for something that was by no means easy: being Paul Drury—that is, being the public persona of Paul Drury and making it look natural and easy.

This evening he inserted a videotape into his VCR. He turned off the sound. He didn't want to hear the narration. He knew what he would see on the screen. He had seen it hundreds of times. It never failed to move him. What it showed in all-too-vivid color was something that could not have happened, that was impossible—yet, had happened. He watched his own taped copy of the Abraham Zapruder film taken in Dallas on November 22, 1963.

The film was on his tape twice: once at its normal speed, which ran in about twenty seconds, then one frame at a time, each frame on the screen for a full second.

The Lincoln limousine moved slowly along Elm Street. The young President grinned and waved from the open rear seat of the limousine. His thick brown hair moved in the wind. The longer hair of the young and beautiful Jacqueline

Kennedy moved more, below her pink hat. The couple were pleasantly surprised to receive so cordial a welcome in Dallas, and their elation was plain on their faces.

President Kennedy's grin disappeared abruptly, and he grabbed at his throat with both hands. As the car moved, street signs intervened between the limousine and the Zapruder camera, but the sequence was all too plain.

Mrs. Kennedy realized something was wrong. She turned toward her husband, her smile gone, replaced by a horrified stare. The President slumped toward her. Then suddenly the President's head jerked convulsively, and a part of it exploded away.

It was impossible. It couldn't have happened. Ten thousand theories had been advanced to explain it, but it remained impossible. It couldn't have happened. It was a nightmare from which he, Paul Drury, would waken. It was a nightmare from which the nation would awaken. President Kennedy was alive! He was in Washington! He was—

Thirty years, almost. Almost thirty years.

Drury switched off the tape as the one-second frames continued. He tipped his chair back and stared at the ceiling, taking a minute to adjust his emotions. Then he sat up and began to tap on the keys of his computer keyboard. An idea . . . He wanted to see if his files contained anything more . . .

He was tired, though. Dammit, he was tired! Soon he would be fifty years old. He'd bought success—and paid a high price for it.

3

The studio audience for *The Paul Drury Show* didn't get a warm-up. No one came out and told them jokes to fill the thirty minutes before airtime that they sat in the studio. They had nothing to look at but one another and the busy technicians moving cameras about on the floor as if they had never done this show before, tugging cables, moving lights. For those who had never seen it before it was fascinating, but the fascination did not endure. When they'd seen one camera moved they'd seen them all, and by broadcast time the audience was restive, touchy.

Then—

"Ladies and gentlemen! KWLF Los Angeles and the Wulf Network proudly present the one thousand one hundred sixteenth edition of *The Paul Drury Show!* And now, ladies and gentlemen, PAUL DRURY!"

A black curtain parted, and Paul Drury stepped out into the glare of a spotlight. He stood there for a quarter of a minute or so, bowing in response to the applause of the studio audience, then strode to his right and took his seat in a high-backed black-leather armchair facing a black-leather couch on which his three guests would sit. As the applause continued, Alicia Drury came forward and clipped a microphone to the lapel of his slim double-breasted dark gray suit. This was an element of the form-u-la: that the technology of broadcasting was to be fully visible on the screen. The audience would see microphones clipped on the guests. The applause light came on, and they applauded the statuesque Alicia, recognizing her as the former wife and longtime friend and associate of the host. She brought out his microphone and no other. He raised his right hand, and she hit it lightly with a fist, both of them grinning— another bit of the form-u-la.

A tall glass stood on a small round table beside the armchair. It was an open secret, meant to be known to the audience, that the glass really did contain Scotch and soda, not ginger ale or iced tea. The guests too would have their drinks, on the low table before their couch. Attendants would walk onto the set and replace any glass that became empty—not during commercial breaks but during the show.

On a twenty-six-inch-high pedestal lectern in front of Drury's chair a ring binder lay open. Lying on the white pages was a pair of half glasses: reading glasses.

Paul Drury was six feet five inches tall. An important element of his success was that he was a commanding figure and personality. His light brown hair was darkened by a hairdresser. The studio makeup artist darkened his eyebrows before he went on camera.

A camera focused on Drury's face. "Good evening, ladies and gentlemen," he said in the low, mellifluous voice that was said to be another element of his success. "Welcome to the eleven hundred sixteenth show. We're coming up on five years of five-nights-a-week shows shortly—which is four years and eleven months more than anybody ever thought we'd last."

The studio audience dutifully laughed.

"Tonight we are doing our forty-eighth show relating to some element of the continuing controversy over the 1963 assassination of President John F. Kennedy. As I've said on the air many times, I was a witness to the assassination, standing on Dealey Plaza that fateful day, a boy of nineteen, a university student. Some people say I am obsessed with it. But if I am, apparently you are, too, since our shows about the assassination have always been among our most popular. And it's difficult, isn't it, to realize that this year will mark the *thirtieth* anniversary of that fateful day. It's difficult, too, isn't it, to realize that if President Kennedy were alive today—which God grant he could be—he would be *seventy-six* years old!"

The studio audience and television audience didn't guess where Drury's eyes went as they shifted, but Tim and Alicia behind the glass in the control booth knew very well. Drury had glanced at the director, Marvin Goldschmidt, who was making circling motions with both hands, indicating that Drury should go on a little faster, so as to get his guests introduced before it would be necessary to take a break for commercials. Poor Goldschmidt had begun to learn, but it had not yet entirely soaked in, that for the most part Drury was his own director and would not vary his pace, even if it meant they had to skip one or two commercials. It took a strong, secure television personality to survive causing commercials to be skipped, but Drury had done it more than once.

To this point Drury had ad-libbed, glancing at his own notes in his ring binder, but now he signaled for the TelePrompTer to roll, and he began to read—

"We have with us tonight three men who have interesting perspectives on the Kennedy assassination. I would like to introduce first Mr. Blake Emory, who has devoted countless hours to reviewing every aspect of the events of November 22, 1963. A retired detective lieutenant of the Kansas City police force, he made the assassination his avocation from the day it occurred, his vocation since his retirement. He is

the author of six articles on the assassination and this year
will publish a book outlining what an experienced investi-
gator has concluded from his extensive review of the
evidence. Welcome Mr. Blake Emory!"

Emory walked onto the set. He was short and solid,
conspicuously a man who had been tough and wiry in his
time. His white hair was brush-cut. His face was flushed. It
was also flat, as though he had boxed and had his nose
crushed more than once. He went to the couch, sat down,
and frowned at the young woman who came over to attach
his microphone.

"Mr. Jackson McGinnis was on Dealey Plaza on November 22, 1963, as I was. He witnessed the assassination, and
his story remains to be told. Welcome, please, Mr. Jackson
McGinnis!"

Almost as tall as Drury, wearing a coffee-with-cream-
colored suit and yellow socks, McGinnis came onto the set
with the bouncy air of a boxer entering a ring. His
yellowish-gray hairpiece was obviously a wig. Maybe seventy years old, he held his mouth open to get breath. He
smiled at the studio audience.

"Finally, ladies and gentlemen, Dr. John Trabue, professor of history at the University of Texas at Austin, and a
fellow of the Lyndon Johnson School of Public Affairs.
Professor Trabue is this year a visiting professor at the
University of Southern California. Welcome, please, Professor Trabue!"

The slight, apparently timid professor walked out and
went to the couch, glancing neither at Drury nor at the
studio audience. He held his mouth in a controlled little
smile. His dark hair covered little of his pate. He wore
gold-rimmed glasses, tinted green; and he carried with him

a folder of papers. He wore a dark-blue three-piece suit, and his shoes were brown.

"Ladies and gentlemen, these three men, each of them an expert in his own way on the mysteries surrounding the assassination of President Kennedy, will talk to us, and we will take your telephone calls—immediately following these . . . commercial . . . announcements!"

Drury beckoned to Marvin Goldschmidt to come over to him, and he gesticulated, giving the director instructions. He had shaken hands and chatted with his guests in the waiting room, and now he all but ignored them. Unsure of themselves, they did not chat with one another, but sat staring at Drury and the lights and cameras.

Tim and Alicia sat on stools behind the panels in the control room. "How do you like that?" he said to her, nodding at one of the monitors where the commercial now airing was on display. "Ford. A real breakthrough to get an automobile company as a sponsor."

"Much good may it do us," she muttered.

"Well . . ."

A door opened and Charles Bell came into the control room and took the third tall steel-and-black-vinyl stool. Bell was a heavy investor in Paul Drury Productions. In effect, he owned the show, though his ownership meant little, since PDP would be worthless if Paul Drury should ever decide to leave.

Bell nudged Alicia with his elbow. "Tonight?" he murmured without turning to look at her. She did not answer, and he raised his voice slightly. "Tonight?"

She nodded almost imperceptibly.

"For damn sure," said Bell through clenched teeth.

She shrugged.

Bell was a Texan, but he was nobody's image of a Texan. He did not look like the caricature Texan, did not dress the part, and did not speak like the parodied Texan. He was ruddy of complexion, jowly, and graying in his fifties. He was short. His exquisitely tailored dark blue suit draped gracefully over his ample figure.

"Live," said Goldschmidt's voice over the speaker in the control room.

Drury began to speak. "Tonight, ladies and gentlemen, we have with us three people who may be described as experts on the Kennedy assassination. Many of you will remember Professor Trabue. This is his fourth appearance on this show. You may remember Mr. Blake Emory, who has appeared with us twice before. New to us tonight is Mr. Jackson McGinnis.

"Mr. McGinnis, you were present on Dealey Plaza when President Kennedy was assassinated. You say you saw something that has nowhere been reported. Why don't you tell us what that was?"

McGinnis swallowed and nodded. "Well, sir," he said. "I worked at that time for the City of Dallas. In fact, I worked all my life for the City of Dallas. I was the foreman of a crew that would clean up the area after the President went by. There was lots of folks out to see the President go by, and my fellers would pick up what trash they dropped, so's the place would look nice, the way it's supposed to. You know the county buildings are there, and the monuments and fountains, and we always tried to keep the grass clear of trash.

"Anyway, where I was, I was on the south side of Elm Street, that is, between Elm and Main, in the little triangle-shaped park there. I was pretty near to the curb, just one little girl standin' in front of me, and I could see over her without no trouble. So I had a good place to see the President go by."

McGinnis, though he was conspicuously nervous and kept rubbing his hands on his suit jacket as if he were rubbing the sweat off his palms, spoke with bouncy self-confidence, showing a toothy smile to the studio audience and the cameras.

"And just before he got to where I was, I saw him jerk his hands up and grab his throat, and I heard a shot. There wasn't no question where that shot come from. It come from the School Book Depository Building. I mean, you could hear where it come from plain as anything. I looked up at the building, but you couldn't see no rifleman. He'd ducked back in. I looked back at the President. He had his hands up to his throat, and he looked awful. Then the whole top of his head blew off, just blew off. And there was no doubt where that shot come from. If that shot had missed Mr. Kennedy, it might of kilt me, or somebody standin' close to me."

"Where did that shot come from, Mr. McGinnis?" asked Drury, who until now had said nothing. His face had filled the screen half the time McGinnis was talking: a study in intent skepticism.

"Up there on the north side of Elm Street there's what they call a pergola," said McGinnis. "It's another one of the monuments. You know, a half circle, like, closed behind, open in front, made of concrete. Sort of like a bandstand, only not. It was a perfect place to shoot from. Close to the street. High up, so you could shoot over the crowd. And a feller with a rifle fired from up there. I happened to be right in line. I seen him."

"After he fired, what did he do?" asked Drury.

"Couple of fellers took the rifle from him, and they walked off, out of the pergola and I figure down into the parking lot behind it."

"Mr. McGinnis," said Drury, "if the pergola was a perfect vantage point from which to shoot President Kennedy, wouldn't that have been apparent to the Secret Service and the Dallas police, too; and wouldn't the pergola have been guarded?"

"It wuz," said McGinnis. "Guarded *fer* him, so's he could get off his shot. See, I figured those fellers that took the gun and led the rifleman away was police of some kind. But they wasn't. There was never a word said about it. That was all covered up."

"Thank you," said Drury. He reached for his glass and took a sip of Scotch. It was a gesture of skepticism, as his regular audience knew, and the group in the studio tittered. "Mr. Blake Emory, you were a police detective in Kansas City at the time of the assassination. You took an immediate interest in the crime, read everything you could about it, went down to Dallas to visit the site, and interviewed witnesses. When you retired seven years ago, you made research into the assassination of President Kennedy your full-time work. You are a detective experienced in criminal investigation. You are the author of six articles on the assassination, and this year, the thirtieth year since the assassination, you will publish a book on the crime.

After a short break, we will hear what you think of Mr. McGinnis's story."

In the control booth, Bell turned to Tim and Alicia and said, "Bullshit."

"Fortunately," said Alicia.

"Sooner or later—"

Bell interrupted Tim. "No. Tonight."

Tim nodded. "If we can. There are a thousand ways he could screw us up."

"My part's in place," said Bell.

Tim looked through the glass and nodded toward Paul Drury. "The goose that laid golden eggs," he said.

When the commercials were over, Blake Emory began. "In all the research I have done on the assassination," he said, "I never before heard of a shot fired from the pergola. I firmly believe that a shot, maybe two, came from the Grassy Knoll, maybe one or two from the underpass. But, as you said, Mr. Drury, the pergola was a perfect place from which to fire a shot, and it was guarded by Secret Service agents as well as plainclothes detectives of the Dallas force."

"That there's just the point," said McGinnis. "The cops was *in on it,* the Secret Service was in on it, and lord knows who all else."

"Professor Trabue," said Drury, "you've made a specialty of the Kennedy assassination, as a professional historian. Has anything you have read or heard suggested shots fired from the pergola?"

"Well, as you know, Mr. Drury," said Professor Trabue, "I am a firm believer in the accuracy and completeness of the Warren Commission Report. In the twenty-nine years since it was published, I have not seen a shred of credible evidence that supports any alternative theory. Commission-bashing and conspiracy theories have become a lucrative industry. I am willing to take any alternative theory you wish, from the Garrison charges in New Orleans to the Oliver Stone movie, and I will show you where they depend on facts that are not facts and make quantum leaps in logic. People are obsessed with conspiracy. They don't want to believe anything inexplicable happens except by some deep, dark conspiracy. Lee Harvey Oswald killed President Kennedy, Mr. Drury. I am sorry that spoils some people's fun and other people's livelihoods, but that's it, plain and simple."

"I got a question for the professor," said McGinnis.

"Ask it," said Drury.

"Where'd you say you're a professor at?" asked McGinnis.

"The Lyndon Johnson School of Public Affairs, University of Texas," said the professor. "This year I'm a visiting professor at USC."

McGinnis smirked. *Lyndon Johnson* School," he said with a self-satisfied smirk. "That explains that."

"What *does* it explain, exactly?" said Drury, reaching for his Scotch.

"He works for the *Lyndon Johnson* School," said McGinnis confidently. "I don't s'pose there's a grown-up person in this country doesn't know Johnson was one of them that wanted Kennedy killed and done what he could to make it happen."

"Mr. McGinnis," said Drury. "I am curious about something. President Kennedy was assassinated thirty years ago, almost, and only now are you telling us you saw the rifleman fire the shot. Why didn't you report what you saw to the Dallas police, to the Secret Service, to the FBI, or even to the newspapers?"

"I done," said McGinnis. "Working for the City of Dallas, I knew enough about the Dallas police not to go to them. I figured the Secret Service had to be in on it. So I went to the FBI. I figured Mr. Hoover'd be interested. The agent there in Dallas, he took my statement, and I never heard no more about it."

"As a matter of fact, Mr. McGinnis," said Drury, "you did go to the Dallas police." He flipped pages in his ring binder. "On March 4, 1964, almost four months after the assassination, you went to the Dallas police. Their report says— and I quote—'Jackson McGinnis, 864 San Diego Street, claims to have seen shot fired from concrete pergola north of Elm Street. Claim inconsistent with statements of numerous other witnesses. Sergeant Chaney, Officers Gilchrist and Temple were in concrete pergola at time of assassination, saw no rifleman.'"

"Well, I forgot that. I guess I did go to the Dallas cops and tell them what I seen," said McGinnis.

"Why did you wait until March to report what you saw?"

"You got no idea what it was like in Dallas right after the assassination—"

"As a matter of fact, I do," said Drury. "I lived there. I was going to school there."

"Well— I don't think that date on that report is right. That's another thing they'd do, make up a different date so's to make it look like I didn't come in right off."

"The FBI agent who interviewed you reported that your

account was contradicted by the statements of too many other witnesses."

"Well, who wuz they?"

"Mr. Emory," said Drury, "how many shots do you conclude were fired on Dealey Plaza that day?"

Emory, as much as McGinnis, was startled by the abrupt change of subject. "I can identify six," he said. He spoke irresolutely, though whether it was from being so surprised or because he was not entirely sure of his statement was impossible for the audience to tell. "You know, a bullet plowed into the ground there in that park where Mr. McGinnis says he was standing. A Dallas police officer guarded that spot until an FBI agent came and dug out that bullet. But that bullet's missing. The FBI claims it doesn't have it."

The conversation went on, mostly now among Drury, Emory, and the professor. McGinnis was subdued, even sullen. Emory asserted that Oswald could not have fired the two shots that hit Kennedy—one maybe but not two. He described it as an impossible feat of marksmanship.

"You've changed your mind on that," said Drury.

"I don't think so."

"Well, you were interviewed by a Dan Paccinelli, a reporter for the Kansas City *Star,* in 1968 and you said, I quote—'That would have been a difficult shot, sure, but not impossible.' So which is it, Mr. Emory, difficult or impossible?"

In the control booth, Alicia turned to Bell and said, "That damned computer. He can pull out anything anybody ever said."

Emory was not fazed. He smiled. "Let's call it 'nearly impossible,'" he said.

After the next commercial break, Drury began to receive telephone calls.

A woman from Seattle: "The fact is, you're completely off the track, all of you. President Kennedy is not dead. In the summer of 1963 he was diagnosed as suffering progressive brain damage from the syphilis he'd had since about 1938. The assassination was staged. He's alive today in a hospital in England. Of course he doesn't know who he is or where he is, and—"

"Thank you, Seattle," said Drury as he cut off the call, letting the audience see a chopping motion and a flash of impatience on his face.

A man from Baton Rouge: "I have a question for Professor Trabue. Do you fear that the work of careful historians like yourself will be lost in the public mind? I mean, a movie like the Oliver Stone thing has a hundred times bigger audience than you can ever have; and, in spite of the fact that it's all based on speculation, it's the only version of the assassination that a lot of people are ever going to have."

"That troubles me very deeply," said Professor Trabue.

"Question for our caller in Baton Rouge," said Drury. "This is the forty-eighth show we've done on the assassination. We try to give time for every point of view. Do you think we're part of the solution or part of the problem?"

"I'm not sure," said the man in Baton Rouge. "I believe Professor Trabue is correct, that the Warren Commission was thorough and accurate, but there's so much money to be made from playing loose with the facts—"

"Can I ask you to keep watching us?" Drury interrupted. "This is only the forty-eighth show. We've got more to reveal. We may have some surprises for you."

A young woman from Columbus, Ohio: "I'd like to know

what each of your guests thinks about the proposition that Kennedy had to be killed because he was about to order a withdrawal of our troops from Vietnam."

Drury signaled Professor Trabue to answer first, and the professor said, "There is no evidence whatever of that. None whatever. In the absence of evidence, I am not prepared to believe any such preposterous accusation."

Drury pointed at McGinnis, who said, "That's *my* whole point. Lyndon Johnson wanted Kennedy killed so's he'd get the presidency and could keep the war goin'—from which he and a lot of others were making tons of money. It's simple as that," he concluded, confidence restored and self-satisfied.

"Mr. Emory—"

"I don't think there's much doubt that Lee Harvey Oswald was something different from what the Warren Commission thought he was. For example, when Oswald was a marine he contracted gonorrhea. The Marine Corps medical report on that says specifically that he contracted the disease in the line of duty and it wasn't his fault. Now, what duty could he have possibly been performing that would cause him to catch a venereal disease? What else besides intelligence work? He was an intelligence agent, and it is possible he was ordered to assassinate President Kennedy."

"The Warren Commission," said Drury, "specifically found that Oswald was not an intelligence agent."

"The commission overlooked a lot of evidence," said Emory. "A lot has come out that wasn't available to the Warren Commission."

"The Warren Commission didn't *want* the evidence," said McGinnis. "The Warren Commission was part of the cover-up. After all, who was Earl Warren, anyway? A com-symp, as everybody knows."

Drury flipped pages in his ring binder. A murmur went through the studio audience, most of whom knew that flipping those pages usually meant that Paul Drury was about to crush someone. "I wasn't going to bring this up, Mr. McGinnis," he said, "but the employment files of the City of Dallas indicate you were not employed in the Street Sanitation Department on November 22, 1963, indeed that you were not hired by that department until August 1965."

"They got *that* mixed up," McGinnis snorted, but his complaint was drowned out by applause from the studio audience.

In the control booth, Bell asked Alicia, "If he knows the guy wasn't there, why'd he bring him on the show?"

"Don't you watch the shows much?" she asked. "It's something audiences love. He sets up a patsy, then shoots him down. McGinnis makes a pretty crude patsy, but that's his role. Paul let him say something absolutely outrageous . . . then WHACK!"

"Comic relief," Bell suggested scornfully.

"Emotional release," said Alicia.

Calls kept coming in. Calls were one of the most popular parts of *The Paul Drury Show*. Ideas the show would not have dared to dignify with guest invitations came in on the telephone lines. How Drury handled them, and how his guests did, gave the show its special, off-the-wall, entertaining flavor.

Toronto: "Look. Marilyn Monroe was worth a hundred million to the people who owned her contract. Kennedy had her killed. Anybody who lost that much money was going to blow away the guy who made him lose it."

Stamford, Connecticut: "Have you ever heard of the Society of the Illuminati? Nothing happens those guys don't sanction. You ought to read up on it."

Tampa, Florida: "If Bobby Kennedy had been elected President of the United States in 1968, he'd have used the power of the office to find out who really killed his brother and who covered up—which is why *he* was murdered."

Charleston, West Virginia: "When you put together the power of the Mafia, Wall Street, the CIA, the FBI, the Pentagon, the defense industries, and Fidel Castro . . . They could kill anybody and get away with it."

The end of the hour approached, and Drury broke for commercials. Afterward he summed up—

"Mr. Jackson McGinnis has brought us an interesting new insight into the assassination—which unfortunately doesn't seem to hold up. As was said by a young American student studying for the priesthood in Rome, in a college where students were supposed to speak only Latin, *'Haec opinio non tenet acquam.'* Even so, we are grateful to Mr. McGinnis for appearing and giving us his stories and his views. Who knows? He may yet prove right.

"Mr. Blake Emory's extensive research is interesting as always, and we are grateful to him, as we are grateful to Professor John Trabue who always capably represents the orthodox view of the Kennedy assassination.

"We ourselves have been working for a long time on a documentary show based on all we have learned from these forty-eight hour-long shows. We are using a computer to assimilate a vast body of material. I am looking toward the actual thirtieth anniversary of the assassination to do a different kind of show, with pictures and commentary, that may change forever the way we look at the assassination of President John F. Kennedy.

"Tomorrow night our topic will be cigarette smoking, whether it's as bad as they say and what demands non-smokers are entitled to make on people who like to smoke. Our guests will be the Surgeon General of the United States, Mr. Stuart Milliken of the Tobacco Institute, and Renee Laurentan, world-known authority on social behavior.

"Until then . . . Remember to . . . USE YOUR HEAD! Paul Drury . . . GOOD NIGHT!"

T W O

As soon as the light went off on the camera, Drury
ripped off his microphone and was up from his chair,
striding off the set without a nod or a backward glance at
his guests or the crew. As he rushed out of the studio and
along the concrete-paved hall toward his dressing room, he
jerked off his necktie. Inside the dressing room he slammed
the door and began to throw off his clothes. He kicked off
his black Gucci loafers at the same time that he was
shrugging out of his jacket. He tossed everything aside, on
a couch, on the floor: suit, shirt, underpants, socks . . .
Naked, he grabbed open the glass doors of a shower. His
body gleamed with sweat. It streamed down him. He waited
impatiently for the water to warm up so he could adjust it to
something short of ice-cold; and as soon as it was ready he
stepped under the gushing stream and closed the glass
doors.

"Orrghh!" he blubbered into the water striking his face.
"Jee-zuss! Shlooof! Orrghh!"

The dressing-room door opened. A diminutive young
woman entered, carrying a tall glass filled with ice and
seltzer water, with only a touch of Scotch. She went to the
shower, opened the door, and handed Drury the glass. He

took the drink in his left hand, seized her wrist with his right, and held her while he drew her halfway into the shower and kissed her on the mouth.

"Karen! Oh, God!"

When he let go of her, her clothes were wet, her hair was wet, and the floor under her feet was wet.

Drury tipped back the glass and drank half its contents. He paused for a moment, then drank the rest of it and handed her the glass.

She took the glass to his dressing table and put it down. She snatched a towel from a rack and dried her face and hair. That done, she began to gather up Drury's clothes. She did it gingerly. Even the gray suit was damp with his sweat.

Karen Bergman had an uncertain title and position in Paul Drury Productions. On the screen credits she was listed as "Assistant to Mr. Drury." She was a sort of secretary and did a little typing. She ran endless errands. Her job, really, was to be around, within call, to do whatever he wanted done. When they were alone, she called him Paul; and when they were not she called him Mr. Drury.

She was a drama graduate of UCLA and still hoped, at twenty-seven, to land a dramatic role, preferably in a series. Her only appearances on camera, though, had been walk-ons with no more than a line or two to speak. When Drury spotted her and offered her this job she had been working as a curtain-puller on a morning game show, where her function had been to dress in a tight black skirt and well-filled white blouse and wiggle onto the set on cue to pull the cord that opened a curtain and displayed what a contestant had won—this accompanied by a squeal of surprise and delight if the contestant did not squeal convincingly enough. She had called herself the third-string Vanna White. On *The Paul Drury Show,* she was the blond young woman who came out and clipped on the guests' microphones. Also, she brought out his fresh Scotch and soda if he needed it. Occasionally he leaned over and brushed a quick kiss across her cheek, on camera. Audiences seemed to think that was a generous, paternal gesture.

The black skirt and white blouse had followed her here. Drury liked the costume, and she wore it, with only minor variations, on the set and off. The skirt remained tight, but not so much that she had to walk unnaturally as she'd had to do on the game show. Her hair was artificially lightened. Her eyes were blue, her face very regular, without a flaw. Her figure was of course stunning—compact, since she was not more than five feet four. Drury had told her once she would have succeeded better as an actress if there had been something—just anything—wrong with her.

Marvin Goldschmidt knocked once and came in. *"Magnifique!"* he said.

"There was too goddamn much light on McGinnis," said Drury from the shower. "He looked like a light from heaven had descended on him and he was about to start climbing Jacob's ladder."

"I thought so too," said Goldschmidt, "but the light-level guy said no, and I must say it looked okay on the monitors. It went out on the air okay. Just looked like that in the studio."

"If you say so. Take a look at the tape. Be sure."

"Got it," said Goldschmidt.

Tim and Alicia came in, without knocking. "Looked good," said Tim.

Alicia sat down on the couch. She said nothing. She planted a hard, censorious stare for a moment on Karen's wet blouse, which was transparent, showing her bra. Karen saw the stare and returned one of her own, defiantly.

Drury threw back the shower door and stood wet and stark naked before his producer, assistant producer, director, and assistant. Karen handed him a towel, and he began to dry himself. "Guys and gals are working on that tobacco crap," he said to Tim. "Right?"

"Right," said Tim.

"Well, be damned sure they do. When I come in tomorrow afternoon, I want a full briefing, no shit, no shortcuts. I was on Dealey Plaza when Kennedy was shot, but I wasn't with Sir Walter Raleigh when he discovered tobacco. That guy from the Institute will have his case researched and briefed, and he'll be ready to field any question. I've gotta be in the same position. No sleep tonight."

"There's a limit, Paul," said Alicia.

"They can go to bed when we go on the air tomorrow night," said Drury, rubbing himself vigorously with his big white towel. "And sleep till Monday. Friday night's the Shirley MacLaine thing, and I don't need research for that. That's personality stuff, and I can handle that without anything besides the minimum curriculum vitae on each guest, but tomorrow night has got to be meticulously prepared."

Karen handed him a pair of dark blue slingshot underpants, and he stepped into them and pulled them up. He dropped his towel into the water just outside the shower stall.

"You committed to that show on the abortion pill?" Tim asked.

"What'm I gonna do?" asked Drury. "Our business is to sort out fact from fiction. Let's just be damned sure we're neutral on the subject. Hey! On that show, don't pencil in any dumb farts. Two guests, or four. Scientifically respectable. Evenly divided. Okay?"

Tim nodded, and Alicia nodded.

"So okay, guys. Gotta get a bite of din-din and some sleep. See ya tomorrow."

Karen handed Drury a pair of socks, and he sat down to pull them on.

In the hall outside, Tim and Alicia encountered Bell. He confronted them grimly.

"Tonight."

Tim nodded. "Okay. Tonight. Tonight's the plan. We're ready to go."

"Except that the guy's unpredictable," said Alicia. "If he decides to sleep tonight in Karen's apartment, the plan's down the drain. Other than for something like that—"

"Tonight!" grunted Bell. "We've put it off too goddamn long."

Hollyridge Road is a rough-paved narrow twisting strip of asphalt running along a high ridge of the Santa Monica Mountains. It is bounded on both sides by expensive homes, one of which was the home of Paul Drury.

When Tim Edmonds and Alicia Graham Drury arrived there a little before ten o'clock, they had walked almost a mile along the ridge from the last spot where they felt it was safe to park their car. Hollyridge Road was patrolled, not just by the LAPD but also by a private security force hired by the homeowners, and cars parked along the road were always investigated. So were people walking on the road, and every time they had seen headlights they had scurried off into the cover of the brush that was encouraged to grow to anchor the soil and prevent landslides.

They had rehearsed this walk and knew how long it would take. They had rehearsed, too, their means of entry into the house. Alicia had lived there for two years and knew the estate well. She knew the house was protected by an elaborate alarm system, but she also knew how to disable the system without setting off the alarm. Inside a steel box, disguised as a mailbox, was a machine something like the cash machines at banks. You could insert a plastic card with a magnetic code into a slot, then punch in a code number on the little round keypad below. That disabled the system for three minutes, time enough to get inside the house. Once you were in, you could turn the system off by using the card and a different number in a control box in the kitchen. But you didn't have to do that. The system detected motion outside and any touching of the doors or windows. Once you were inside, you would normally leave the system active, since it didn't detect motion inside the house.

It was an expensive system, but it served Paul Drury's requirements: sophisticated security coupled with easy access for his professional and household staff, plus a few of his friends. When Alicia left the house for good, she had handed her card to Paul, in the presence of his attorney. No one had guessed she had kept another card—which she had taken from his bureau drawer some time before, knowing he kept several on hand and did not keep exact count of how many he had. Paul had not bothered to change the code, which he could easily have done. After all, their divorce had been reasonably amicable.

The only approach to the house was up a short stone driveway to the double doors of the garage. To the left was a wrought-iron gate which opened onto the lawn and to the swimming pool and cabana. The driveway was brightly lighted. It was visible, though, only from the windows above, not from neighboring houses. Alicia and Tim walked up the driveway, through the gate, and onto the lawn. Pulling on gloves before they touched anything, they went first to the side door of the garage, unlocked it by using the magnetic card in a slot, and looked in, to be sure Paul's car was not there. They entered the garage and used a door inside as their entrance to the house.

Paul's taste in home furnishings was like his taste in office furnishings. He liked the clean-lined modern. He also liked space, and his living room would have been thought by some to be sparely furnished, that it might have contained twice as many couches and chairs as were there. If the lights had been on, they would have displayed his taste in paintings, which included some neorealistic nudes, male and female.

They went first to Paul's desk, at one end of the living room. The drawers were locked. Tim, who had been in the house many times and knew where things were kept, returned to the garage and pulled a small crowbar off its hook on the garage wall. He used it to pry open the desk. The bar shattered the frame and veneer of the handsome piece of furniture, and when he wrenched the center drawer open, bits of wood fell on the carpet.

With gloved hands, Alicia began to pull files from the drawers and toss them on the floor.

Tim interrupted her. He clutched her to him and kissed her. "I've never loved anyone half as much as I love you," he said. "I didn't know it could be like this."

She returned his kiss. "Neither did I, my own darling," she whispered, then turned back to rifle through the drawer.

"Have you found it? For God's sake, have you found it?" he asked excitedly as she paused in her search.

She handed him a tiny blue envelope of heavy paper.

Tim stared at the envelope in the dim light, then opened it. "What bank? What bank?"

"What's it say?"

"It says 'Mosley,' which is the name of the company that made the damned vault! What bank? The key doesn't do us any good if we don't know what bank!"

4

Paul Drury was at dinner with Karen Bergman.

She had changed out of her wet clothes. Sitting across a small table from him in La Felicità, she was wearing tight silver lamé pants and a loose-woven white cotton sweater. Anyone who glanced at her more than casually could see through the open weave of the sweater that she wore nothing beneath it. The sweater was something else Paul liked, and she wore it when they went to reasonably private places.

He was now wearing gray slacks and a classic blue blazer with monogrammed buttons, over a white Ralph Lauren golf shirt.

They had all but finished their dinner. Both of them had had angel-hair pasta under a creamy sauce of shrimp and crab and lobster meat. They had all but finished their bottle of wine, too.

"Will I be coming home with you?" she asked him.

"Not tonight. I'm absolutely wrung out. That show exhausted me. I worked the formula, but— Well, it isn't easy, you know."

"I know."

He clasped his hands under his chin, so tightly his knuckles turned white. "I'm having difficulty focusing on anything," he said. "More and more, I'm dominated by the November special."

"I'm not asking you to tell me the answer," she said, "but do you really know who killed Kennedy?"

Paul Drury sighed. "I'm not sure. I know somebody was hired to do it and was there and could have done it. That is, he could have fired a shot, maybe two. I don't know that he did, not for sure."

"What about Lee Harvey Oswald?" she asked in a whisper.

Drury shrugged. "I don't think there is any doubt Oswald fired at least one shot, maybe two, maybe even three. And he may have hit Kennedy once. But there were more shots. That's the point. There were more shots." He flexed his shoulders and grunted. "If I only knew—"

"Paul . . . I could help relax you tonight. You can go to sleep while I'm doing it."

He put his hand on hers. "Friday night," he said. "The Friday show is easy. Friday and Saturday . . . and Sunday."

"Swim?"

"You bet. A good time. Just a good time." He beckoned to the waiter. "I'm sorry, baby, but I'm going to have a cab take you home. I've gotta hit the sack. I'll probably sleep in my clothes."

"Oh, Paul, it's not even eleven o'clock!"

"Sorry."

5

He was lucky he hadn't gone to sleep driving, Drury reflected as at long last he turned into his driveway, deactivated the security system, and hit the button that opened the garage door. He eased his big, dark green Mercedes into the garage, switched off the lights and engine, and opened the door. He walked to the door into the house and put his card in the slot.

"H'lo, Paul."

"What . . . ? What the hell?" asked Drury as he jerked his

head to the right and saw Tim Edmonds. "Where were . . . ? What are you doing here . . . ?"

Alicia stepped up behind him. She had been hidden on the far side of the second car in the garage: the vintage Lamborghini Drury drove only for fun, never to the studio. Tim had been hidden there, too, and had stepped out in front to distract Drury as Alicia moved around the rear of the Mercedes and slipped up behind him.

Clutching a pistol in both hands, Alicia put it to the back of Drury's head and pulled the trigger. The small-caliber pistol made a small, sharp crack that echoed inside the garage but probably not beyond. As Drury collapsed, she fired a second shot into the back of his head. With him flat and silent on the garage floor, she squatted beside him, unfastened his watch, reached into his jacket pocket for his billfold, and pulled a heavy gold ring with a huge diamond from his finger.

Tim brushed past her, opened the door of the Mercedes, and leaned across the front seat to pull a small black box from under the seat on the passenger side.

Alicia opened the door into the house, and they hurried up into the dark living room. For a minute or so they stood behind a large window, watching the area. They saw nothing. From all indications, no one had heard the shots in the Drury garage.

They deactivated the security system for three minutes at a station in the kitchen, left the house through the kitchen door, slipped around the pool in the shadows of the cabana, and returned to the gate that opened onto the driveway.

As they walked back along Hollyridge Drive, to where they had left their car, they were frightened three times by approaching headlights, and three times they scurried off the road and hid. When finally they reached the car—a rented green Oldsmobile that was unlikely to be remembered—they literally flung themselves onto the seats, physically exhausted, emotionally drained.

"Not finished," Alicia whispered.

"I hope we're not too late for dinner, Roberto," Tim said to the proprietor of Cocina Roberto. "It's after eleven-thirty."

"We serve until one o'clock, Señor Edmonds."

"Wonderful! Let's start off with margaritas and with some guacamole."

"Certainly, Señor. And welcome to you also, Señora Drury. It is always good to see you."

Alicia and Tim were silent as they drank their margaritas and dipped chips in the guacamole. From time to time, Tim glanced at his watch.

"Relax," she said after a while. "It worked out fine, and there's just one more thing to do."

"Do it," said Tim. "I want it off my mind."

Alicia nodded and left the table. She went to the women's room. A woman was there, repairing her makeup, and Alicia went inside a toilet stall and sat down to wait. After a minute the woman left. Alicia went immediately to the pay telephone near the door—a telephone thoughtfully provided by Roberto for women who wanted to make calls without their dates knowing. She punched in a number and waited, pulling a Sony Walkman from her purse while the telephone rang four times.

"Hello. This is Bill McCrory. I can't take your call right

*now, but if you will leave your name and number, I will get
back to you as soon as I can. Please wait for the beep."*

Alicia pressed the PLAY button on the Walkman.

*"Hi. This is Paul. Make a point of calling me first thing in
the ay-em, please. Kind of important."*

Back at the table, she smiled at Tim Edmonds and said,
"Done. Done and done."

THREE

At 9:00 A.M., Thursday, June 3, rain was falling on Los Angeles. Officer Ted Dugan, LAPD, was irritated. A three-year man on the force, his duty this morning was to stand at the end of a driveway on Hollyridge Road and turn away reporters and assorted curious. Some of the reporters were pretty damned pushy.

And now here came . . . God almighty! A wheezing old heap of junk, God-knew-what: battered, silver paint showing rust in some places, crude brushed-on repair work on the right front fender. Only one windshield wiper was working, fortunately the one in front of the driver. Dugan stepped out and raised his hand imperiously. He'd be damned if he let—

But hold on. Wait a minute. Dugan stared at the license plate: 044 APD. Somewhere in the back of his mind he had a fix on that number—044 APD. The driver stopped, rolled down his window, and showed a shield.

My God, it was Columbo! Lieutenant Columbo! That was the license number he'd been told to look out for: on the ancient Peugeot driven by Columbo. The man in the car was short. He badly needed a haircut; his dark hair was disheveled and falling over his ears, collar, and forehead.

His eyes—narrow, set inside a pattern of lines—were sharp and intense; yet somehow he looked distracted and not entirely sure he had come to the right place.

"Can y' help me out a little, Dugan?" he asked, reading the officer's name from the board on his shirt.

"Yes, sir. Of course."

Columbo pulled the car a little to one side. It still half blocked the driveway, but the paramedics' squad wagon, which was parked at the garage door, red and blue lights flashing, could squeeze past. So could any of the three police cars on the driveway. He got out, dragging from the rear seat a large sheet of once-clear plastic. "Car leaks a little when it rains," he explained to the tall blond Officer Dugan. "Put this plastic over it to keep out the rain. Like a raincoat for a car. Right? Raincoat for the car. Don't want rain drippin' on the seats."

It would have, without the plastic. The convertible top had tears and would have let in water by the gallon—*had* let in some water during Columbo's drive up from the city. The lieutenant himself had come prepared for rain. He was wearing a wrinkled short raincoat, stained and frayed, on the verge in fact of being called shabby. He tossed the plastic over his car and walked around it, smoothing it down.

"If a wind comes up, I'd appreciate your keeping that from blowing off, Dugan. Just put a couple rocks on it."

"Yes, sir."

Columbo glanced around. He stood in the rain and frowned at the house. The facade it presented to the street was the garage doors. The house, Spanish-style stucco with a red-tile roof, was beyond the garage and above it as the land sloped sharply up. He could see why the main rooms of the house would face west—because from the windows the view would be out over Los Angeles and the Pacific. From the driveway he could see the roof of the cabana and so surmised that a swimming pool lay on the flat land at the top of the slope. The house was not a mansion; that was not the right word for it. It was a villa.

"My, this is some place, isn't it? Imagine the money y'd have to have to live in a place like this! But I've seen the man's TV show. The man earned what he had. And now—" The lieutenant shook his head. "Tragedy."

Officer Dugan had heard the name Columbo often. He'd heard all about him. Even so, it was difficult to believe this was Columbo. Below the bottom of the stained raincoat, a thread hung down the lieutenant's leg, inspiring in Dugan an all but irresistible urge to reach down and tear it loose.

"Where's everybody?" Columbo asked. He glanced around at the six official cars drawn up on the street and in the driveway. "They removed the body?"

"No, sir. The body is in the garage. Most of the people are in there, I imagine."

Columbo looked around. It looked to Dugan as if the man were oblivious to the rain falling on him and wetting his unruly dark hair. "How do you get in?" he asked.

Dugan pointed to the gate—not a gate that was part of the security system, just a decorative gate, low, wrought-iron painted white. "Through there and into the side door of the garage."

2

Columbo walked to the gate. For a moment he fumbled with the latch. Finally he got it open, then went through and up a paved walk to the garage.

The officer outside had been right. The body of Paul Drury lay on the garage floor, and half a dozen people milled around it, some staring at it and others intent on examining the cars and the garage clutter.

"Lieutenant!"

Martha Zimmer came toward Columbo. Her rank was detective, LAPD, and she was wearing the badge exposed on the pocket of her white blouse. She had to. Otherwise, men were not readily disposed to accept the fact that she was a detective. She was short. To use the term most often applied to her, she was "squat." Her dark hair was cut short, her apple-cheeked face was plump, and she wore no makeup. Her weight might not have been acceptable to the department except for two things: first, that she was an intelligent, effective officer; second, that she had just borne her second child and had gained weight during her pregnancy.

"H'lo, Martha," said Columbo. "Welcome back. I hear everything went okay. How you feelin'?"

"Perfect," she said.

"What we got?"

Martha nodded toward the corpse lying facedown on the concrete floor of the garage, his head in a dried pool of blood. "That's Paul Drury, the journalist talk-show-host fellow. The medical examiner has made a very preliminary finding that he's been dead since before midnight last night. This is his car. It looks like he came home, used his radio controller to open the garage door, and was shot in the back of the head, twice, before he could get in the house. He's absent his billfold. The house has been ransacked."

"How'd the assailant or assailants unknown get in here?" Columbo asked.

"Don't know. There's an alarm system, but it didn't work."

Columbo nodded. He reached into his raincoat pocket and pulled out the cold, half-smoked stub of a cigar. "Gotta match?" he asked.

Martha smiled and handed him a book of paper matches. "Keep them," she said.

"Who found him?"

"A Mrs. Badilio," said Martha Zimmer. "She's the house-keeper. You get into the house with a sort of credit card that has a PIN you can use to work the alarm system. She's got one of those cards and used it to get in."

"You talked with her?"

"Just for a moment. She's not in very good shape."

Columbo used one of the paper matches to light the cigar. He looked at a man standing beside the body. "Hi, Doc," he said. "What ya figure?"

"Preliminary . . ." cautioned Dr. Harold Culp. "Very pre-liminary."

"Oh, sure," said Columbo. "Understood."

Dr. Culp was a man of forty, forty-five maybe, and if he were the former he was prematurely gray and prematurely turning bald. The round tanned bare spot on the back of his head was not wide enough for the bald spot of a tonsured monk; it was more like the size of a yarmulke. He wore horn-rimmed bifocals.

"There are two small bullet wounds at the back of the head and low," said Dr. Culp. "No exit wounds. The bullets are still inside the head, somewhere in the brain. There is considerable powder residue around one wound, very little around the other. One shot was fired with the muzzle almost pressed against the head. The other was fired from a foot or so away. The size of the wounds suggests a small-caliber weapon, even as small as a twenty-two."

"No big noise," said Martha Zimmer.

"What do you figure was the time of death?" asked Columbo.

"Before midnight," said Dr. Culp. "State of the body. State of the dried blood." He nodded emphatically. "It could have happened as early as ten last night. At the very outside, not after twelve-thirty. But that's a preliminary estimate, remember."

Columbo glanced around the garage. "My, look at that other car the man had. That's a Lamborghini. That's an expensive foreign car. That one's a classic. I drive a foreign car, y' know. My car's a French car. Not a Japanese car—not that I got anything against Japanese cars—but my car was built in France, and they sure know how to build cars over there. Uh . . . The door's open on the Mercedes, but the interior lights aren't on. Why is that, y' s'pose?"

"The battery is down, Lieutenant," said a uniformed officer. "Rose, Lieutenant. I responded to the call and was the first officer on the scene. The car door was open when I came in, and the battery is dead."

"That's odd, don't y' think?" asked Columbo. "I mean, the man got out of his car, it looks like. He walked to the front of the car and up to the door to the house. What's that in his hand there? A plastic card? Credit card? Why . . . ? Oh, I see. Slot. Door opens with a card, not a key. Anyway, why would he leave the car door open?"

Columbo reached for the button that opened and closed the garage door. He pressed it. As the door rumbled up, a bright light came on.

"See, he didn't need the light inside the car. So why would he walk away from his car and leave the door open?"

"Why would he?" asked Martha Zimmer.

Columbo shook his head. "He wouldn't. The killer opened the door to get somethin' out of the car. *He* left the door open. He was nervous and in a hurry. Besides, what'd he care if the battery ran down in Mr. Drury's car?"

Columbo reached inside his jacket and pulled out a small notebook. He checked his pockets. "You got a pencil to spare, Martha?" he asked. "I want to make a note of this. What was in the car that the killer wanted? Can you think of any other reason why that car door was left open and the battery was left to run down?"

Columbo made a note with the pencil Martha had handed him. Then he pointed toward the house, and the two of them went in.

"My, what a place! Isn't this *elegant!*" he said of the kitchen, which was equipped with two microwave ovens besides a conventional oven, a dishwasher, huge Sub-Zero refrigerator, electric stovetop, electric grill, glass-enclosed refrigerated wine cellar . . . "How'd you like to cook a dinner in here, Martha?"

A uniformed sergeant came into the kitchen. "Lieutenant," he said briskly, "there are two friends of Mr. Drury outside. They'd like to come in. One's the ex-wife."

"Oh, sure," said Columbo. "Don't let the woman go out to the garage, though. She shouldn't have to see that."

Tim Edmonds and Alicia Drury came into the kitchen and were introduced to Columbo.

"We came up here as soon as we heard," said Tim. He had walked up the driveway in the rain, and drops of water gleamed in his blond hair. His long Burberry raincoat was spotted. "I guess there's no hope that we were told wrong."

"If you were told that Mr. Drury is dead, you were told right," said Columbo.

Alicia put her hands over her face and sobbed. She, too, wore a Burberry coat, almost identical to Tim's.

"How did it happen?" asked Tim.

"Murder," said Columbo. "Shot in the head. Sometime last night. Midnight, give or take an hour."

Tim looked at Alicia. "When we were at Cocina Roberto," he said.

She nodded. "My God! While we were having a good time, he . . ." She put her hands to her face and sobbed again.

Columbo spoke to Tim. "The lady is Mr. Drury's ex-wife, as I understand. What's *your* connection?"

"I'm— I *was* his producer."

"And a friend, too, I bet. Huh? Listen, Mr. Edmonds, I need somebody to take a look at the body. I wouldn't want to ask the lady to do that, but—"

"I'll do anything I can to help," said Tim solemnly.

"Well, that's nice of you, Mr. Edmonds. I know this isn't easy. Right this way. Well, I s'pose you know the way. You've been in the house before, haven't you?"

"Many times," said Tim.

3

"Yeah. Well, there he is, sir. A gruesome sight, I'm sorry. This is how he was found. Lyin' there, facedown. The car door was open, the way it is now. The battery had run down, because the door was open all night."

Tim Edmonds shook his head convulsively and covered his face with his hands. For a moment Columbo wondered if he would vomit. "I can't believe it," Edmonds whispered hoarsely.

"Does anything look odd about the body?" asked Columbo. "Anything look different?"

"What do you have in mind?"

"I don't know. That's why I'm askin' you. Just . . . does anything about him look different from what you'd expect?"

Tim forced himself to stare at the corpse for most of a minute. "Well . . . Where's his ring?" he asked.

"There's a good question. What ring?"

"Paul wore a heavy gold ring with a big diamond in it. It's missing. And— Okay, his watch is missing."

"Was that expensive jewelry, Mr. Edmonds?"

"The watch was a jeweled Vacheron Constantin."

"And that's expensive?"

"That's expensive, Lieutenant. Several thousand dollars. And the ring had to be worth several thousand. You know show-biz people. The watch was elegant. The ring was flashy. But that was Paul: a combination of the elegant and flashy. That was his personality. Is his billfold missing?"

"Right. The officers looked for that. Did he usually carry a lot of money?"

Tim Edmonds shrugged. "I never noticed that he carried more than other people carry."

"What might have been in the car that a robber would want?" asked Columbo.

"I don't know. I haven't the slightest idea."

They went back inside the house. Alicia had accompanied Martha Zimmer into the living room, where the contents of a desk were strewn about the floor. The exquisite leather-topped desk had been splintered to force it open.

Alicia sat staring at the mess. "What the devil could someone have wanted?" she asked, speaking to no one in particular.

Martha Zimmer spoke. "Aside from this . . . the desk, the perp doesn't seem to have gone into any other rooms."

"Yeah?" said Columbo.

He squatted beside the desk. It was a handsome wooden desk, not an antique but an expensive piece of office furniture in dark wood. It was one of those desks with a lock in the center drawer, and when the center drawer was locked all the drawers were locked. The wedge end of a crowbar had been pried in between the top of the center drawer and the desktop, and the wood had been broken to defeat the lock. The small crowbar was lying on the floor.

"Isn't that odd?" said Columbo. "Why would a burglar leave his crowbar here? Anyway, Martha, did you ever know of a professional housebreaker to use a crowbar? They've got a special tool: thinner, not so long, easier to hide under a coat. Right?"

"I guess I've investigated fifty housebreakings," said Martha. "I've never seen a crowbar before."

"'Course . . . Is Mrs. Badilio able to talk to us?"

"She's pretty weepy," said Martha. "But—"

Mrs. Rosa Badilio, who had been within earshot in the kitchen, had overheard the conversation and now walked into the living room. "I can answer questions," she said. Her voice was impaired by shock and weeping, but it was firm.

"You don't have to right now," said Columbo. "I just need to ask one for now."

"I can answer any," she said.

Mrs. Badilio was a Hispanic who commanded English well but spoke with an accent. She was a woman of about forty, short and plump. Her black hair had been turned a sort of reddish brown by something she put on it.

"All right. Why don't you sit down there? Now, as I understand it, you found Mr. Drury."

"Yes, sir. I come to work at eight o'clock. My husband drives me here and comes back for me in the afternoon. Mr. Drury hardly ever is out of bed by that time, so I come in with my own card that works the alarm and the locks. I let myself in through the kitchen door. Because I let myself in with a card, the alarm does not go off. As soon as I am inside, I turn off the alarm. Always then I look in the garage to see if both cars are there, which tells me if Mr. Drury is at home. Sometimes he isn't. I opened the door between the kitchen and the garage and I saw— You know what I saw."

Mrs. Badilio lowered her head and sobbed for a moment.

Columbo stared at his cigar. It had gone out. He stuffed it in a pocket of his raincoat. "Mrs. Badilio, have you noticed anything that might tell us how the murderer got into the house? Any doors open? Any windows? Did you close any door or window?"

Mrs. Badilio shook her head. "If any window had been open, the alarm would have gone off."

"Right. Okay, the desk was broken open with a crowbar, that one lying there. Do you think you ever saw that tool before?"

The woman studied the crowbar for a moment, then said, "Mr. Drury kept a few tools hanging on a pegboard in the garage. I think he had a tool like that. That could be it."

Columbo marched through the kitchen and opened the door into the garage. He strode back to the living room. He nodded. "If he had a crowbar hanging out there, it's missing."

"That's probably it, then," said Tim Edmonds. "The burglar used Paul's own crowbar to break open the desk."

"Yeah . . . What could he have been lookin' for in there?" asked Columbo.

"Computer disks," said Alicia.

"How's that?"

"Computer disks. Paul kept all his information, about everything he was doing on the show, on computer disks. The big computer at the office has the equivalent of thousands of volumes of information stored in it. But he carried a laptop computer home with him. One of the little disks out of that computer could hold as much information as a four-hundred-page book. Sometimes he copied data from the main computer onto one of those little disks, so he could read the information at home."

"And you think he had some of those disks in one of the drawers there?"

"I don't know, but he might have. So whoever killed him might have wanted those disks," she said.

"What kinda stuff might have been on one of those disks?" asked Columbo.

"Well . . . to give you an example," said Tim, "tonight he was going to do a show about smoking and health. I don't know if he had some special, damaging information he meant to disclose. You never knew for sure. He was very private about these things. You see, the secret of his success was the way he used information. He accumulated it, put it in his computer, and used a search program to pull out any fact he wanted."

"My, that's fascinatin'. We sure could use one of those machines, couldn't we, Martha? That's the way *our* business is—all kinds of facts, little details, trying to remember them all, organize them, and make some kind of sense out of them. Sorry. I run on and on. Anyway, where is this laptop computer?"

"It's either in his office," said Tim, "or was here and was stolen off this desk last night, or it's in his car."

"Mrs. Badilio," said Columbo, "I need to know if anything else is missing. Any valuables. Have you looked around any?"

"I looked at the silver," she said. "It's there. Other things . . . Little television is okay. I can't see that anything's missing."

"We looked around the house," said Martha. "No other theft is apparent."

Columbo nodded thoughtfully. He reached into his raincoat pocket, took out his cigar, stared at it, then returned it to the pocket. "'Murder most foul,'" he mumbled.

"What?"

"Oh, uh, Shakespeare wrote that. That's what this is. A

case of premeditated murder, all planned in advance and carried out according to plan."

"Then you don't think it's possible," said Tim, "that Paul simply surprised a burglar. After all, his ring and his watch were taken. And his billfold."

"That was done to make it *look* like a simple burglary," said Columbo. "I wouldn't be surprised if nothing was taken from the desk either, that the desk was broken open to make it look like the murderer came in the house lookin' for something. Anyway . . . This is what they call murder by lyin' in wait."

"What does that mean?" asked Tim.

Columbo gestured, laying out the floor plan of the garage in his own imagination, even if no one else could see it. "Mr. Drury uses his controller to open the door, right? Probably he aims the controller through the glass of the sun roof and closes the door right away. He gets out of the car and walks up to the door between the garage and the kitchen, with his card in his hand. At this point he's shot in the back of the head."

"But—"

"The light came on when the door opener was triggered," Columbo went on. "Forgive me, sir. I interrupted you."

"No. Go ahead," said Tim. "This is interesting."

"The murderer was waitin' in the garage. So why didn't Mr. Drury see him when the door went up? Because he was hidin' behind the Lamborghini. When the door came rumbling down again, making a lot of noise, he scurried across the back of the two cars and came around the left side of the Mercedes. Mr. Drury's attention was all fixed on gettin' the card into the slot. Maybe he'd had a little to drink and had to fix his attention hard on that. The murderer gets right up behind him and shoots him in the back of the head. Then, just to make sure, he shoots him a second time."

"And why wasn't this a burglar, maybe somebody who'd seen Paul's expensive jewelry?"

"Because somebody got in with a plastic card," said Alicia. "Otherwise the alarm system would have gone off. Which makes suspects of everybody who knew him well enough to have had access to a card. It makes *me* a suspect, because I once had a card. That puts me in a very limited little group, doesn't it, Lieutenant?"

"Oh, no, ma'am. Not really. No matter how sophisticated a security system, a clever criminal can find a way to break it—steal a card, bribe somebody at the security company, and so on. On the other hand, I suppose I should say, yeah, you're inside a *very big* circle of suspects. Everybody who worked with him and could have had business problems—"

"Meaning me," snapped Tim.

Columbo shrugged. "No offense, sir. You see, what I gotta do is eliminate all the possibilities. All of 'em. If I don't, somebody'll say I didn't investigate right. I mean, maybe you wouldn't mind tellin' me where you were last night."

"Alicia—that is, Mrs. Drury—and I had dinner at Cocina Roberto."

"Uh-huh," said Columbo, scribbling a note. "Cocina . . . Roberto. Mexican place, huh? I bet they make good chili."

"I . . . don't know, Lieutenant. I never ordered it."

"Oh. Well, anyway, what time did you get there and what time did you leave?"

"We got there a little after eleven-thirty and left a little after one."

Columbo made a note. "'A little after eleven-thirty . . .' How long's the drive from here to Cocina Roberto?"

"I'd guess twenty minutes to half an hour."

"'Twenty . . .' Okay, I don't have to hold you folks up any longer. I'll be stoppin' by your office later."

As Alicia and Tim walked down the driveway under a shared umbrella, Tim chuckled. "What a dolt! If we could have picked a detective to investigate this case, we couldn't have done better than him."

"Did you see the body?" Alicia asked quietly.

"It doesn't look any different."

"You're right about the detective. I checked to see if he had his shoes on the right feet."

"Uh, Mr. Edmonds! Mrs. Drury!"

They looked around. The unkempt detective was trotting down the driveway after them, without an umbrella. By the time he caught up his face already gleamed with water.

"Sorry. I'm sorry to trouble you, but I need to clear up one little point. Nothin' . . . Just one little thing."

"Certainly, Lieutenant," said Tim with feigned patience.

"Thank ya. Let's see. The show went off the air at nine-thirty. Right? And you arrived at Cocina Roberto a little after eleven-thirty? Can you tell me where you were those two hours? Just one of those little things I'm supposed to get into my notes."

Tim glanced at Alicia. "Well, Lieutenant," he said, "I guess we can count on you to be discreet, can't we? The truth is, Mrs. Drury and I are . . . How shall we say?"

"Say we're in love, Tim," said Alicia, tightening her arm around Tim's waist. "Everyone knows, Lieutenant. It's happened since the divorce, and everyone understands that, too."

"So we drove out to Blocker Beach," said Tim. "You

understand? For privacy . . . And we, uh . . . You understand."

"You, uh—"

"Right. Okay?"

"Sure. Okay. I didn't mean to intrude on your privacy.
That fills everything in as far as you're concerned, and I
probably won't have to ask you anything more."

FOUR

"You got a call waiting, Lieutenant," said Dugan, the uniformed officer on the driveway, as soon as Columbo had watched Alicia and Tim drive away in a black Porsche.

Columbo walked over to the black and white patrol car. He sat down inside and picked up the microphone. "You callin' Columbo?"

"Is this Lieutenant Columbo?" asked the dispatcher.

"Yeah."

"Please call 555–2147. That's 555–2147."

"Okay."

Back inside the house, Columbo went to the kitchen phone and punched in the number.

"Attorneys Dunn and McCrory."

"Hi-ya. This is Lieutenant Columbo, Los Angeles Police. I had a message to call this number."

"Oh yes, Lieutenant. Mr. McCrory would like to speak with you. One moment, please."

Columbo pulled the cold cigar from his raincoat pocket and this time lit it, judging this would be the last time for it and he'd have to buy some cigars sometime this morning.

"Lieutenant Columbo? This is Bill McCrory. Headquarters told me you are in charge of the investigation into the death of Paul Drury. I have a little piece of information that might be helpful."

"Information is the name of the game, sir. We'll be grateful for anything ya got."

"Okay. Briefly, I was Paul's lawyer—not on everything but on matters involving Paul Drury Productions. I heard of his death on my car radio as I was driving in this morning. When I got in the office, I checked the recorder I keep on a separate private line here. There was a phone message from Paul, asking me to call him first thing this morning. Okay? The important thing is, my phone recorder time-stamps all the messages. This one is time-stamped eleven forty-seven last night. The news story on the radio said the time of his death wasn't clear. Well— He was alive at eleven forty-seven."

Columbo frowned and shifted his cigar to the left corner of his mouth. "That's very helpful, sir. That's very helpful."

"Paul Drury was not just a client, Lieutenant. He was a friend. If there's anything I can do to help solve the mystery surrounding his death, please call on me."

"Could I do that? Would you mind if I came by your office?"

"Why, not at all. When would you like to come?"

"I'm just about finished here at the house. For now. Would it be inconvenient if I came by, say, in the next half hour?"

"That will be fine, Lieutenant."

Dunn & McCrory occupied offices on the top floor of a glass office cube on Wilshire Boulevard. When Columbo arrived there, the rain had stopped, and his plastic car cover was in the trunk. He stopped half a block away, ran into a newsstand, and bought a breast-pocket package of cigars. When he reached the reception room at Dunn & McCrory he was puffing contentedly on a fresh cigar.

"You're Lieutenant Columbo?" the secretary-receptionist asked skeptically.

"Yes, ma'am," he said, showing his badge. "Columbo, LAPD. Mr. McCrory is expecting me."

She took him into the office and introduced him.

McCrory's office was a veritable grove, decorated with a dozen big potted plants plus a fifty-five-gallon saltwater aquarium in which colorful fish swam in a jungle of white coral. The desk was kidney-shaped: glass top on glass pedestals.

"Well, this is certainly a beautiful office y' got here, sir," said Columbo, looking around. "It must be restful to work in this kind of an atmosphere—I mean, with all the plants and the fish, just like bein' outdoors, except it doesn't rain in here."

"That's exactly the point, Lieutenant," said McCrory. "It reduces tension."

Columbo walked over to peer into the aquarium and did not see the skeptical shrug McCrory gave his secretary before she closed the office door. She returned the shrug, putting a finger to her upper breast to signal that she had seen the man's badge, otherwise she would not have brought so tousled and eccentric a character into his office.

"I wish Mrs. Columbo could see this aquarium. She loves this kinda stuff, but she can hardly keep a goldfish alive. Hasn't got a green thumb for it, as you might say."

"Maybe it's the cigar smoke, Lieutenant," said McCrory.

"Huh? Oh, sorry," said Columbo, turning away from the tank and stepping toward a chair. "Y' mean I shouldn't blow smoke around the fish. I see your point. Well. I don't want to take too much of your time." Reluctantly, he crushed the fire out of the cigar, in a heavy glass ashtray, and shoved the still-warm butt into his raincoat pocket.

McCrory was an apple-cheeked man with thinning blond hair. He wore a blue-and-white-checked jacket over a yellow golf shirt, with butter-yellow slacks. He didn't look like a lawyer. That was explained by the photographs on his walls: of show-business personalities, who had autographed their portraits. He was a show-biz lawyer.

"Let me play my phone-recorder tape for you," he said. He stood and bent over the machine.

Columbo leaned forward and watched as the lawyer pressed buttons and started the somewhat complex telephone-answering machine.

"You see, Lieutenant, I keep a private line here in my office, so clients with something confidential on their minds can call me without even going through the receptionist or my secretary. Only a few people have the number. When I have a client in the office, I just turn down the volume on the thing, and it answers the phone and records the message without the client sitting across my desk hearing anything. It's on twenty-four hours a day and seven days a week. Here's what I heard this morning—"

The first voice from the machine was that of Paul Drury. *"Hi. This is Paul. Make a point of calling me first thing in the ay-em, please. Kind of important."*

Then a mechanical voice from the machine said, *"This message received at . . . eleven . . . forty . . . seven . . . P.M. Wednesday . . . June . . . two."*

Columbo nodded. "And that was his voice, for sure?"

"For sure," said McCrory.

"Well, that's interestin'. The medical examiner's preliminary finding is that Mr. Drury died before midnight. Eleven forty-seven. That cuts it pretty close."

McCrory shrugged. "The machine's accurate, Lieutenant. At least it always has been."

"Look, I know those tapes have to be expensive. But would you mind letting me take that one . . . as evidence?"

"Not at all."

As McCrory fumbled with the machine, finding the way to remove the incoming-messages tape, Columbo frowned and ran a hand through his hair. "Can you think of any reason why anyone would want Mr. Drury dead?" he asked.

"Lots of people wanted Paul Drury dead," said McCrory. "I'm quite sure he never blackmailed anybody, but he made public a lot of information certain people did not want made public."

"F'r instance."

"Do you remember when Orange International tried to take over Smathers Petroleum? Orange offered every Smathers stockholder a share of Orange for a share of Smathers, plus a bonus of $12.75 a share. Remember?"

"Uh . . . I don't follow the stock market, sir."

"Well. Paul Drury did a show about Orange International. He showed that a share of Orange plus the $12.75 was a bad deal for a share of Smathers. I mean, the Orange officers had inflated salaries and perks, plus golden parachutes. What was more, Orange had a huge potential liability arising from an oil spill. Paul dramatized all this on a show about the disastrous securities manipulations of the eighties. The Smathers stockholders saw the show, didn't accept the Orange offer, and the takeover collapsed."

"Isn't that interestin' . . ." said Columbo as he accepted from McCrory the tape he had finally managed to remove from the machine.

"It gets still more interesting," said McCrory. "Guess who *did* take over Smathers."

"I'm afraid I wouldn't know."

"Bell Explorations. See the connection?"

"No, sir, I'm afraid I don't."

McCrory smiled tolerantly. "Charles Bell, the chairman of the board of Bell Explorations, is the chief stockholder of Paul Drury Productions."

"Oh! I get it. You figure he used the Drury show to shoot down the Orange bid so he could pick up Smathers for himself."

"Exactly. I'm not sure Paul understood it at first. I imagine he really thought he was doing a show along the lines of the Milken-Boesky market manipulation story."

"But would the Smathers people hate him enough to kill him?" asked Columbo.

"Probably not. But tonight he was going to do a show on the hazards of cigarette smoking. There are people in the tobacco industry who are capable of murder."

"What about things closer to him, that *I'm* capable of understandin'? Like, what was the cause of the divorce?"

"Only that they should never have married in the first

place," said McCrory. "Paul had a big ego. He was promiscuous. Another possibility— A jealous husband. A jealous boyfriend."

"But Mrs. Drury, she—"

"She got a generous settlement. Anyway, she and Tim Edmonds are a pair. But Alicia is no angel, Lieutenant. She's an addictive gambler. She may be something worse."

"I'm afraid I'm going to have to ask ya to spell that out, sir."

"There are stories that she is—or was—mob-connected. Rumors. I can't substantiate them. But there are stories."

"Are you thinkin' that maybe the death of Paul Drury was a mob hit?" asked Columbo.

"I couldn't say that. I'm suggesting a line of inquiry."

Columbo rose. "I sure do thank ya, Mr. McCrory. I won't take any more of your time right now. I'll return your tape as soon as possible."

McCrory came around his desk and extended his hand. "Don't worry about the tape," he said. "And call anytime." He reached past Columbo and opened the door.

"Thank ya. Thank ya," said Columbo. He stepped out into the reception room. "Oh. Just one more thing. One little thing kinda bothers me. Why would Mr. Drury call you at eleven forty-seven? He didn't expect to find you here, did he?"

McCrory turned up his palms. "I don't know. Maybe it was just something on his mind. Maybe he was afraid he'd forget it."

"Umm. Did he ever do that before? I mean, did he leave messages on your recorder late at night?"

"Once or twice before, I guess."

"Well, thank ya, sir. Thank ya. I'll try not to bother you

any more. I know your time is valuable. And, uh, I'd appreciate it if you didn't tell anybody else about the call and the tape."

The offices of Paul Drury Productions and of Tim Edmonds Productions were in another square glass office building, this one on La Cienega, only two blocks from the studio where the show had been done. Though the rain had stopped and the sun was hot, Columbo still wore his raincoat.

As he walked from the parking lot to the front entrance of the office building, he hummed a tune under his breath. He didn't know what it was called, but the words that passed through his mind as he hummed were—

> *This old man, he played one.*
> *He played nick-nack on my thumb.*
> *With a nick-nack patty-whack,*
> *Give a dog a bone.*
> *This old man came rolling home.*

He had something else on his mind as he rode up in the elevator: that he was glad he was a homicide detective and not one of the laborers in one of these faceless, graceless buildings. There was another song. How'd it go? "And they're all made of ticky-tacky and they all look alike." This one was made of green glass, as about half of them were. That was the only way they differed: green glass or smoky glass. Columbo had worked hard to get the job he had, and the struggle had been worth it, even if it just kept him from having to work in one of these cubes.

"We thought you'd be here before we were," Tim Edmonds said in the reception area of Paul Drury Productions.

"Oh, I had another call to make," said Columbo.

"Well, who would you like to see?"

"Anybody. I don't want to be too much trouble. I know everybody has to be feelin' awful."

"Well, maybe you'd better talk to Karen Bergman. She may have been the last person to see Paul alive. You can use Paul's office. I'll send her in."

Paul Drury's office was dominated by a huge desk, some eight feet long and five wide. The top and the vertical panels were of green marble. The desk was absolutely uncluttered. Green leather boxes with lids contained, apparently, the papers he had been currently working on. A pen-and-pencil set sat on the front of the desk. A computer monitor and keyboard sat at each end of the desk, and Columbo was amazed to see that holes had been drilled through the marble for the cables that obviously connected to the computers out of sight below. The floor of the office was of a green marble similar to that of the desktop. Couches and chairs sat on oriental rugs laid on the marble. Behind the desk the marble was bare, so Drury could wheel his chair from one end of his desk to the other.

The walls were white and were covered with autographed portraits of scores of celebrated people: every President of the past twenty years, senators, governors, judges, actors, actresses, singers, dancers, and "personalities." Other photos sat in frames on the credenza behind the desk. These were nudes. Columbo recognized Alicia Drury. Her picture, in black and white, was dramatically lighted and even somewhat modest for a nude. Others were not modest at all.

At one end of the room stood a wooden statue of Drury. It was rough, as if it had been carved with an axe, but it was an accurate and not unflattering caricature, though oddly discordant in this room.

The room seemed to be divided into two conference areas, each with a couch and chairs, one set in light-brown leather, one in black. Apparently two meetings could be held in the office at the same time—even three if some people gathered around Drury's desk.

"Lieutenant Columbo."

He turned around and faced a small attractive blonde. "Miss Bergman?"

"Yes. Won't you sit down?"

He chose a chair facing the light-brown couch, and she sat down on the couch. Her tight black skirt crept back, exposing six inches of her legs above her knees. He noticed, but his attention was fixed more on her face. It was puffy. She had been crying.

"Uh . . . Mr. Edmonds suggests you may have been the last person to see Mr. Drury alive. Other than the murderer, of course."

"I may have been."

"Why don't you just tell me. Your way."

The young woman shrugged. "It's the usual story," she said sadly. "Trying to make a career in this rotten business. I slept with Paul. But there was more to it than just that. I really cared for him. I know he cared for me, a little. Last night—"

"Tell me about last night," said Columbo, pulling out his notebook, checking his pockets for a pencil, finding one at last.

"We went to dinner. At La Felicità. Paul was very strung-out, very tired. I don't know if you'll understand this, but Paul would lose three or four pounds while he was on the air. In an hour. Sweat. He'd gain it back as he took in fluids again, but when he came off the set he was dehydrated and exhausted. Last night more than usual. I offered to go home with him after dinner and help him relax. He begged off, saying we'd spend the weekend together. He didn't even drive me home. He called a cab for me."

"What time was that, ma'am?"

Karen frowned at Columbo's word "ma'am." "Quarter to eleven, about. I remember saying, My God, it's not even eleven o'clock."

"And you never saw him again."

She shook her head.

"He said he was too tired to drive you home, said he was too tired to . . . How should I say it?"

"You don't have to say it. We know what I mean. He was too tired even for that. I mean—"

"How far is it from this restaurant where you ate to his house?"

"Uh . . . Say twenty minutes' drive. To take me home he'd have had to drive twenty minutes more each way, which would have made an hour for him to get home. That's why he called a cab."

"So he could have been home by eleven-oh-five, eleven-ten?"

"Sure."

"And if he was as tired as he said, he could have been in bed asleep by eleven-fifteen, eleven-twenty."

"Right."

"Well, Miss Bergman, he made a telephone call at eleven forty-seven. To his lawyer."

"I don't believe it."

"He reached one of these answering machines that makes a note of what time it is when a call comes in. The machine says he called his lawyer at eleven forty-seven."

"From where?"

"Well, of course we don't know."

"There's something damned screwball here, Lieutenant," said Karen Bergman. "Paul was a fraud in a lot of ways. But I knew him pretty well. He was *tired!* He couldn't fake that with me. Besides, he wasn't a man to turn down what I was offering—"

"Unless he had an appointment to meet somebody," Columbo suggested.

"Another woman . . . ?"

"Well, I wouldn't say that, ma'am. But I'd give a lot to know what happened between, say, quarter to eleven when he left you and eleven forty-seven when he called his lawyer and said he wanted to talk about something important first thing in the morning."

"A whole hour," she said.

"That's the point," said Columbo. "And then, according to the medical examiner, he died within forty-five minutes at most after he made that call."

"By twelve-thirty . . ."

"What's more, he almost certainly didn't make the call from home. Because he was killed in his garage, with the card that works the locks on his house in his hand. He'd just come home, it looks like."

"Between eleven forty-seven and twelve-thirty," she said. She shook her head vehemently. "No. There's something screwball. It's not like Paul. He wouldn't have—" She stopped. "Unless I didn't know him at all."

"Miss Bergman, I'm gonna ask you not to tell anybody about the eleven forty-seven call."

"All right. But I tell you there's something screwball about it."

Columbo reached into his raincoat pocket and took out the cigar he had allowed to become cold. He struck a match and lit it. "Ma'am," he said, "I was wonderin' if you know anything about a little computer Mr. Drury carried around. What they call a laptop."

"Yes. It's a Zeos notebook computer."

"Where is that little computer now, do you know?"

She shook her head again. "The last time I saw it, it was in the car."

"When was that?"

"Last night. When we went into dinner at La Felicità, he shoved it under the seat. He always shoved it under the seat when he left it in the car. Sometimes he locked it in the trunk, but usually he just shoved it under the seat. He trusted the valet parker at La Felicità."

"Would there have been information stored in that computer?"

"Absolutely. A lot of information. He had a sixty-megabyte hard disk in that computer. Sixty megabytes would be something like seventy-five to a hundred books, depending on how fat they are."

"That much! I wish Mrs. Columbo could see a machine like that. She took a night course at the university about computers, got very interested in 'em. Sixty-five— All the information he had on some subject could have been in that little computer."

"A *copy*, Lieutenant. Just a copy. He kept all the original files in the computers under his desk. The disk drives in those two could hold twenty times as much."

"Twenty times! Two thousand volumes. Four thousand."

"No. *Two* thousand. The two computers were what the technicians call redundant. That is to say, they backed up each other. If something happened to one, the information would be in the other."

"Where are the files? I mean, where are the papers with all this information?"

Karen Bergman shook her head. "There is no paper," she said. "Oh, there are probably some notes lying around, plus some photographs; but Paul saw no reason to store a warehouse full of crumbling paper. With redundancy, he saw no need to keep paper. He was scornful of people who filled file drawers."

"Interestin' . . . Tell me, ma'am, do you know how to run this system?"

She nodded. "I did a lot of research for him."

Columbo pointed toward one of the computer terminals on the marble-top desk. "Uh— Would you mind showin' me how it works?"

She rose from the couch, walked behind Drury's desk, and switched on the power on one of the monitors. "The computers are up twenty-four hours a day," she said. "The technicians tell us that's better for them than being powered up and powered down all the time. We do power the monitors down overnight to save the screens. They haven't been powered up yet today, for obvious reasons."

Columbo came around and stood behind her.

The monitor, which looked much like a television screen, though the resolution on it was immeasurably finer, came to life, at first greenish and dull, then in brilliant colors.

The young woman typed CD/FOLIO. For most of a minute the screen was blank, while a grinding sound rose from the computer under the desk. Then a message appeared on the screen—

GENERAL SYSTEM FAILURE READING DRIVE C:
ABORT, RETRY, FAIL?

Karen Bergman snatched up a telephone and punched a number. "Geraldo, get in here! I'm in Paul's office, and I'm getting a system-failure message on the number-one computer. I'm going to try number two."

The technician was in the office before the second system displayed the same message. He took Drury's chair and struggled with both computers while the young woman paced the office.

"Is this somethin' serious?" Columbo asked.

"His life's work . . ." she whispered. "My God! All the information about the Kennedy assassination! A whole *library* of irreplaceable information about the Kennedy assassination!"

After five minutes of nervous key-tapping, the technician leaned back in defeat, closed his eyes, and blew a loud sigh through a wide-open mouth.

"Geraldo . . . ?"

"The hard disks have been *wiped,*" the technician muttered. "You know what that means? If the data had just been erased, we could have recovered most of it. But this was a wipedisk, the way the CIA and Defense Department erase disks: so you can't ever get back what was on them. There's not a *byte* of data left in either of these computers."

FIVE

I

They sat at a lunch table in the bar at the Topanga
Beach Club—Alicia, Tim, and Bell. It was a country club
without golf, having instead an olympic-size pool with
diving bay, tennis courts, squash courts, and a bowling
green—all overlooking but separated by a wall from the
public beach. The lunch tables had a view of the ocean. Bell,
who had not been at the office, was wearing lemon-yellow
slacks and a pale blue polo shirt carrying the club initials,
TBC.

"Boy! Boy! Busboy!"

Charles Bell snapped his fingers at the young man
hurrying toward his table.

"Yes, sir?"

"Clear these empty glasses. And we want more popcorn.
And tell our waiter we want another round of drinks."

"Yes, sir."

Bell shook his head at Alicia and Tim. "Service gets
worse here every year," he said. "A few years ago we had
blacks, but I guess they're all out mugging people and
selling drugs. At least they could be taught to serve a table
properly. Do you see *anything* on this menu that appeals?"

The busboy—Korean perhaps, or Vietnamese—acted as

if he did not hear any of this and hurried to clear the table.

"It would be appropriate, Charles," said Alicia, "if you looked a little bit distressed. After all, our good friend is dead."

"Murdered," added Tim.

"There's no way to replace him," said Alicia. "The show simply won't go on the air tonight. They're running an old *Beverly Hillbillies,* followed by a *Sanford.*"

"After an appropriate announcement," said Tim. "I taped that before I left the office."

"All right," said Charles. "It came off perfectly. He's dead. The data bases are gone. I made the call that activated the virus after you didn't call to say you'd failed. You *did* get the laptop?"

"I got it," said Tim.

"What'd you do with it?"

"Smashed it open with a hammer. Got the disks out. Smashed them to bits with the same hammer, on my garage floor. Ground the bits through the garbage disposal in the kitchen."

Bell smiled. "Overkill."

"Please . . ." murmured Alicia.

"Did you find the key?"

"Yes, but . . ."

"But?"

"The envelope has the box number on it," said Tim. "But not the name of the bank. The key is stamped MOSLEY, which is the vault manufacturer. We know he had a box, but we don't know in what bank."

"It doesn't make much difference," said Bell. "You got the key, so the police may not know he had a box. We couldn't have used the key ourselves and opened it, because we couldn't have duplicated his signature. In any case, in the absence of the information erased from his disks, the photos in the deposit box are nothing but a lot of snapshots."

"I hope you're right," murmured Alicia.

"What'd you do with the pistol?"

"What we said we'd do," Tim answered. "It went into the trunk of a Buick waiting to be smashed in the hydraulic press. I went by the junkyard this morning to make sure the Buick had been squashed. It had been. It's on a flatcar now, with fifty other smashed-down cars, on its way to be melted at a steel mill. The pistol will get melted along with the rest of it."

"What time did you get home?" asked Bell.

"Four-fifteen," said Tim. "I don't like that part of it. The Los Angeles detective on the case already asked where we were between the time we left the studio and the time we got to Cocina Roberto."

"What did you tell him?"

"I told him we were out on the beach doing you-know-what. He seemed to buy that okay. I wouldn't want him asking where we were between one-twenty and four-fifteen."

"Romantic drive in the mountains," said Bell. "Parked. Went to sleep in each other's arms. You don't have to prove where you were. *They* have to prove where you were."

Their waiter approached carrying a tray with another round of drinks.

"We'll order," said Bell brusquely.

"Yes, sir."

"I'll have the open-faced fried shrimp sandwich. I assume that's with ginger mayonnaise."

"Yes, sir. And would you care for a chilled white wine?"

"Definitely. Choose one for us. Something very dry."

"Yes, sir."

"I'll have the same," said Alicia.

"Yes," said Tim. "I will, too. But bring us also an order of the roasted zucchini with yogurt, to share."

The waiter bowed and hurried away.

"The detective," said Bell. "You say he's an idiot?"

Alicia grinned. "Charles, you wouldn't believe it!"

Columbo crushed crackers into his bowl of chili. He had ordered extra crackers.

"Listen," he said to Martha Zimmer, "you gotta know where to go to get chili like this. You can't get it just anyplace. I don't know what they do, how they do it . . . I just know they make it *great!* I come from N' York, you know. You can't get chili like this in N' York. Not that I ever saw. I s'pose it's the Mexican influence. The Mexicans prob'ly know the secret of it. I don't get it at home. Mrs. Columbo, she tries, but she can't get it right like this. Y' gotta come to a place like this to get the great chili."

He picked up his bottle of root beer and took a swig.

Martha wasn't having chili, said it gave her heartburn. She took a great bite from the mustard-covered hotdog she had ordered and nodded at Columbo's dissertation on the chili.

"The man from the alarm company ever show up?"

"Umm-hmm."

"Have anything to say?"

Martha chewed for half a minute, then swallowed. "He checked it all over. The alarm system was working fine. Those people are no amateurs. He said the only way anybody could have gotten into that house was with one of those magnetic cards."

"How'd it work exactly?"

"You put the card in the slot in the fake mailbox. The machine read the magnetic numbers and then waited for you to punch in four more numbers. If you did it right, that disabled the alarm system for three minutes, which was enough time to get to a door and do it again, so's to get inside. After you got inside, the system would reactivate itself, but that didn't make any difference so long as you didn't bump an outside door or a window. It's a motion detector outside and a peripheral system inside."

"Could somebody have swiped one of Drury's cards temporarily and have had a copy made?"

"Not likely but not impossible. But it wouldn't do you any good unless you knew the other four numbers. There's no such thing maybe as an absolutely secure system, but this one comes close."

"Figures. The guy was obsessed with security, it looks like."

"Officer Rose, responding to the call from Mrs. Badilio, set off the alarm by pounding on the front door with his nightstick."

"Yeah?"

"Anyway, it was no robbery, you know," said Martha. "No burglary. The perp came to kill Drury, plain and simple."

Columbo nodded.

"The perp took his billfold and ring and watch to make it

look like robbery. And I wonder if he didn't break open that desk and scatter the papers for the same reason."

"Whatta you figure's the motive?" asked Columbo.

"To stop a show he was gonna do sometime soon," she said. "To stop him from exposing something."

"You got it figured. All his computer data banks were erased last night. Plus, the murderer stole a little laptop computer out of his car."

"What's next, Columbo? Whatta you want me to do this afternoon?"

"Check with the Bureau of Motor Vehicles and find out all you can about three cars: Edmonds's, Mrs. Drury's, and Bergman's. Drive to Bergman's apartment and see how long it takes to drive from there to La Felicità and from there to Drury's house. Also, see how long it takes to drive from Cocina Roberto to Drury's house. Check with Roberto and see when Mr. Edmonds and Mrs. Drury came and when they left."

"Okay. Oh listen, Columbo. I got a message for you. Captain Sczciegel says to tell you you absolutely have to get over to the police range and requalify with the pistol, which you're six months overdue on doing."

"First thing I'll have to do is find that revolver. I guess it's gotta be in the house someplace. Hid it, you know. Always hid it, so the kids wouldn't get to it. I think it's in the top of the guest-room closet. Maybe Mrs. Columbo knows where it is."

"Sczciegel's serious."

"Yeah. Listen, Martha, maybe you could give me a lesson or two with the thing. I don't wanta shoot myself in the foot."

"Sure. We can go someplace and pot bottles."

"I'd appreciate it."

"You on your way to visit the corpse?" asked Martha.

"I don't see any way to get out of it," said Columbo.

Columbo did not like to go to the morgue. He did not like to see bodies cleaned up and laid out for autopsy. It was bad enough seeing them lying where they were found, but seeing them in the morgue was worse. The only worse thing was seeing them all made up and laid out in caskets.

"Would ya mind not doin' that for a few minutes, Doc?"

Dr. Harold Culp had the electric bone saw in hand and was about to open the body of Paul Drury, from throat to crotch. He smiled wryly. "I didn't know you were squeamish, Columbo."

"I just ate an awful good bowl of chili, an' I don't wanta leave it here on the floor. I mean, if you can spare a minute—"

"Sure," said the doctor, and he switched off the whining little saw.

"You find anything surprising?" Columbo asked. "Anything you didn't expect?"

Dr. Culp put his hands on his hips and stared at the corpse for a moment. The naked body lay on its back. It was wet. The doctor and his assistant had just hosed it down again, to wash off blood and other fluids, which had run down the drain in the autopsy table. The head had been opened and the pieces of skull pushed back into their approximate original positions, so that the head looked like a cantaloupe that had been dropped and unskillfully put back together.

The doctor reached for a stainless-steel bowl on the wheeled table and handed it to Columbo. "There are your bullets," he said. "Twenty-two hollow points."

The little bullets were totally deformed and looked like irregular lumps of lead, with only tiny cylindrical tails showing what had been the rear end of each and what the caliber had been. The noses had been cast with short round holes in them, so the bullets would do just what they had done: spread open and deform, tearing bigger holes than they would have done if they were not hollow-point slugs.

"One bullet went in through the occipital lobe, through the parietal lobe, and into the corpus callosum. The angle was about twenty degrees below horizontal."

"Umm . . ." Columbo muttered. "That suggests whoever shot him wasn't as tall as he was."

"He's six feet five," said the doctor. "Not many people are as tall as he was."

"Okay. Whoever shot him wasn't as tall as he was but wasn't an awful lot shorter. Right?"

"I would guess whoever shot him was six feet tall."

"Yeah. That pretty much eliminates one suspect," said Columbo.

"Hmm?"

"A young woman. Cute little thing. For her to have shot Drury in the back of the head, she'd have had to hold the gun above her eyes."

"Okay. I'll guess that was the first shot. The second shot went in through the temporal lobe, up through the limbic lobe, and all the way into the frontal lobe. The angle of that penetration was sixty degrees above horizontal. My guess would be that when the first shot hit him, he began to fall and maybe paused with his head against the door, and when the second shot hit him his head was bent forward, his chin maybe all the way down to his chest."

Columbo turned down the corners of his mouth and ran his hand across his hair. "Those two shots must have scrambled his brains," he said with a sigh.

Dr. Culp nodded. "I see a lot of head wounds. I always hate them. The greatest thing in the world, the brain; and to see it torn apart like this— Well . . . I hate it, Columbo. I just goddamn hate it."

"No other wounds on him? Bruises?"

"No."

"Okay . . . I don't wanta stay and watch you do this, but when you get him open will you be able to make a judgment about how long his food had been in him? I mean, the state of digestion. He left the restaurant where he had dinner about a quarter to eleven. Will you be able to tell how far digestion had progressed?"

"Right. I can give you a pretty good estimate."

Columbo nodded. "What I figured. I think I'll leave you to that wonderful work."

Dr. Culp grinned. "Suit yourself. What'd he have to eat, y' know?"

"I can ask."

Dr. Culp's grin broadened. "I can find out before you can."

"Yeah. So good luck. I— Oh. There is one more thing. Can you tell me how long it had been since he had a sexual experience? I mean an orgasm."

"No. I can tell you if he ejaculated within the last few hours of his life."

"I'd like to know."

"Well, hold on, you squeamish bastard. I can tell you in two minutes. Just hang on. Help me turn him over, Eduardo."

With the assistance of the morgue attendant, Dr. Culp turned the body facedown. As Columbo stood back and averted his eyes, Dr. Culp forced the stiff legs of the body apart and made a small, neat incision. Drained of blood, the body did not bleed.

"Here y'are, Columbo. Seminal vesicles. Full. An ejaculation empties them, or mostly so. Then the testes fill them again, but that takes a while, as most of us know, to our sorrow." He shook his head. "I don't think Mr. Drury had sex in the last few hours of his life."

"Thanks, Doc."

Columbo returned to the offices of Paul Drury Productions, and once more, they gave him Drury's big, handsomely furnished office as his investigation headquarters.

Tim Edmonds led him into the office. "I didn't expect to see you again today, Lieutenant," he said.

"Well, I didn't want to bother you again today, sir; but, y' see, I'm an untidy person, one of those people that just can't get organized, and I can't seem to, in one visit, get all the stuff I need. And this morning I forgot to ask you if you could give me a list of the shows that would have been done over the next few weeks, maybe months, if Mr. Drury hadn't been murdered."

"I see. You think maybe someone killed him to prevent his revealing something on the air?"

Columbo fished a half-smoked cigar from his raincoat

pocket and began to search other pockets for a match. "That's one of the lines of inquiry I have to pursue," he said. "It's obvious he wasn't killed by a burglar, so I have to look for another motive."

"'Obvious' he— Is it really so obvious, Lieutenant?"

"Oh, yeah. I mean, I could tick off on my fingers the reasons why it wasn't a burglar. But *you* know. You're smart enough to see that right away."

Columbo sat down. Edmonds remained standing, leaning against Paul Drury's marble-top desk.

"Well, uh, you're an experienced police detective, so I guess what's obvious to you isn't so obvious to me. But I can of course give you the list. I suppose the fact that all his files were erased out of the two computers is pretty persuasive that it was no simple robbery."

"Right. Did anybody ever *threaten* to kill him?"

Tim nodded and showed a weak smile. "About four times a week, on average."

"Did he keep any record of those threats?"

"Yes, he did. In the computer."

"No paper copies?"

"Paul laughed at people who kept paper files. He said one time you might as well chisel your records on rocks as—"

"But what happened could happen."

"That's right, Lieutenant. But if he'd kept paper files, someone could have poured kerosene in all the file drawers and struck a match."

"Speaking of a match—"

"There's a lighter on the table."

Columbo used the lighter. "Seems like a man's life got erased," he said thoughtfully.

"No clues, Lieutenant?"

"Oh, lots and lots of clues. Just gotta put 'em together."

"Is there any other way I can help you, Lieutenant?"

"Well, maybe I ought to talk to Mrs. Drury. Maybe to Miss Bergman. I'm afraid I'm makin' a pest of myself, but I—"

"Not at all, Lieutenant Columbo. Don't think of it that way. Our time is yours. Anything we can do to help you find out who killed Paul, we'll gladly do. I'll tell Alicia you want to see her."

Columbo was scribbling a note to himself when Alicia Drury came in. His wife had asked him to pick up a tub of I Can't Believe It's Not Butter on his way home and he didn't want to forget. Alicia Drury was wearing a black dress. That was not what she had been wearing earlier, and Columbo guessed she had gone home and changed into mourning. She sat down where Karen Bergman had sat when Columbo interviewed her just before noon, and she lit a cigarette.

"I'm sorry to be bothering you again, Mrs. Drury, but there are some things I've gotta clear up."

"Of course."

"Since it's clear enough that Mr. Drury was not killed by a burglar, I've gotta find another motive. Lookin' at the shows coming up, can you think of anything he might have been gettin' ready to reveal that—"

"Someone would kill him to prevent," she finished his sentence.

"That's what I've got in mind."

"Let's face facts, Lieutenant. Paul was not an investigative reporter. Virtually everything he used came from published sources. Occasionally something came up in a letter or a phone call—I mean, some new information. What was unique about his show was the way he *used* information, brought it up out of the computer and related this to that, something else to something more, and made a picture. He was . . . a *clarifier*. Then a publicist. He was also a great tooter of his own horn."

"I see."

"Of course—" She shrugged as she tapped ash off her cigarette. "'He who tooteth not his own horn, the same shall not be tooted.'"

Columbo grinned. "Who said that, ma'am?"

"John L. Lewis."

"Really? Isn't that interestin'? Are you saying Mr. Drury was really no expert on the Kennedy assassination?"

"He was a cataloger of facts. He did no research on his own."

"But he was there when the assassination happened."

Alicia shook her head. "He was on Houston Street, at the corner of Houston and Elm. He got a very good look at the President when the car slowed down to make that sharp turn onto Elm. But when the shots were fired, there were trees between him and the car. He heard shots. He didn't see anything. By the time he ran through the crowd and got over to Elm, the limousine was through the underpass and out of sight, on its way to the hospital. I have no doubt he was moved emotionally, and he would never forget the experience, but he was not a witness to the assassination. He all but made his career out of saying he was a witness, but he wasn't. Men tell the truth in bed, Lieutenant."

Columbo nodded. "Don't they just? Anyway . . . I've still gotta look for somebody with motive to—"

William Harrington

"There are plenty of nuts, Lieutenant. He got a lot of threats. A nut—"

"No, ma'am," said Columbo, shaking his head.

"What?"

"It couldn't have been a nut, ma'am. The murder was carefully planned and meticulously carried out. Whoever killed Mr. Drury had a card that worked his alarm system and unlocked his doors."

"As I told you, I once had a card. You should check with McCrory, Paul's lawyer. I handed over my card on the day I moved out, in McCrory's presence."

"Whoever killed Mr. Drury had been in the house before," said Columbo. "He knew where to find the crowbar. I mean, you'd look for tools in the cellar, wouldn't you? Not in the garage."

"I don't know, Lieutenant. I guess I find that conclusion a little bit facile."

"Too easy? Well, maybe so, maybe so."

Alicia Drury dragged hard on her cigarette, then crushed it in an ashtray—having gotten only four or five such deep, hard drags from it. "Just as a matter of information, Lieutenant Columbo," she said crisply, "the divorce between me and Paul was friendly. We decided we'd made a mistake. We didn't have a big fight, and we didn't try to ruin each other in court. You can ask anyone. Paul made me a generous settlement, kept me on as assistant producer, and continued to promote my career."

"Ma'am, I didn't ask about your personal life."

"But now you know, and you can check. If you want to know who had a card that controlled his alarms and locks, I suggest you ask Karen Bergman. He gave his girlfriends cards."

"Miss Bergman didn't kill him, ma'am."

"How can you be so sure of that?"

Columbo shook his head. "She'd have had to climb on a stool or a stepladder. Miss Bergman is too short to have fired the shot through the brain at the angle the shot took."

Alicia stared at him for a long moment, then nodded. "Then maybe you should talk to Bobby Angela. Her relationship didn't work out so well."

Columbo pulled his notebook from his raincoat pocket. For a moment his face was blank, and then he frowned and said, "Bobby Angela? You mean the country-and-western singer?"

"The same. Bobby Angela. Quite a kid, Lieutenant."

"She was on the Drury show," he said, making a note.

"Right. Accusing her father of incest. She and three others that night. One of the worst shows we ever did. Sleazy. Paul usually wouldn't descend to that. He said it was a big social problem."

"So what was the relationship?"

"Stormy," said Alicia. "And it broke up with ugly words. Tabloid stuff. If she had a card, I bet she didn't hand it back to him the way I did mine."

Columbo turned down the corners of his mouth and nodded. He thrust the pen he'd been using back in its holder on the desk. "I sure do appreciate your suggesting this line of inquiry," he said. "I mean, if nothin' comes of it, still I'll have got to meet Bobby Angela. Wait'll I tell Mrs. Columbo about that!"

"I hope it's helpful, Lieutenant."

"I bet it will be, ma'am. And I won't trouble you for more of your time right now. I'm sure grateful."

Alicia rose and went to the door of the office. "Anything else I can do, just call," she said.

Columbo stood respectfully. "Well . . . Actually, there is just one little thing," he said. "Doesn't amount to anything. Just a matter of making the record complete, y' understand."

"Yes, Lieutenant," said Alicia, now impatient.

"Uh, well . . . Do you like to gamble, ma'am?"

"What's that got to do with anything?" she asked acerbically.

"Oh, nothin', I don't think. Just tryin' to get all the facts in line. So . . . Do you, in fact, do some gambling?"

"I make an occasional trip to Las Vegas," she said coldly.

"Las Vegas. Just an occasional trip."

"Just an occasional trip, Lieutenant."

"Yeah . . . Well, I can understand that. I play pool. Play a little nine-ball now and then, for a dollar a rack. A little adventure, what y' call. Relaxes the nerves, doesn't it? Ever lose more than you could afford, ma'am?"

"I can't afford to lose *any* money, Lieutenant, so anything I lose I can't afford. Okay?"

"Sure. That's the way it is with me, too. Mrs. Columbo, she gets real upset if I lose ten dollars at nine-ball. I can understand that. I sure can understand that."

"Anything else, Lieutenant?"

"No . . . 'Course, you never had to leave Vegas *owin'* any money."

"Of course not. Those people want too much interest."

"Right."

S I X

"Do you mind if *I* ask *you* a question?" asked Bobby
Angela. "Why in the world are you wearing that raincoat?"

"That's a very good question, ma'am," said Columbo.
He glanced around. He had caught up with the famous
country-and-western singer beside a hotel swimming pool,
where she had just finished modeling for a photographer for
Playboy, and was now tanning in a white bikini and sipping
a gin and tonic. In the middle of a group of people wearing
nothing but swimming clothes—some of them the skimpi-
est imaginable—he was a curious sight. "Y' see, I carry a
lot of stuff in my pockets, like my notebook and pencil and
cigars and— Well, it's a lot of trouble to transfer all that
stuff over to my other pockets. Line of least resistance, y'
might say. Yeah, that's what my wife says of me: that I like
to take the line of least resistance."

The singer smiled. He knew she was only nineteen years
old, but it was not easy to believe that. She was womanly,
not girlish. Her black hair was cut short and styled to curl
under her ears and along her upper cheeks. Her eyes were
brown. She wore dramatic dark-red lipstick. Her legs were
long and slender.

"I've never before had the honor of a visit by a homicide detective," she said. "You want my alibi for last night?"

"Well . . . not necessarily," said Columbo. "Of course, if you have one, it wouldn't hurt anything."

Bobby Angela raised her finger and summoned a waiter. "What would you like to drink, Lieutenant?"

"Technically, I'm on duty—"

"What would you drink if you weren't?"

"Maybe a beer."

"Maybe a Scotch?"

"Well, ma'am . . . In fact, I do like Scotch. Bourbon, too. In fact, I—"

"A Chivas on the rocks for my friend," she said to the waiter. "And let's do this gin and tonic again."

Columbo sat on the lower part of a chaise longue. He moved to an aluminum-and-vinyl armchair. "My," he said, "this here's a nice pool. Inviting. I wish I had some swim trunks with me."

"They have paper ones," said Bobby Angela. "Wear once, throw away."

"Well, uh . . . Maybe not this afternoon. Uh, you *did* know Mr. Drury?"

"Intimately. He was a real bastard. And I don't have an alibi and can't prove I didn't kill him."

"Did you have one of those cards that work his alarm and door locks?"

"I *have* a card. You want it?"

"Let's go back to what you said, miss. You said he was a real bastard."

"An ego, Lieutenant. He didn't think he was God. He thought God was inferior to him. He thought he could snap his fingers and God would do what he said. Make it rain. Send thunder. He was not a nice man, Lieutenant Columbo. I didn't kill him, but I'm not going to tell you I'm sorry he's dead."

"You say you've got no alibi. Where were you when he was killed?"

"When was he killed?"

"That's a good question. Let's say between ten o'clock and twelve-thirty."

"I have no alibi for that time. I was at home. I went to bed about eleven."

Columbo reached into his pocket, felt the stub of a cigar, then decided that lighting a cigar here at the side of this pool would only add another element to the incongruity of his appearance. "I don't have you on the list of suspects," he said. "Should I?"

The young woman drew a deep breath. "He was abusive," she said. "When I was seeing him, I was eighteen years old. If my father knew what he did to me, he'd have killed him—in spite of what my father did to me. On the other hand, I suppose I should admit Paul helped me make it in show biz."

"I take it your relationship with him was after he was divorced from Mrs. Drury."

"Last year. It was just last year. You want me to tell you about it?"

"Well, uh . . . You don't have to go into the *details,* if you know what I mean."

"Okay. I met him in Las Vegas. I was doing a gig there, in a bar at the Piping Rock Hotel, not out on the big stage. You ever catch my act? Anyway, Paul came in, listened through a coupla songs, and sent up his card. Was I surprised! Would I see him after the show? *Paul Drury!* Of course I'd see him. I guessed what he'd want, and he probably guessed what I'd want."

"Was Mr. Drury a gambler? Did he bet much on the tables?"

Bobby Angela shook her head. "He just wasn't much interested in it. I saw him play a few hands of blackjack once or twice. He just wasn't much interested in gambling. Well . . . In another way, he was interested. He was thinking about doing a show, exposing the way the odds are rigged against the suckers. Somebody talked him out of doing it."

"Who talked him out of it?"

"Alicia. She argued that not one percent of the people of the United States ever gamble in a casino and the other ninety-nine percent could care less what the odds on the tables are. She was still his assistant producer, you know, and he still accepted her judgment on a lot of things."

"Would you say she killed that idea?"

"Right. He told me she did. It bothered me, because I didn't think Paul would come to Vegas anymore, and I was going to be working there for a while yet. But he did come, on weekends. She'd come with him. It was odd. They'd come in together, just like they were still husband and wife, but as soon as they were in the hotel they'd separate and wouldn't see each other till they caught the same plane back."

"Did *she* gamble?"

"I—"

Bobby Angela paused while a waiter brought their drinks. Columbo glanced around the pool. He recognized three celebrities and guessed there were several more. He guessed a woman across the pool was Barbra Streisand, though he knew he could be wrong. A striking, tall, gray, deeply wrinkled man looked to him like James Arness but maybe wasn't. The crowd was a mix of people who came here to be recognized and people who came to recognize them: luminaries and would-be luminaries and tourists come to gawk. Both kinds stared at him. He'd flashed his shield to get in here, and the word was around, apparently, that Bobby Angela was being questioned by a Los Angeles police detective.

"He said she gambled. I never saw her do it. He said she gambled too much and lost more than she could afford."

"Is that so? She lost more than she could afford? That's interestin'."

"Is she a suspect?"

"Well . . . miss, y' gotta understand that in a thing like this *everybody's* a suspect. If I ask questions about somebody, it doesn't mean that person's *particularly* a suspect, more than anybody else."

Columbo took a sip of his Scotch. It was the dark, smoky kind of Scotch, the kind he liked. "I understand you play the guitar when you sing."

She reached into a copious round bag sitting beside the table and pulled out a video cartridge. "There," she said. "You can catch my act."

"Well, thank you! That's very generous of you. I'll watch it tonight. Mrs. Columbo'll love it, too."

"The outfit I was wearing in Vegas is what you see on that tape," she said. "Shiny little black vinyl shorts. See-through blouse. Net stockings. High heels."

"Yeah? An' you play the guitar?"

"I play the guitar."

"Gettin' back to Mrs. Drury. Not that she's the lead suspect or anything. But if she didn't gamble, what was she doin' in Las Vegas those weekends when Mr. Drury was with you?"

"She had friends there," said Bobby Angela. "I'd see her sometimes at dinner with a man."

"Same man? Always the same man?"

"Never the same man twice. Always a high roller, if you know what I mean."

"Are you sayin' she was pickin' up guys? Or lettin' herself get picked up?"

"That's what Paul thought. He didn't like it. She had one particular friend. I never saw them at dinner together, but I sometimes saw them together during the day. Phil Sclafani. Everybody knew him. Paul didn't like it that his ex-wife was seeing Phil Sclafani, either."

"Sclafani? Who is he?"

"You know how stories get around. There are all kinds of stories about who he is. He lives in the penthouse of the Piping Rock, where I was working. His father lives up there, too. Actually, it's the old man's penthouse. His father is Joe Sclafani. Of course, the story is that . . . They're connected."

"Mob connected?"

"Don't quote *me* on it. I mean, I can't afford to have hostility from those people."

"But you think Mrs. Drury is a good friend of this Phil Sclafani?"

"I don't know how good friends they were. If they were— Well, if they were lovers, they didn't look it. When I'd see them at lunch together, she usually looked miserable."

"That's very helpful, Miss Angela," said Columbo. He took another sip of Scotch. "I appreciate it."

"Fancy seeing you, Columbo. You got something you want to talk about?"

Columbo dragged fire from a match into his cigar. In Ben Palermo's office he had no hesitation about it. Ben was an FBI agent. "I figure when I need information, the thing to do is go see the man that prob'ly has it."

"Or a fellow New Yorker, hey?"

"Well, New York boys do make the best cops. The worst crooks, too."

The FBI provided its agents with starkly utilitarian offices, just like the LAPD provided its officers—which was one reason why Columbo went to his office only when he couldn't avoid it. He didn't like gray steel office furniture any better than he liked office work.

"Who you got in mind?"

"Whatta ya know about a coupla guys in Las Vegas who call themselves Sclafani? There's Joe Sclafani, apparently, and Phil Sclafani."

"The Sclafani Family," said Ben.

"They're the Sclafani Family?"

"What's left of it. Joe Sclafani is of course Giuseppe

Sclafani. He's gotta be eighty-five. He was at the Apalachin meet in 1957. Philip is his eldest son. He's sixty or so."

"When I was a cop in New York, Giuseppe Sclafani was a legend," said Columbo. "He's still alive and livin' in a penthouse in Vegas?"

"The penthouse of the Piping Rock Hotel—named, incidentally, for Meyer Lansky's casino at Saratoga Springs."

"Giuseppe Sclafani . . ." Columbo muttered, shaking his head. "Still alive! The only one. Carlo Gambino, Albert Anastasia, Joe Profaci, Vito Genovese, Bugsy Siegel, Meyer Lansky, Frank Costello . . . all dead. Hey, Ben! Fill me in on the Sclafanis, huh? They'd already left New York when I was on the job there. Gimme a briefin', will ya?"

Ben Palermo leaned back in his chair. He was Columbo's age but looked older. His yellow hair, always thin, was all but gone except above his ears and around the back of his neck. His complexion was pink. He wore silver-framed glasses.

"Let's look at Giuseppe Sclafani's curriculum vitae backward," said Palermo. "He's been in Las Vegas since about 1964, and he's built up a highly profitable business there. He had to start small, because he'd lost six fortunes in Cuba. He'd built a casino hotel in Havana, using his own money and some from investors, plus some from the Batista government. In October 1960, the Castro government confiscated all the American hotels, including Giuseppe Sclafani's and Meyer Lansky's."

"It broke Meyer Lansky," said Columbo. "I mean, both ways: money and health."

"But not Joe Sclafani," said Palermo. "It just made him mad. When he came to Las Vegas he made his presence known by having a couple of guys killed. It was understood he had sanction for it, too: from The Commission. Why not? Here was a guy who'd been at Apalachin. People stepped aside and made room for him in Vegas."

"I remember stories about what he did in New York," said Columbo.

"If the stories say he killed a lot of people, our files say the contrary. He was a friend of Meyer Lansky. It was Lansky that got him involved in Havana. Before that, Sclafani was a partner in two of Lansky's casino operations: one at Saratoga Springs and one in Broward County, Florida. He and Lansky shared a business philosophy: that the best way to make a dishonest dollar was in gambling, avoiding violence and publicity, and Lansky wouldn't work with a man who didn't accept that philosophy. Except for a few girls that worked the casinos, they weren't involved in prostitution. The Sclafanis weren't involved in loan-sharking, which requires leg-breaking to collect. They weren't in drugs. They were in the waterfronts rackets: corrupt unions, skimming shipments. They took a percentage off what came in through Brooklyn. They broke a few heads when they had to, but it wasn't the Sclafani way."

"He's a Sicilian, as I remember," said Columbo.

"Well, I said I'd give you his biography backward. He was brought to this country from Sicily in 1924, by Salvatore Maranzano."

"The Castellammarese connection," said Columbo.

"Right. Maranzano brought young Sicilians over here to form a cadre of tough young guys absolutely loyal to him. Sclafani delivered whiskey for him and collected the money. For a while. Then Maranzano recognized in Giuseppe Sclafani a young fellow too smart to use as nothing but an errand boy. He promoted him, gave him a territory. Of course . . . two things happened. Maranzano was murdered in 1931, and Prohibition was repealed in 1933. Sclafani made his peace with Luciano and was allowed to look for new businesses. That's when he made his connection with Meyer Lansky."

"What about this Piping Rock operation? Is it legit?"

"As legit as any Las Vegas casino. You don't have to cheat to make money out of a gambling casino. The odds take care of that. You want to tell me why you're asking about all this?"

"The Paul Drury murder," said Columbo. "The ex-wife seems to be a close friend of Phil Sclafani. Somebody told me to look out for a mob connection, and then somebody else told me she's a buddy of Sclafani."

"The Vegas office has Sclafani under surveillance," said Palermo. "We'd still like to have the ass of a guy who was at Apalachin, who's a member of The Commission. We don't give up easy, and for ten years we've been looking for a way to make a conspiracy charge stick. We know pretty much everybody he sees. I'll ask the Vegas office to run through their surveillance reports to see if the name Alicia Drury comes up. Any others?"

"Tim Edmonds. Karen Bergman. Drury himself, for that matter."

"We've made a mistake," said Alicia. "We've made a mistake, so be damned careful."

She sat beside Charles Bell in his custom-built silver-gray Cadillac convertible. He had spotted a parking place and pulled into it. They sat facing the Santa Monica beach. The sun glared. Surfers were working the curlers on an incoming tide. She was still wearing the black dress that had impressed Columbo as a mourning dress. Bell was wearing the lemon-yellow slacks and pale blue polo shirt he had worn at lunch.

"Let's not spoil a happy occasion," he said.

He opened the glove compartment and pulled out a small silver bowl, the kind in which nuts might be served at a formal party. Reaching into the back seat, he picked up a leather attaché case.

"Appropriate, don't you think? Churches burn their mortgages in silver bowls. Or so they say. May I borrow your cigarette lighter?"

Alicia reached into her purse and took out her lighter.

Bell opened the briefcase and took out a small document that lay on the top of other papers. He showed it to her.

"There. That's it, of course. And that's the deal: sixty-two thousand dollars. You kept your part of the bargain. I'm keeping mine."

She nodded solemnly.

He tore the document to bits and dropped all the pieces but one into the bowl. That one he held in his left hand. With his right he snapped the lighter and got a flame. He touched the flame to the single piece, got it burning, and dropped it in the silver bowl with the rest. The flame spread, and in a moment all the bits of paper were afire. He smiled, and she frowned, as they watched the paper burn. After a minute, nothing was left but some black and gray ash, with a few tiny orange sparks still glowing. Bell grinned. He held the bowl outside the car and leaned out to blow into it. The ashes rose from the bowl, were caught in the wind off the Pacific, and swirled away, tiny and scattered and invisible.

"The bowl is yours," said Bell gallantly, handing it to her. "A memento."

"Thank you," said Alicia glumly.

"Now, what mistake have we made?"

"Lieutenant Columbo is not a fool," she said. "He's figured out that Paul was shot by somebody more than six feet tall. Something about the angle of the shots."

"Twenty percent of the adult population of Los Angeles is more than six feet tall."

"Not the point. The point is that he figured it out. He decided in a minute there'd been no robbery. Taking Paul's watch and ring was foolishness. He—"

"Alicia. Suppose he cracks your alibi. Suppose he figures out that you *could* have been in the house at eleven-ten. That doesn't prove you were. He can't find the pistol, that's for sure. He doesn't know how many people had cards—"

"I told him Karen had one, and he said she would have had to stand on a stool to shoot Paul."

Bell smiled tolerantly. "He hasn't got a motive. That's the big point. Why in the world would *you* have wanted to kill Paul Drury? The motive is so many steps away from you, so far apart, that he'll never make the connection."

"Everything depends on that."

"And on one more thing," said Bell ominously. "You don't lose your nerve, and you don't crack. I'm confident of you, Alicia. I worry about Tim, though."

Alicia drew a deep breath and sighed. "If I were convicted of murder— Well, if I were, he would be, too. Anyway, we'd never see each other again. That's what Tim couldn't stand."

"The man is desperately in love with you, isn't he?"

She nodded.

"He must remain in love with you for the rest of your lives, Alicia. That's what's going to keep you out of the slammer. It's what's going to keep all of us out. Tim must never falter. You must never give him reason to have pangs of conscience, never let him learn to resent you for getting him into a homicide, never let his love flag. I'm sure you know how to handle it. You could do worse than Tim Edmonds. You did once."

"All right. You're going to see Columbo. Remember what I told you. He's not as dumb as he acts."

"I guess this is my day," Columbo said to the maitre d' at the Topanga Beach Club. "This is the second time today I've been invited to sit beside a nice swimmin' pool and—"

"You were *invited* here, sir?"

"Oh, yeah. I shoulda said that right off. I'm Lieutenant Columbo, police. I'll be a guest of Mr. Charles Bell."

"I see. Yes, Mr. Bell is expecting you. Won't you let us check your coat, sir?"

"Uh, well . . . I guess I should let you do that. People kinda stared at me when I sat down beside that other pool with my raincoat on. Let me get, uh . . . Let me get this cigar out."

Columbo's jacket was dark gray, his slacks light gray, and his loosely knotted necktie was dark blue with tiny red dots. The cigar butt bulged in his jacket pocket. "Well, isn't this a nice place?" he said to the maitre d' as the man led him toward a deck overlooking both the pool and the beach on the opposite side of the highway. "I bet some really nice people are members here."

Charles Bell rose.

"Lieutenant Columbo, sir," said the maitre d'.

Bell seized Columbo's hand and shook it in a firm grip. "I'm pleased to meet you, Lieutenant. I wasn't surprised when you called and am glad you agreed to come here. I thought this would be a nice place for us to meet. Have a seat. Let me order us a round of drinks."

"Thank you, sir. As to the drink, I'd better be careful about that. I had a double Scotch early this afternoon."

"In that case, let's have a bottle of nice chilled white wine, and I'll order a platter of hors d'oeuvres."

"Well, sir, if you don't mind, I'd really rather have red."

"Great! Red it will be. I like it better too, truth be told."

Bell summoned a waiter and gave his order.

"This sure is some nice place," said Columbo. "I wish Mrs. Columbo could see it."

"Why don't you phone her and invite her to join us for dinner? I'd be happy to have you and Mrs. Columbo as my guests."

"That's more than kind of you, sir, but this is one of the nights when my wife goes to a class at the university. One of these days she's gonna have a college degree."

"Then maybe we can make it another night. Anyway, I asked you to meet me because I want to offer any help I can. The death of Paul Drury is a damn nasty thing, and I'm hoping you'll track down the killer and bring him to justice as quickly as possible."

"That's what I hope too, sir."

"Do you understand my connection with Paul Drury?"

"I have some word on that, but I'd rather you told me."

"All right. My father was Austin Bell, late of Dallas. He made a considerable fortune in the oil business, which I was lucky enough to inherit. I found Dallas a little provincial and decided to try to expand my horizons. I looked for investments in fields outside the oil biz. To make a long story short, I decided to invest in Paul Drury Productions. I'm the major investor. My investment just became worthless."

"I can see why you're anxious to have the killer brought to justice."

"Without Paul Drury there is no *Paul Drury Show*. Do you have any idea who killed him, Lieutenant?"

"I got some ideas, sir. Y' understand I can't talk about it yet."

"Of course not. Is there any information I can give you?"

Columbo glanced away from Charles Bell for a moment, to watch a tall blonde in a blue bikini and high heels walk by. "Aside from his show, what kind of man would you say Mr. Drury was?"

"He was what a man in his line of work has to be," said Bell. "Egomaniacal. Manipulative. Basically something less than honest. What else can I say?"

"Women?"

"Alicia. Karen Bergman. Jessica O'Neil. Bobby Angela. In the past two or three years."

"Jessica O'Neil? The actress?"

Bell nodded. "During his marriage. While he was still married to Alicia. Cause of the divorce."

Columbo nodded, turning down the corners of his mouth.

The waiter arrived, bringing a tray of hors d'oeuvres that included a dip of crab meat and shrimp and a small bowl of caviar. Also on the tray were two small glasses of vodka, chilled to thickening.

"This is a *spécialité de la maison,* Lieutenant," said Bell. "Ice-cold vodka with caviar. I took the liberty of adding it to our order."

"Fish . . . fish eggs," said Columbo dubiously. "That's . . . uh, that's very nice, sir. Y' know, I enjoy any kind of food that's from the sea."

Bell spooned caviar onto a cracker and handed it to Columbo. He did one for himself. *"Prosit!"* he said as he bit the cracker in half and followed it with a sip of the vodka.

Columbo imitated him.

"You like it, Lieutenant?"

"Oh, sure. That's wonderful. A man could get a quick headache, though—drinking anything that cold."

"That's why we only take sips."

As they ate the caviar and drank the vodka, Bell asked Columbo about his background and elicited the somewhat vague information that the detective was from New York.

"Myself, I grew up in Texas," said Bell. "Went to school there. Paul made a big point about being on Dealey Plaza on the day of the Kennedy assassination. I was there, too. To tell the truth, I had a better view of what happened than he did."

"You saw it happen? That's very interestin'."

"A sorry day, Lieutenant. A sorry day for our country."

"Oh, yeah. For sure."

The red wine was a Bordeaux, heavy and musty. Although Columbo's experience with wines ran more to Italian reds, he recognized the Bordeaux as distinguished, and he enjoyed the experience of drinking a wine that probably cost the Texan more than fifty dollars for the bottle.

The conversation turned to the Dodgers and the Lakers, fishing, politics, and the weather.

"I really . . . really have gotta be goin'," said Columbo eventually. "I can't tell ya how much I appreciate this wonderful snack. It's been very kind of you, sir, very kind."

"My pleasure, Lieutenant. If there is any information I can give you, please—"

Columbo rose. He smiled and nodded and gave his hand to be shaken. "Yes, sir. Yes, sir. Thank ya again."

"Best of luck, Lieutenant Columbo."

"Thank ya. Uh . . . Y' know, now that I think of it, there is one other thing I guess I ought to ask. Little thing that's come up. Probably doesn't mean anything."

"What is it?"

"Well . . . This probably doesn't mean anything, but the name Philip Sclafani has come up. Who's Philip Sclafani, sir? Do you know? And what has he got to do with anything?"

"I never heard that name before, Lieutenant," said Bell, suddenly coldly emphatic.

Columbo nodded. "Well, good. Didn't figure you would have. Just somethin' I've got to clear up, for my report. Thanks again, sir. And good evening."

SEVEN

It was a joke at headquarters that Columbo never sat down at his desk. He just stood beside it, they said, and read his mail and made phone calls. In fact, he did sit at his desk, more than he wanted. He had reports to make, and he had to sit at a typewriter and hunt and peck. This morning, though, he did not sit. Smoking his first cigar of the day, he stood and read the papers from his in box—

—A reminder that he had not made reservations for himself and his family to attend the annual picnic of the LA Detectives Chapter, Police Benevolent Association.

—Three sheets of instructions on how to fill out Form 2301–11(d), report of damage to a police vehicle.

—A memo from Administration, complaining that many detectives were not fully complying with the standing procedures for time reports.

—Revised Procedure 1167–201(b)(3) on how to package for evidence any controlled substances seized.

—A sealed envelope.

He opened the envelope and found a fax:

Columbo: The Grassy Knoll

4–June–1993. 09:11. Total p. 01.
Lieutenant Columbo, LAPD
Benjamin Palermo, Los Angeles Office,
Federal Bureau of Investigation.
Confidential.

A review of the surveillance reports on Philip Sclafani, complied by our Las Vegas office, discloses that on seventeen occasions between 01–01–92 and 04–12–93 Alicia Graham Drury was observed in the company of the subject. Except for one occasion, all contacts were meetings at breakfast or lunch. On one occasion AGD was observed in conversation with PS in the lobby of the Piping Rock Hotel. On each occasion, the two persons were alone, although others stopped by their table occasionally.

The surveillance reports do not mention any of the other three persons you named.

Feel welcome to inquire further.

He found also in his box a pink telephone slip saying that Dr. Culp had some information for him.

"Columbo."

He looked up from his reading to see that Captain Sczciegel had walked up and was addressing him.

"Good mornin', Captain. Fine day."

"Any leads in the Drury murder?"

"Uh, yes sir. Yes, sir. I've got leads."

"It wasn't a burglary?"

"Oh, no sir, it certainly wasn't a burglary. It was cold-blooded murder."

Captain Sczciegel, who pronounced his name "SEE-gel," ran his hand over his bald head. "That means you've got to look for motive," he said.

"Yes, sir."

"You got any ideas?"

"Oh yes, Captain. Y' see, Mr. Drury was in the business of making public information people didn't want made public. Put another way, he gave a lot of publicity to information that people would rather everybody forgot about."

"And you figure somebody killed him to prevent him from doing that. Doesn't that give you a hundred suspects, Columbo? Or a thousand?"

"No, sir. No sir, it doesn't. Because the murder was committed by somebody who had a magnetic card and the code numbers that disabled the alarm system and opened the doors to Mr. Drury's house. Not only that, the murderer was familiar with the house and knew some of Mr. Drury's habits."

"I've got to give the chief a statement he can make public. Can I say we're checking leads and feel confident we'll make an arrest within a few days?"

"Well . . . I don't know if I'd say 'confident.' I don't want ya to think I'm guaranteein'—"

"How about something like, 'Police are checking a number of promising leads and feel they will break the case before long.' How's that?"

"I'm no expert on talkin' to reporters, sir, but that sounds better to me."

"All right. Now, I don't like to interrupt your work on this case with an administrative technicality, but you've simply *got* to stop by the firing range and requalify with your service revolver. I'm getting heat about it."

Columbo nodded emphatically. "I'll do it, Captain. I got that pistol out last night and cleaned and oiled it. Detective

Zimmer is going to give me a quick lesson with it; then I'll—"

"God, Columbo. I'm going to pretend I didn't hear you say you got it out. You're supposed to carry it."

Columbo turned up his hands.

"All right. Never mind. Just go over and qualify."

"Yes, sir."

"Oh, and Columbo, one other thing. Have you ever thought about buying a new raincoat?"

"Yes, sir. I *have* thought about it. I do think about it. But I just haven't got around to it. I keep puttin' it off. It's not like it was urgent. This one's got a lot of wear left in it."

In the coroner's office, Dr. Harold Culp was at his desk. "Sit down, Columbo," he said. He put a finger on a jar that sat on the desk. "Guess what that is."

"I'm not sure I want to know," said Columbo, staring at a repugnant lumpy varicolored mass and deciding he was glad whatever it was was sealed inside glass.

"That, my friend, is a part of the contents of Paul Drury's digestive tract. That particular sample is from the stomach. I have others from the intestines. And all of it is evidence."

"Yeah? Y' mean it tells me what I want to know: how long he lived after he ate at La Felicità?"

Dr. Culp nodded. "What you see in that jar did not enter his stomach more than half an hour before he died."

"You sure of that? I have evidence that says he was alive at eleven forty-seven."

"Then he finished eating about eleven-seventeen," said the doctor emphatically.

"But a witness says he left the restaurant before eleven. A quarter to eleven, about."

"If that is correct, he was dead by eleven-fifteen or eleven-twenty."

Columbo ran his hand through his hair. "This is mystifying." He shook his head. "Y' see, the eleven forty-seven time isn't dependent on the word of a witness. It's the time put on a phone call by a recorder that time-stamps incoming calls. I wonder if— Well. What had he been eating?"

"I thought you'd never ask. That's pasta, mostly. Some crab meat, some shrimp, and some lobster meat. Red wine. Coffee."

"Coffee. Meaning he'd finished his dinner."

"No dessert," said Dr. Culp.

Before Columbo entered the elevator to go up to William McCrory's office, he stubbed out his cigar and put it in his pocket. People gave him dirty looks when he smoked in elevators. When he entered the room with the lush plants and the saltwater aquarium, he shook the lawyer's hand and said, "Well, sir, you notice I'm not smoking a cigar, out of deference to your aquarium. I sure wouldn't want my smoke to harm your tropical fish."

McCrory laughed. "That's thoughtful of you, Lieutenant," he said. "Have a seat."

"If y' don't mind, I'd like to stand here and look at your fish tank. Those fish sure are beautiful!"

"When things get tense, I turn and watch the fish," said the apple-cheeked lawyer. "It's therapeutic."

"I bet it is."

"Well. What can I do for you?"

Columbo broke himself away from the aquarium and sat down facing McCrory's desk. "Something very peculiar has come up. The medical examiner checked the contents of Mr. Drury's stomach and is scientifically certain the man died within half an hour after he finished his dinner. I'll be checkin' the restaurant, too, but Miss Bergman says they left there as early as a quarter to eleven—anyway, *before* eleven for sure. He sent her home in a cab. The doctor is very positive. You see the problem."

"How could he have called me at eleven forty-seven? Hmm? There's the problem."

Columbo nodded. "Is there any way somebody could have tampered with your machine and set the time on it wrong?"

"Someone would have had to come into my office after I left here Wednesday afternoon, set the time wrong, then come back before I came in yesterday morning and set it back again."

"There's no way to tamper with it by telephone? Y' know you can change some things on those machines by calling in and beeping codes."

"You can't change the time, Lieutenant. Not without coming in and doing it. Not on this machine."

"No . . ."

McCrory smiled and shrugged. "Of course, *I* could have done it, to make an alibi for myself or somebody else."

Columbo shook his head. "No . . . For that to work, Mr. Drury would have had to cooperate by calling in here and leaving that message. It's hardly likely, is it, that he'd help you make an alibi for his murderer?"

McCrory smiled and shrugged. "No way. Not the Paul Drury I knew."

"Okay. Yesterday you told me Mrs. Drury may be mob-connected. I'm going to ask you to be more specific."

"I said I couldn't prove it."

"I don't ask ya to prove anything, sir. And I'll keep what you tell me confidential. But I'd like to know if you had anything specific in mind."

"Paul told me she was cozy with a Mafioso in Las Vegas. He didn't like it."

"Was this during their marriage?"

"Partly. Sometimes she went to Vegas when he couldn't or wouldn't go. That really upset him."

"Why'd they get divorced, sir?"

"Things like that. Plus, he was seeing another woman."

"Jessica O'Neil."

McCrory smiled and chuckled. "You don't miss much, do you, Lieutenant?"

"It's the only way I can possibly succeed in my work, sir—just plug away, plug away, and be thorough. I read a lot about detectives who figure things out by being brilliant, and I've known a couple or three who can do that; but me, all I can do is work hard, find out all I can, and, like you say, don't miss much. Does the name Philip Sclafani mean anything to you?"

McCrory's smile broadened into a grin. "I'm damned glad *I* didn't kill Paul and have you on my case," he said. "Yeah, Sclafani's the name Paul mentioned."

"You got any idea why this fellow Philip Sclafani would want Mr. Drury killed?"

"No. After Paul and Alicia were divorced, she saw Sclafani openly, and Paul knew it. He was going to Vegas to see Bobby Angela, and Alicia'd fly over with him and see Sclafani openly. Paul called him a 'greaseball scumbag' and things like that, but I don't think there was ever a confrontation between them."

"Well . . . I'm taking too much of your time, Mr. McCrory. I'm just still puzzled about the time of that telephone call. That's a big conflict in the evidence."

"I can't explain it, Lieutenant. I wish I could."

"Thank you so much for your time, sir. I'm very grateful. I hope I won't have to bother you again."

Outside the office, Columbo pulled his cigar from his raincoat pocket, then stared at it for a moment, remembering he was about to get into an elevator. He returned it to the pocket. He'd light it out on the street.

Martha Zimmer was waiting outside La Felicità when Columbo arrived. As Columbo approached her, she pulled off her sunglasses. As usual, she wore a blue blazer and a white blouse over her ample upper figure, with her detective's badge displayed on the blouse pocket. Today she was wearing a pleated gray skirt. They went inside. He showed his badge and introduced himself to the hostess, and she picked up her telephone and called the owner to come out from his office.

"My, isn't this a nice place?" Columbo said to Martha as they waited. It was in fact a handsome small restaurant, the kind of place an aggressively urbane man like Paul Drury would have found, appreciated, and patronized. It was Italian in tone, yet determinedly Southern-California-American: dark wood, wrought-iron sconces, fire-engine-red tablecloths, candles inside amber-colored glass.

"I bet the food is better than the décor," said Martha.

The proprietor came out: a tall, rather suave man with a bushy black mustache.

"I'm Vincent Conte, Lieutenant Columbo. What can I do for you?"

"We're investigating the death of Paul Drury, Mr. Conte. We've got just a couple of simple questions. This is Mrs. Zimmer. She's a detective, too—LAPD."

"Would you like to sit down in the lounge? Can I offer you a drink?"

"Well, maybe a root beer," said Columbo.

"I'm afraid we don't have root beer," Conte said. "Coca-Cola?"

"Oh, fine. She'll have the same."

The bartender had overheard and squirted the two Cokes into glasses, which he brought to their booth.

"Mr. Conte, I imagine you know Mr. Drury ate here and died not long after he left, Wednesday evening."

"I know. A tragedy. I have lost a friend, too. He dined here once a week, regularly."

Columbo nodded. "We have conflicting stories about when he left here. Can you tell me what time he left?"

"I can tell you exactly when he left. He asked us to call a cab for his young lady about ten-forty. The cab arrived within five or ten minutes, and they left. I stepped out to see that everything was in order. He put the young lady in the cab and got into his own car. I'd had the valet parker bring it out at the same time when I called the cab. That had to be—"

"A quarter to eleven?"

"Within five minutes of it."

"What had he eaten for dinner?"

"A specialty we call Pasta Felicità. It is an assortment of

shellfish—lobster, crab, shrimp—in a white wine sauce with herbs, over angel-hair pasta."

"Wine?"

"Montepulciano."

"Did they eat dessert?"

"No. They ordered coffee but no dessert."

"How about the young lady, sir. Do you know who she was? Do you know her name?" Martha Zimmer asked.

"Her name is Miss Karen Bergman. She worked for Mr. Drury and had been here with him twice before."

"Did they argue? Did you see any tension between them? Anything like that?"

"No. I thought them an affectionate couple."

"Well, that's very helpful, sir. We appreciate it."

"Would you and Mrs. Zimmer be my guests for lunch, Lieutenant?"

"That's very kind of you, Mr. Conte, but we've got things we have to do. Maybe another time."

"Anytime, Lieutenant. I will be honored."

What they had to do was drive up into the mountains and find a secluded ravine where Columbo could fire a few shots from his revolver, on the sly. He drove the Peugeot, and in half an hour they found a spot they considered suitable: along a small stream, with a steep bank on the other side so slugs could not escape and create a hazard. Martha took off her shoes, and waded across the stream to line up half a dozen tin cans she had brought for targets.

Martha had left her blue blazer in the Peugeot, and her own revolver hung in a soft shoulder holster in her left armpit. She remained barefoot because she didn't want to put on her shoes again until her feet were dry.

Columbo stared at the uneven line of cans, frowning and puffing nervously on the stub of a cigar. "In all my years on the job, in New York and LA, I never fired a single shot. Never drew my gun."

"You had to qualify with a service revolver to get your shield," said Martha.

"I got the idea the range officers always took it easy on me."

"Well, go ahead and shoot a can."

He had carried the Colt revolver down from the car. He pulled it out of his raincoat pocket and took aim at one of the cans. He pulled back the hammer, steadied his aim, which wavered anyway, and finally pulled the trigger. The revolver barked and jerked, and the bullet kicked out a hole in the bank above the cans—two feet above them.

"Y' see? I never could get onto this. I never learned to swim, either."

"Aim with both arms, Columbo. You're allowed to use both arms. And don't extend your arms so far your elbows are stiff. Leave a little flexibility."

"I can use both hands? Awright, then!" He drew back the hammer, aimed again, this time with his left hand locked around his right wrist. The bullet hit the water and threw up a big splash.

"It's only twenty-five damned feet," muttered Martha. She pulled her own revolver from her holster. "Look, Columbo. Stand with your feet a little apart, like this." She fired without pulling back the hammer first. A can leaped in the air. She fired a second shot, and another can leaped.

Columbo pulled out his cigar and threw it away. He

mimicked her stance and fired again. His slug kicked a hole in the bank, between two cans.

"Y' got the elevation," said Martha. "Now get the windage, and you'll knock down a can."

Columbo took the stance again. His tongue came out of one corner of his mouth, and he fired. A can fell over. He'd knocked the sand out from under it.

"The targets at the range are bigger," he said.

"Yes, and they're twice as far away."

He spread his legs and thrust the revolver forward, this time steadying it by closing his left hand around his right and the grip. He tried closing his left eye and sighting with his right, then his right eye and sighting with his left. He pulled back the hammer. He hesitated for a long moment, then fired.

A can leaped, then rolled into the stream.

"Good enough," said Columbo. "Quit while I'm ahead."

"One shot out of five? Not good enough. We ought to put at least a box of ammo through that gun."

"I'd be deaf," said Columbo as he shoved the pistol into his raincoat pocket. "Anyway, I've got to go see Jessica O'Neil."

"Whatta ya want me to do?"

"Go back to the Drury house with a team and search for a hidden safe. Remember, the guy was clever and may have hid it someplace where nobody would think to look."

EIGHT

"It's very nice of you to give me your time this afternoon," Columbo said to Jessica O'Neil.

"When a police detective comes to your door and sends in word he wants to talk to you about a murder, you *make* time, Lieutenant."

"I still say it's nice of you, ma'am. Some people don't like to do it."

"Well . . . Come out on the deck. I'm studying a script. C'mon. We'll sit in the sunshine while we talk."

Jessica O'Neil was an unusual actress, according to what Mrs. Columbo had read about her in *People* magazine and told Columbo over breakfast one morning. Her father was a financier in New York. She was the heiress to a considerable fortune, had studied art at Wellesley, then had come to California and studied acting. She was a painter. Probably the paintings he noticed as they walked through the house were her own work. In appearance she was not unusual. She was just pretty, as he appraised her. She was no great beauty, certainly not a beauty contrived by a makeup artist; she was just a very pretty girl, with a friendly face and dark-brown hair. She was wearing a man's vest undershirt and a pair of blue denim shorts. He pretended he didn't notice she was wearing nothing under the shirt. He was not a man to ogle, but he was not blind nor was he indifferent to a woman's charms, either.

"I'm sorry I'm interruptin'—"

"Don't be sorry. You're here about the murder of Paul Drury. That's scary. I want to see it solved. Can I offer you a drink? I'm having iced tea, but I've got just about anything."

"Iced tea. That's very nice."

Jessica O'Neil called into the kitchen as she and Columbo walked toward the deck and told the maid who had answered the door to bring iced tea for the lieutenant.

The redwood deck overlooked a swimming pool on a terrace below, and beyond that it overlooked in the distance the beaches at Malibu and the Pacific beyond. The air was unusually clear that Friday afternoon, but a line of thunderstorms was visible at sea. Rain was likely before evening.

"I saw one of your pictures," said Columbo.

"Really? Which one?"

"Ironweed."

"Then I have nothing to hide from you, do I, Lieutenant?" she asked with an amused smile.

She referred to the fact that in that picture she had appeared more than briefly in the nude. "Uh . . . No, ma'am, I guess you don't." He hoped she hadn't meant to tell him she had noticed his eyes on her undershirt.

"I thought I was in love with Paul Drury," she said soberly. "In fact, I didn't just think it; I was—for a time. He was married to Alicia, but that didn't make any difference. My father warned me about Paul. My father said he was a cheap little adventurer."

"Did he give you one of those cards that let you into his house?"

"Yes. I still have it. Do you want it?"

Columbo shrugged and turned down the corners of his mouth. "No, it doesn't make any difference. The codes were changed yesterday."

"I was in New York when he was murdered. I flew east on Sunday and came back yesterday afternoon—in case you want an alibi for me."

"I wasn't goin' to ask you for one, ma'am. Do you mind if I light up a cigar?"

"Not at all."

"Gotta match?"

Jessica O'Neil grinned. "When the maid brings your iced tea, I'll send her in for one."

"I hate to put people to a lotta trouble."

"That's what she does for a living, Lieutenant: run errands. What can I tell you about Paul?"

"Why don't you just give me a short account of the relationship. I mean, I don't have to have details, if you know what I mean. Just tell me the story, sorta sketch it out."

"I met him at the J. Paul Getty Museum. That would have been in April of 1991. It was a coincidence. I was there. He was there. We recognized each other. We struck up a conversation, and before it was over he asked me to go to dinner with him. We went to dinner that weekend—Saturday night, I think it was. He worked hard all week and was big on weekend dates."

"Where was Mrs. Drury that Saturday night?"

"In Las Vegas. He resented her leaving him on weekends. That's what made him feel free to have dates."

"How long did you continue to have weekend dates with Mr. Drury?"

"A little more than a year."

"Go on, ma'am. I shouldn't have interrupted."

Jessica O'Neil sighed. "He was divorced in December of 1991. I thought he'd ask me to marry him then. Or soon. But he didn't. That's what broke us up, really. Also, when my father saw that Paul was not going to ask me to marry him, he began to pressure me to break it off."

The maid brought the iced tea, and Jessica O'Neil told her to bring a lighter.

"What'd your father have against Mr. Drury, specifically, if you don't mind sayin'?"

"A whole lot of things," she said. "You know how it is with men in banking: they exchange information. He'd found out a lot of things about Paul."

"Like what, ma'am?"

"He said Paul was not securely funded, that he was apt to go bankrupt if any little thing happened. Also, he didn't like Paul's chief investor."

"Charles Bell?"

"Yes. Charles Bell's father was Austin Bell, who died in 1989. Austin Bell was one of those Texans my father despises: a swaggering superpatriot, member of the John Birch Society and all that. My father met him at least twice. He absolutely detested him. The story is told that Austin Bell funded the training and equipping of Cubans for the Bay of Pigs invasion. Among the last things he did, which annoyed my father, was make an immense contribution to the Oliver North defense fund—saying Ollie North was one of the last great American patriots. My father loathed Austin Bell. And he didn't think any better of his son."

"Is Charles Bell involved in all this kinda stuff?"

Jessica O'Neil shook her head. "Not that I know of. Paul didn't know of it if he was, I can tell you that."

"Well, I guess a man's politics—"

"There was more than that," she interjected. "The word was around in New York financial circles that Austin Bell was a silent partner in some things a Texan might get away with but an ethical New York banker wouldn't dare touch."

"Please be specific about that, ma'am."

"My father believes— I have no idea what the source of his information is. My father believes that Austin Bell was a silent partner of Meyer Lansky's in the Riviera Hotel in Havana. If he was, he lost a scad of money, because the Castro government confiscated the hotel and didn't pay a cent in compensation."

"Lansky's dead . . ."

"Meyer Lansky died in 1983. Austin Bell died in 1989. My father believes that any money Charles Bell has is tainted—so any investment in Paul Drury's business was tainted, too."

"Isn't that an odd combination, ma'am?" Columbo asked. "I mean, extreme right-wing politics and a connection with a man like Meyer Lansky?"

"Not necessarily, if you think about it," said Jessica O'Neil. "Austin Bell would have hated the Castro regime as an ideological matter—and he would have hated it more because of the loss of his investment in the Riviera."

"That makes sense."

"I told Paul something of what my father thought. Not all

of it. Paul just shrugged it off. 'Money is money,' he said. Meaning he didn't care where Charles Bell got the money he invested in Paul Drury Productions."

"Did Mr. Drury confide in you, ma'am?"

She grinned. "Paul was a pillow talker. Especially when he thought he could make an impression. Look, Paul knew I had money. He knew my father was scornful of him. He told me things he thought would make him look good. He told me he was going to break the mystery of the Kennedy assassination. Thirty years after it happened, he would broadcast the greatest television show of his career and reveal who really killed President Kennedy."

"How'd he figure he was gonna do that?" asked Columbo.

"Computer technology. He said he already had in his computers' memories the greatest existing library of information on the assassination. And he was going to get more. With his computers he could match this fact to that fact and compare and compare . . . until he built a case that would prove who really killed John F. Kennedy."

"Did you tell your father that?"

"Yes, and my father said Paul was an egomaniacal nut."

"What'd you think, Miss O'Neil?"

"I'm more computer-oriented than my father. Generation gap, you know. I didn't think it was impossible Paul could put together a case, by using his computers to compare and compare . . . The way he said."

"Well, we have to forget what he might have done that way," said Columbo. "His computer library got somehow erased. Permanently. Beyond recovery. Every bit of it."

"That's what I read in the papers."

"If there was somebody shaking in their boots, they can stop shakin'," said Columbo.

"Not necessarily," said Jessica O'Neil.

"Not necessarily . . . ?"

"They have to find the pictures," she said.

"Whatta you mean?"

"He had pictures. And they weren't in his computers. I don't understand this exactly, but when you put images—pictures instead of words—into computer memory, it involves something called pixels. I guess they're dots, you know, like in a newspaper engraving. Well, each one of those pixels uses computer memory, and it adds up to so much memory that storing more than a few pictures in a computer is not very practical—not in the present state of the technology. So his pictures were not in the computers."

"Then where were they?" asked Columbo.

"Ask me another question first," said Jessica O'Neil. "Ask me how I know."

"How do you know?"

"He knew I was skeptical that he could solve the Kennedy problem. He knew my father was scornful. One night he showed me two photographs taken on Dealey Plaza. 'See that man?' he said. 'See that guy with the rifle? That man could have killed Kennedy.' It was clear enough. A man with a rifle, standing beside a tree. I mean, who knows if that's the man who shot the President, rather than Oswald up in the School Book Depository building? But there was a man with a rifle standing beside a tree, with another man standing beside him, as if he were keeping lookout for the rifleman. I've since looked at the published pictures. Those men had to be standing on what they call the Grassy Knoll."

"So where are the pictures?" Columbo demanded.

"In the house, I supposed. In a safe. In a safe at the office. In a safe-deposit box in a bank. Buried in a box in the yard."

"Are you suggesting that something about the assassination of President Kennedy could be the motive for the murder of Paul Drury, thirty years later?"

"Look at it this way, Lieutenant. The assassination has become a multimillion-dollar industry. Books. Movies. Television series. Suppose Paul was in possession of absolute evidence, proving who *did* kill Kennedy? The millions would dry up. *Nobody* wants to know who killed John F. Kennedy anymore. If we ever find out for sure, it destroys the industry."

"But he showed you pictures? Did he tell you where he got these pictures?"

"He was on the air once a month if not more, exploiting his own niche in the industry. He got endless publicity. People sent him letters, diaries, clippings . . . and pictures. The world is full of people who think television personalities are the court of last resort; if you can just convince some TV character that something is true, you've proved it's true. That was *The Paul Drury Show*. He got evidence and faked evidence. Part of his formula was exposing faked evidence. You ever watch *The Paul Drury Show*, Lieutenant Columbo?"

"Frankly, ma'am, I never watched it when I could avoid it. Mrs. Columbo liked it, especially his Kennedy shows, so I did see some of them. But on the whole the kind of show he did was not to my taste. Anyway, I do appreciate your time. I won't take any more of it."

2

"Yes, sir. Yes, sir. I appreciate your time. Look, there is something you can do for me in the Drury murder case."

Columbo was on the telephone, talking to the office of the district attorney, specifically to Assistant District Attorney Jonathan Lugar.

"It's possible . . . I don't know for sure, but it's possible that Mr. Drury had a safe-deposit box in some bank. The problem is, we don't know what bank. I wondered if that's not somethin' the DA's office can find out faster'n we can at LAPD. The information could nail the murderer of Mr. Paul Drury. Yeah. Well, I sure do appreciate your cooperation."

3

Martha Zimmer sweated as she faced Columbo just before five o'clock. "Thank God I'm not nursing my child," she said. "What kind of schedule could I keep?"

Columbo smiled at her. "Should I apologize because I trust you more than other detectives?" he asked.

"Columbo . . ."

"Well I do, Martha. Find anythin'?"

They stood in the living room of the Paul Drury house on Hollyridge Road. She was in charge of a team of uniformed officers who had been searching the premises for a hidden safe or a safe-deposit box. Two of them had metal detectors.

Martha Zimmer shook her head. "You want we should empty the swimming pool and check under the floor of the pool?"

"No, we won't need to go that far. And you don't need to

stay any longer. I want this house locked up with the alarm system set. Tell the precinct to run a car by here every half hour all night, at irregular intervals. I gotta rush on down to La Cienega. People are waiting for me."

"How is it going, Lieutenant Columbo?" asked Alicia Graham Drury. "The newspapers say you have leads."

She stood talking with him in the reception area of the Paul Drury office. It was closed, and the doors were locked, but he had knocked and had been admitted. A few cartons sat around. The staff had already begun to disassemble the office.

"Yeah, yeah. We have leads, ma'am. Probably most of them are worthless, but that's the way you get to the bottom of these things: by checkin' out all the leads."

"Do the leads suggest who killed Paul?"

Columbo made a swaying gesture with his right hand. "Sort of," he said.

Alicia was wearing faded blue jeans and a blue cotton shirt. If she had gone into mourning yesterday, that had lasted less than twenty-four hours. She was smoking a cigarette. She flipped her hand in a gesture of nervousness or impatience, and ash fell to the floor. "You are not, I imagine, ready to say where your leads are taking you."

"Oh no, ma'am. No. The leads wouldn't support a charge. Not yet."

"Well, good luck, Lieutenant. Is there anything more I can do for you?"

"No, ma'am. I came by to see some other people. I don't wanta bother you any more than I have to."

"Well . . . You can use Paul's office again. If you need anything more from me, I'll be here a few more minutes."

She opened the double doors into Drury's office. Columbo stepped in, again impressed by the lavish office. "Oh, Mrs. Drury," he said, turning around to speak to her before she left the reception area. "There is one other thing. Nothing important. Routine question. Do you happen to know if Mr. Drury had a safe-deposit box?"

"I'd like to know," she said. "We haven't found his will. I called Bill McCrory today and asked him. He doesn't know. What's more, he doesn't have the will. What bearing does it have on anything?"

"None that I can think of," said Columbo. "Just part of the routine. Y' know, a big part of my work is routine."

She nodded and walked out of the reception area. Columbo went into Drury's office and sat down. In a moment Drury's secretary came in.

"You're Miss Whistler, aren't you?" Columbo asked.

Leslie Whistler was an attractive redhead, stocky and busty, wearing a white blouse and a black skirt. She nodded.

"I have a few routine questions, Miss Whistler. I'd appreciate it if you'd think of my questions and your answers as confidential. First, did Mr. Drury have a safe in the office?"

She shook her head. "No."

"No locked cabinet where he could keep confidential things?"

"No, sir."

"All his confidential information was kept on the disks in his two computers?"

"So far as I know, Lieutenant. Of course, you had to know the password to get into his computers."

"Did anybody besides Mr. Drury know that password?"

"Quite a few people did. Researchers . . ."

"And when those disks were erased, everything was lost?"

Leslie Whistler nodded. "Mr. Drury said more than once that people could break into this office and corrupt paper files. In other words, someone could steal papers, substitute other papers, or even pour kerosene into the file cabinets and burn up everything before the fire department could get here. He said computer files were just as secure as paper files. Nothing was safe, he said. No kind of records were absolutely secure against tampering or destruction."

"What about photographs?"

"I don't know what he did with those. He had some. We do have file cabinets, and we've been through everything. The pictures aren't in them."

"Meaning that he kept some records somewhere outside the office."

"At home, I suppose," she said. "I understand the house has been sealed by the police. When we get in, we'll find the pictures."

"Probably. Okay, Miss Whistler, I wanta ask you to listen to a tape."

Columbo fished out of one of the deep pockets of his raincoat a small tape recorder/player, furnished him at headquarters. It would play the tape from McCrory's answering machine. He held up a finger and pressed the PLAY button.

"Hi. This is Paul. Make a point of calling me first thing in the ay-em, please. Kind of important."

Leslie Whistler put both hands over her mouth. Her face reddened.

"Is that his voice, Miss Whistler?"

"Yes. Absolutely."

"Sounds right? Sounds like something he'd say?"

"Lieutenant, if I've heard him say exactly that one time, I've heard him say it fifty times. If he wasn't coming in the next morning, he'd usually tell me, saying he was going to work at home the next day. Lots of mornings I'd come in and find a message like that on my recorder. He'd got some idea in the night and wanted me to type it up first thing in the morning. That's how he'd say it: 'Call me in the ay-em.' It's eerie!"

"You don't hear anything wrong with it?"

She shook her head. "Play it again, I—"

"Hi. This is Paul. Make a point of calling me first thing in the ay-em, please. Kind of important."

She sighed. "If I've heard those exact words once, I've heard them fifty times."

Columbo nodded. "Right. 'Call me first thing in the ay-em.' It was almost like a formula with him, wasn't it?"

"Yes, it was."

"But that's all he'd say? He didn't say *what* was important?"

"Actually," she said, "he usually added something, like 'I want to send a letter to Humphries.' In the morning I'd call him and ask him, 'What do you want to say in a letter to Humphries?' That'd remind him of what he'd had in mind, and he'd dictate something or give me some kind of instructions."

"And his voice sounds normal? I mean, on this tape. His voice sounds normal?"

She nodded.

"Okay, Miss Whistler. I'm gonna ask you to keep our conversation strictly confidential. Right?"

"Sure. If you say so."

Columbo's final interview at the Drury office that afternoon was with Geraldo Anselmo, the computer technician who had yesterday discovered that all the disks in the two computers had been wiped. The technician was a very young man, somber, and a little frightened.

"Let me make sure I understand this, Mr. Anselmo. You say you can recover information that has just been erased?"

Anselmo nodded. "When you order a computer to erase a file—that is, a body of data—the computer usually doesn't really erase it. It eliminates it from the disk directory, making it invisible, and it eliminates it from the FAT, the table that tells the computer what space on the disk is available for writing new data. You can't retrieve the file, and the computer has been told to write over it whenever it needs space for new data. But until it is written over, the data is still there, and there are programs that can recover it. If, coming in here Thursday morning, I'd found that the disks had been erased, I could have recovered almost everything. But this wasn't done that way. This was a wipedisk. The disks had been totally blanked."

"How could that have been done, Mr. Anselmo?"

"Three ways," said Anselmo. "First, someone could have sat down at Mr. Drury's desk and done it. Second, someone could have done it from another office, since the computers under Mr. Drury's desk were networked—that is, cabled to terminals in other offices. Not every researcher could get to all the information, since access was controlled by passwords, but half a dozen other offices had some access.

Third, a virus could have been planted in the computers. The computers were linked to outside information sources by telephone. Someone outside could have sent in a virus."

"Tell me about this virus," said Columbo.

"It would have been an outlaw instruction code, probably just a little bit of it, hiding on one of the disks. It could have been set to activate on June 3, 1993, or it could have been set to wait for a signal sent in by telephone. Either way, the virus went active during the night and wiped the disks. In the process, it wiped itself, too, so we can't know what it looked like."

"Does it take a brilliant technician to do this?" asked Columbo.

"Not very. A computer illiterate couldn't do it, but thousands and thousands of technicians could."

"Hackers," said Columbo.

"No. Someone who did this thing, with a motive for doing it."

"Aren't there protections against it?"

"Yes, sir. Two protections. One is to run an antivirus program periodically. I ran ours last Saturday. It is possible for a very ingenious virus to get past antivirus programs, but ours said the machines were clean. Of course, the second is to back up everything, either on tape or other disks. I'm afraid Mr. Drury didn't do that. He didn't want multiple copies of his proprietary information lying around. In fact the work stations in the other offices were disabled so far as copying was concerned. People could read from the files but couldn't copy anything."

"Took an awful risk, didn't he?"

"Yes, sir. I'm afraid he did."

5

After dinner, while Mrs. Columbo was in what seemed likely to be an hour-long telephone conversation with their daughter in San Diego, Columbo took Dog in the Peugeot and drove out to Blocker Beach. Holding eager and happy Dog on a leash, he walked along the road above the beach and watched the hordes of kids frolicking in the sand and in the water.

NINE

I

Paul Drury was buried late on Saturday morning. In point of fact, his body was laid to rest in a vault in a mausoleum. The nonsectarian funeral service was private, but the men and women of the news media crowded the little chapel at the cemetery and then shoved their way forward toward the door of the mausoleum.

"Bastards!" muttered Charles Bell.

Besides Bell, the chief mourners were:

—Alicia Graham Drury, ex-wife of the deceased, dressed in mourning black and clinging to the arm of

—Tim Edmonds, producer of the now-defunct television show that had made the dead man rich and famous, wearing dark blue and glancing nervously at frequent intervals at

—Marvin Goldschmidt, director, who seemed genuinely distressed, eyes misty, and who had given his arm, whether to steady her or himself, to

—Karen Bergman, executive assistant, wearing a tight black skirt and a white blouse, weeping quietly and from time to time fixing hostile stares on

—Bobby Angela, country-and-western singer wearing

black: black ski pants and a black cashmere sweater, short-sleeved, and, finally

—Jessica O'Neil, dressed in a dark green linen suit, her eyes covered by big sunglasses.

The redheaded secretary was there, crying openly. William McCrory, Drury's lawyer, stood throughout the funeral, looking miserable and for once wearing a lawyerly suit. Geraldo Anselmo, the computer technician, hung on the rear of the group, apparently wondering if he should have come.

No member of a family appeared. The news media would wonder if there was a family.

The news people were so focused on the celebrities that they failed to notice Lieutenant Columbo, LAPD, Homicide, standing at the rear of the crowd, wearing a short wrinkled raincoat and smoking a cigar.

"We've got serious problems, and we've gotta talk," said Bell to Tim and Alicia as they left the mausoleum. "I flew over to talk to Phil yesterday. Where'd Columbo get his name? He doesn't like it a little bit that this LA homicide dick mentions his name in connection with Paul's death."

"Who *could* have given Columbo the name?" asked Alicia. "We know damned well none of us did it. Who the devil has he been talking to?"

Bell glanced over his shoulder at Bobby Angela and Jessica O'Neil. "He's talking to *everybody*. Old girlfriends—"

"What could *they* know?" asked Alicia. "Paul didn't know Phil. What could he have told them about Phil?"

"I *don't know*," Bell grunted. "But Lieutenant Columbo asked me if I knew the name Phil Sclafani. It wasn't a social question, for damned sure."

"If you're talking to Phil, send him word," said Alicia. "The word is, cool it! If I didn't tell Columbo about Phil—and I sure as hell didn't—and you didn't tell him about Phil—and you sure as hell didn't—then he doesn't *know* anything about Phil and is just playing games. I warned you about this guy Columbo. He's not as dumb as he looks. Not as dumb as he acts."

"Yes, he is," said Tim. "Dumber."

"He's gotta be under pressure," said Bell. "Pressure's on him from downtown. Paul was killed Wednesday night. This is Saturday, and LAPD hasn't come up with anything. Paul was a public figure. The public wants to know who killed him."

"The news media want to know. It's not the same thing," said Alicia.

"The pressure is just the same, or worse," said Tim. "I'm telling you. Columbo is grasping."

"He's grasping too damned close," said Bell.

"Speaking of—"

Columbo, still hanging respectfully back, only nodded at the three mourners when their eyes met his. Bell broke away from Alicia and Tim and walked toward Columbo.

"Lieutenant! We haven't set that dinner date for you and Mrs. Columbo."

"That's right, we haven't, sir. But I mentioned it to her, and she's sure lookin' forward to that. I hope it's not disrespectful for me to be smokin' a cigar here. I didn't think about it. A funeral— But you probably know how it is with me. I get so wrapped up in what I'm thinking about that I— Well . . . That's *my* problem. This is a sad occasion."

"It's good of you to be here," said Bell.

"Well, you never know what you'll see at funerals. I try to stay way back and just watch from a distance, but sometimes you do see things that tell ya somethin'. People have ways of revealin' themselves at funerals."

"Did you see anything today, Lieutenant?"

"No sir, I didn't. It's a shame, though, that there's no family, isn't it? Or maybe it isn't. Nobody to be really devastated."

"Tim and Alicia and I are going to have lunch, Lieutenant. Why don't you join us?"

"Oh, I guess I've bothered you people too much already."

"We'd love to have you," said Bell.

"Well . . ."

"Come in my car," said Bell. "I'll bring you back here to pick up yours later."

"Oh, I couldn't do that, sir. When you drive a car like mine, you don't leave it around places. I can meet you somewhere."

"All right. Do you know where the Bel Air Country Club is?"

"Yes, sir."

"As soon as you can be there, Lieutenant."

"I don't know why you had to do this," Alicia complained to Bell as they sat down in the lounge where great glass sliding doors gave them a view of the first tee. "If you think you can play games with this man, you're wrong."

Bell looked across the room, where Tim was returning from the men's room. "We were worried about Tim losing his nerve. Are you losing yours?"

"I've got a hell of a lot at risk."

"I told you before, don't lose your nerve. That's the only way we can lose this game. Columbo can't really focus on us till he finds the motive, and he's not going to find the motive."

"He's focused on us already."

"Suppose he is. He can't prove anything."

Tim sat down. "The detective is here. I saw him talking to the parking-lot boy about that car of his."

"Probably telling him to take special care of it."

"I'd buy that car from him if he'd sell it. That old Peugeot's a collector's item."

When Columbo, having declined to check his raincoat, came to the table and sat down, Alicia said, "Charles was telling us that your car is a collector's item."

"Well, I don't know about that, ma'am. All I know is, it's gonna have a hundred fifty thousand miles on it one of these days, and you don't see many cars showin' that much mileage. Of course, I've taken good care of it . . ."

"Wouldn't you like to check your coat?" Tim asked.

"That's a good idea. But I got somethin' in my pocket I want to show you."

He took out the little recorder/player again and pressed the PLAY button. *"Hi. This is Paul. Make a point of calling me first thing in the ay-em, please. Kind of important."*

People at nearby tables turned and stared, wondering why they were hearing a snippet of tape apparently from a telephone-answering machine. Some of them knew Charles Bell and recognized two of his guests, but they seemed to wonder who the odd little man with the tape player might be.

"McCrory's tape . . ." Alicia whispered.

"Do any of you hear anything strange in that?" Columbo asked. "The voice? The words?"

"That's Paul," said Tim. "That was how he talked, the way he worked. He often left us messages like that. Where'd you get that one?"

"From his lawyer," said Columbo.

"Does it have any significance?" asked Bell.

"It might. It just might. Y' see, Mr. McCrory's answering machine says it received this message at eleven forty-seven, but the medical examiner has conclusive evidence that Mr. Drury could not have been alive after eleven-fifteen, eleven-twenty at the most."

"I didn't know medical examiners could fix time of death with that much precision," said Bell.

"Mr. Drury had just finished a meal. The state of the food in his stomach—that is, how much it was digested—fixes the time of death very precisely. We know he finished his dinner no later than a quarter to eleven. Miss Bergman remembers the time. Mr. Conte, the owner of La Felicità, is very certain of it. So there's a strange conflict between the evidence of the tape and the evidence from the autopsy. I mean, *I* think it's a strange conflict. It kept me awake last night, wonderin' how there could be that much discrepancy between what the tape says and what the autopsy says."

"Autopsy!" Alicia shuddered. "You mean that body we just put in a vault was—"

"Yes, ma'am. A very thorough autopsy had been performed. It always is when a person has been murdered."

"Are you saying, Lieutenant," asked Tim Edmonds, "that three days after Paul was killed we still don't know what *time* he was killed?"

"Oh no, sir. We know what time he was killed. Between eleven and eleven-twenty."

"Then what about the tape?" asked Alicia.

"I don't think the tape is very reliable evidence, ma'am. There are always ways to fake tapes."

"Eleven-fifteen . . ." muttered Tim.

"Right," said Columbo. He reached into his pocket and pulled out a small spiral notebook. "That's when . . . Lemme see, here. That was when you and Mrs. Drury were at Blocker Beach."

"Does this promote Tim and me to the top of the list of suspects?" Alicia asked.

"Oh no, ma'am. I guess I'm so used to this business that I forget how things I say can frighten people. No, ma'am. You're no more suspected than you were before. Like I said, there's a very big list of suspects."

"Let me add a—"

Bell was interrupted by a waitress who came to take a drink order for the new man who had joined the party at this table. Columbo ordered a Scotch.

"Do you like Glenfiddich, Lieutenant?" Bell asked.

"I'm not sure I ever had it, sir."

"Make his Scotch a Glenfiddich on the rocks," said Bell.

"Make it a double, since he's behind us, and you can bring the rest of us another round. Lieutenant Columbo, I'd like to add a suspect to your list if I may."

"Always glad to have another suspect, sir."

"Really? Well, I'm surprised you haven't focused more on the people who threatened Paul."

"I haven't done that, sir, because whoever killed Mr. Drury knew a lot about his personal habits and had a plastic card to get into his house. It doesn't look like he was killed by a stranger."

"Let me tell you about someone who *might* have had a card. Does the name Virgil Menninger mean anything to you?"

"No, sir. I can't say it does."

"Virgil Menninger," said Bell, "is the father of Barbara Menninger, better known as Bobby Angela. On a *Paul Drury Show* one night last year, Bobby Angela accused her father of having abused her as a child. I mean, she accused him of incest. He was furious. He called and threatened to kill the girl and Paul, too. He's called several times since, when he was drunk. And he could have had a card. Not likely but possible."

"Why would he have a card?"

"Paul gave cards to his girlfriends," said Alicia. "Karen Bergman has a card, undoubtedly—though I've never seen it. Jessica O'Neil had one. Bobby Angela must have had one. And if she had one, her father could have gotten access to it."

"What does this man do for a living?" asked Columbo. "And where's he to be found?"

"He works in the casinos in Vegas," said Tim. "He plays the guitar and wanted to be a country-and-western singer.

He's worked as a table man for several of the casinos. He's had some trouble, been in jail."

"I'll run him through Records," said Columbo. "'Virgil . . .' Could anybody lend me a pencil?"

"See anything on the menu that appeals to you, Lieutenant?" asked Bell.

"What do you recommend, sir?"

"The seafood salad is good."

"Ah, that'll be fine. That'll be very nice."

The waitress returned with their drinks, and Bell ordered lunch. Bell asked Columbo what he had done in New York.

"Oh, I come from the city, Manhattan: the part close to Chinatown. Very ordinary family. Very ordinary. Big family. I have five brothers and a sister. I was an ordinary kid. I guess my two great interests in life when I was a kid were pinball and pool. When I started goin' around with the future Mrs. Columbo, she told me I had to make somethin' of myself if I wanted to marry her. When I got out of the army, I studied for the police exam and got myself on New York's Finest. Twelfth Precinct. A good old Irish sergeant took a liking to me and taught me. I came to Los Angeles to visit an uncle. My uncle used to play bagpipes with a Shriners band. He made me a pitch to stay here. I applied with LAPD, and here I am; been here ever since. I guess I'm a lucky man. I love my work. Not many of us get to make a livin' doin' what we love to do."

Alicia said her own background was not very different from Columbo's. She was from the Lower East Side. Her family was Greek. She, too, had grown up in an extended family, with two grandparents and an aunt living in the family apartment, together with her own parents, two sisters, and a brother. She had worked her way through CCNY, as a waitress, also as an occasional figure model for art classes. Her degree was in drama and television production. She had married Graham shortly after she graduated and divorced him two years later. Then she had come to California.

Tim was Californian born and bred, as Bell was Texan. Both of them had inherited money.

"Alicia has never been to Europe," said Tim. "I'm going to take her there on our wedding trip."

"Oh, are you two getting married?" asked Columbo. "That's great. Congratulations."

Alicia, who by now was all but finished with her lunch, put down her fork. "We've made no announcement yet," she said firmly. "It's known around, but it's still confidential."

"Your secret is safe with me, ma'am."

She stared at him for a moment, running her tongue around inside her mouth, cleaning her teeth. Then she lit a cigarette. "Columbo, you're a sketch," she said. "Churchill spoke of a modest man with much to be modest about. You're a modest man with no reason for modesty. I'd hate to be a criminal with you on my trail."

Columbo shook his head. "All I do, ma'am, is do my job the best I can."

"Don't overlook Karen Bergman, Lieutenant. I wouldn't be surprised if when we come up with a will, he left little Karen some money. Anyway, the last woman he was with was always the one with the least affection for him."

"I'll keep that in mind. That's an interestin' point. And, uh, I think it's time I went along. I'm sure you have things to talk about. Look, uh . . . let me put down some money, here. I shouldn't let you people buy my lunch."

"No way, Lieutenant," said Bell. "Forget it. We're grateful for your hard work. Here you are, working on a Saturday. We're grateful to you."

"Well, thank ya awful much. I really 'preciate it." He pushed back his chair and rose. "Gee, I guess I never did check my coat. Anyway . . . Thank ya again."

"Good luck, Lieutenant," said Tim. "We hope to see you again soon—and hear you tell us you've cracked the case."

"That's my hope too, sir," said Columbo as he backed away, shoving the little tape player back into his raincoat pocket. "G' bye. Oh . . . Oh, just a quick minute. There is one little thing that's kinda bothered me. Nothin' important, y' understand. Just one of those loose ends that's like havin' a popcorn hull in your teeth that you can't get rid of. Y' know?"

"What is it, Lieutenant?" asked Tim, since Columbo was plainly talking to him.

"Well, sir . . . You told me you and Mrs. Drury went out to Blocker Beach and were there for— What? An hour? Isn't that right? And the reason you went there was to have some privacy. But, sir, wasn't it kinda difficult to find any privacy out there? It's supposed to be closed at sunset, but the fact is, it's choked with kids, on the sand, in the water, having a good time. I just wondered about that. One of those little things that bothers me when I can't understand."

"In places like that you *do* have privacy, Lieutenant. Since a hundred people in a hundred cars are doing the same thing— If you see what I mean."

"Oh. Well, sure, I see what you mean. 'Course. You and Mrs. Drury are adult people with homes where you can have all the privacy you want."

"Ever hear of doing something *romantic,* Lieutenant?"

asked Alicia. "Try taking Mrs. Columbo out there some evening, for the same reason. It'll do something for your marriage."

Columbo nodded and smiled shyly. "Say, I bet it would, at that. Thank ya, Mrs. Drury! Thank ya."

Columbo didn't have a radio in his car, so he stopped at the country club desk and asked for a pay phone. The woman behind the desk looked him up and down and told him, "Our guests don't use pay telephones, sir. Telephone carrel number three is not occupied. You may make your call from there."

Columbo walked inside the little room and closed the door. He picked up the telephone and dialed headquarters. When the operator answered, he asked for Records.

"Records."

"This here's Lieutenant Columbo, Homicide. Want ya to run a name for me. Virgil Menninger. That's with three *n*'s."

"Hold on, Lieutenant."

He glanced out through the window in the door as he listened to the clerk at Records pecking computer keys. There was an ashtray on the telephone table, complete with a book of the country club's matches, so he lit a cigar.

"Lieutenant?"

"Yeah . . ."

"Menninger, Virgil C. How much do you want of this? Born 1950, Texarkana, Texas. Uh . . . He's done time in Texas and Oklahoma. Theft, bunko. He's been arrested in Los Angeles, San Diego, and San Clemente, all on suspicion, dropped. That was suspicion of theft, auto once and theft, bunko twice. Last known address, Las Vegas, Nevada, where he registered for a license to work as a table man in the casinos. That was in November 1986. Clean since then. License granted. Last renewal in November '92. Okay?"

"You have anything on his daughter? Barbara Menninger."

"Hang on."

Columbo smiled at a man staring at him through the door, not sure if he was curious or if he wanted the telephone. The man jerked his head around and walked on.

"Lieutenant."

"Yeah?"

"Menninger, Barbara aka . . . Jesus Christ! Also known as Bobby Angela! She's the—"

"Right. The singer."

"Born 1973, Waco, Texas. Arrested LAPD, January 3, 1992, drunk and disorderly. Released January 4, no charge filed. No other record."

"Well, thank ya. That's very helpful."

He punched in another number, Captain Sczciegel's direct line. "How about authorizin' travel to Las Vegas, Captain? Huh? Well, you know, I thought I'd go over, take in a coupla shows, try my luck at the tables. The Drury murder. That's what, the Drury murder. Right. Understood. Okay, thanks. I'll catch a flight, soon as I let my wife know I'm going."

TEN

The Piping Rock Hotel was far too expensive for a man traveling on an LAPD expense account, so Columbo checked into a modest motel on the edge of Las Vegas. By seven or so in the evening he had overcome the airsickness that had threatened him during the short flight—by drinking strong black coffee and eating three hard-boiled eggs in the motel dining room—and was ready to make his first contact in Las Vegas: a courtesy call on the Las Vegas Police.

A desk sergeant pointed to a hallway and told him to knock on the third door on the right. He did and entered the office of Lieutenant Bud Murphy, a young detective with a shiny bald head and beady brown eyes. He was in his shirtsleeves and wore his shoulder holster and service revolver under his left arm.

"The Paul Drury murder is *your case?*" said Murphy, unable to conceal how impressed he was.

"You know how it is," said Columbo. "I just happened to be the man available."

"Is there some way we can help you?"

"Well, yeah. I'm lookin' for a guy. Virgil Menninger."

"Is he a suspect?"

"No," said Columbo. He shook his head. "What he is . . . How would ya say this? He's a cover for me. Like, an excuse to come to Las Vegas. I do wanta ask him a coupla questions, but what I'm really interested in is the Sclafanis."

Detective Bud Murphy nodded. "So are we. So's the FBI. So's the Gaming Commission. We haven't found a thing. There was a lot of skimming going on around here twenty-five years ago, but even that wasn't proved against the Sclafanis. I wouldn't want to vouch for them, but we don't have anything on them."

"Does Menninger work for them?"

"I can find out in a sec." Murphy picked up a telephone, punched in a number, and spoke briefly to whoever had answered. He turned back to Columbo and said, "Used to work at the Piping Rock. At the Sands now. Also clean."

"The Sands . . . I'm gonna pretend I don't know that."

"Shall I come with you?"

"Not till they figure out who I am."

"Got it, Lieutenant Columbo. Look, it's great to meet you. I'm on duty all night. Give me a buzz if you need me."

Piping Rock was not one of the very biggest, most luxurious hotel casinos in Las Vegas. It was smaller than the best-known hotels. Its stage did not feature the major stars who appeared on the stages of hotels like Caesars Palace or Bally's; nor did it promise the cuisine or the sumptuous appointments of those hotels. It was, on the other hand, a solid, well-maintained, flourishing establishment, busy twenty-four hours a day.

Columbo had left his raincoat in his room and arrived at the Piping Rock wearing a dark-gray suit. It was only when he was inside the hotel that he noticed he had tied his necktie wrong, thin end hanging below fat end. Well . . . couldn't change it now. He lit a cigar and stood in the lobby, getting his bearings.

To the left of the lobby was a dark bar. He could hear music from there. Likely as not, that was the bar where Bobby Angela was singing when she met Drury. He decided to walk in there, to check it out, just to see what kind of place she had worked.

The bar was dark, as he had judged from outside. The only light not on the stage was the dim yellow light over the cash register. A single spotlight on the ceiling glared down on the young woman singing on the little stage, and in its cold light her skin took on a bluish-pink glow. She was attractive. She sat on a stool, wearing black velvet pants and nothing above. She clutched a microphone in both hands. She was singing "Memories" from *Cats,* backed by a guitar and an electronic keyboard.

Columbo stepped up to the bar and ordered a beer. The bartender was quick to bring it and to hand him a bill for four dollars. Columbo frowned over it and handed him four-fifty.

The young woman had a good voice, he judged, and she sang "Send in the Clowns" from *A Little Night Music,* then "Music of the Night" from *Phantom of the Opera* before she took her bows to good applause and left the stage.

"Don't I remember Bobby Angela used to sing in this room?" Columbo asked the bartender.

"One time, yeah."

"I thought so. Friend of the boss, wasn't she?"

The bartender shrugged. "I wouldn't know."

"Well, that sure is a talented young woman that's singin' now. I don't get in often, but I'm glad she's the one on the stage when I did get in. It sure is good to be back. Bobby Angela's dad used to work here. Is he still around, d' y' know? I got acquainted with him when—"

"Never heard of him," said the bartender.

"Yeah. Well, he's prob'ly moved on," said Columbo. "So . . . Guess I better get some chips and try my luck."

He used his VISA card to buy a hundred dollars' worth of chips, resolved to cash in ninety dollars' worth. If they played pool for money in a casino, he would be willing to try his skill. At casino tables, skill had nothing to do with winning. The casino would not cheat. It didn't have to. The odds determined whether or not the house would win in the long run—and it always did. An occasional player might win, but house versus players, the house never lost.

The casino seemed like an acre of room.

The carpet was red. The tables were green, like so many pool tables, which Columbo wished some of them were. Conversation around them was hushed, as players concentrated on the games. They resented shrieks of joy or howls of despair—which were rarely heard.

They were all kinds of people: slender young men in bankers' suits, looking as if they had come out from Wall Street as soon as the market had closed yesterday afternoon; Marlboro man types in blue jeans and checkered shirts, conspicuously not what they dressed to be; Ma and Pa from Indiana, in polyester, her glasses hanging from a chain, his rimless, obsessively intent on the table and their chips; sugar daddies giving juvenile chippies a taste of the big life; narrow-eyed careful gamblers, aware of the odds and still somehow convinced they could beat them, watching, studying, and moving; daughters of fortune, watching for the chance to attach themselves to a winner, knowing he had to be a winner at something else to have the money to come here; and first-timers—soldiers on leave, truck drivers—who had saved for this great, great adventure, young mothers determined to win their way out of . . . out of whatever, optimists, naïfs, suckers.

Columbo had seen them before.

The ceiling was smoky mirrors, and Columbo knew very well that supervisors prowled the gloomy catwalks above, looking down through those transparent mirrors, mostly at the table men, watching for cheating, but also at the players.

A table man could not cheat. He would be searched for chips when he left the floor. The only way he could cheat was by declaring a confederate a winner when he had not really won. The men above watched for that. At the blackjack tables, they watched for card counters. Blackjack was played with two or three decks now, to make card-counting almost impossible. Still, there were a few mathematical wizards who would do it, and when identified they were thrown out of the casinos.

Gaming Commission rules did not allow girl blackjack dealers to work topless. That had been tried many years ago, and the commission had ruled it so distracting to the players that they lost more than the odds would have justified—which the commission ruled unfair. The commission had not ruled it unfair for them to deal blackjack at glass tables, wearing miniskirts and glittery panty hose.

Players could stare at the cards or the dealers' legs—their choice.

Columbo walked among the tables, looking at the players, looking at the games. His twenty five-dollar chips had been handed to him in a little box with a wire handle, and he carried it.

"Carry that for you and bring you good luck," said a young woman.

He looked at her. She was gorgeous: her hair stylishly coiffured, her makeup studiously applied, her strapless white dress molded to her generous but taut figure. "Uh . . . Sorry, ma'am. That's a generous proposal, but I'm afraid I could never concentrate on the cards if you were standing behind me."

"You have to *learn* to concentrate, cowboy," she said. "Everything in life depends on concentration."

She did not press the point further but walked on, leaving him concentrating on his cigar and grinning.

He found a vacant place at a blackjack table and sat on a stool, looking down on the cards, the glass, and the pretty dealer's shapely legs. She dealt him a ten down and a five up. He took a hit, was dealt another ten, and lost his five-dollar chip. On the second hand he was dealt a jack down and an eight up and stuck. The dealer had seventeen and paid eighteen. He was even. The third hand he was dealt a six down and a four up. He took a hit and was dealt a three. He took another hit and was dealt a queen. He was out five dollars.

He walked away from the table and around the big room again. The real players, the gamblers who knew where the odds gave them the best chance, were at the blackjack tables and the craps tables. The tourists, those who weren't at the slot machines in the hall outside, were at the roulette tables.

For a few minutes he stood behind the players at a table and watched them shoot craps. He hadn't played the game since he was a kid. The action was fast and fascinating, and you could lose all your money without knowing just how and when.

He tried another blackjack table and in the course of a few minutes won fifteen dollars. With a hundred ten dollars in his carrier, he went to the window to cash in.

"Don't happen to know a guy by the name of Virgil Menninger, do ya?" he asked the cashier. "Used to work here. I'd like to say hello."

The cashier shook his head. "Never heard the name."

As Columbo left the casino and returned to the lobby of the Piping Rock, a broad-shouldered man with a butch haircut came up to him. "Would you mind telling me your name, sir?" the fellow said, polite enough.

"Who's askin'?"

"My name's Cronin. I'm a security officer for the hotel."

"All right. I'm Lieutenant Columbo, Los Angeles Police Department, Homicide Squad. Wanta see my shield?"

Cronin shook his head. "Is there something we can do for you, Lieutenant?" he asked.

"Well, I'm lookin' for a fella. Used to work here. Maybe still does. Virgil Menninger. Know him?"

"Is he suspected of murder?"

"Oh no, nothin' like that. I just wanta ask him a question or two. Strictly routine kind of thing. Just cleanin' up some loose ends for the record."

"He used to work here. Works at the Sands now."

"The Sands . . . Could ya tell me if he left here for his own reasons? Or . . . ?"

"We had a little problem with him," said Cronin.

"Yeah? What was that?"

"I bet you know," said Cronin.

"Let's see if I do."

"He had a daughter, worked here too. One night she went on television in Los Angeles and said that Virgil— Hey. I got this figured out. You're working on the Paul Drury murder. Am I right, or am I not right?"

Columbo turned down the corners of his mouth, raised his eyebrows, and lifted his chin. "Well . . . I guess I can trust you, can't I, Mr. Cronin? Yeah, I'm one of the guys lookin' into that problem."

"Okay, the broad went on the Drury show and accused her father of having done bad things to her, if you follow me. Boy, Virgil went nuts! She was singin' in the lounge, and he went in there an'— Well, the boss had to let him go."

"The boss bein' . . . ?"

"Mr. Philip Sclafani. Mr. Sclafani's father is the owner of the hotel."

"Oh, yeah. Sclafani. From New York originally. I'm from New York myself, Mr. Cronin, originally. I remember hearin' the name Giuseppe Sclafani when I was a kid. My! He's still alive and owns this hotel?"

"Like a drink on the house, Lieutenant?" asked Cronin, gesturing toward the lounge.

"A beer," said Columbo.

"Whatever you like."

They walked into the lounge, where the topless singer was again performing. She was singing "Don't Cry for Me,

Argentina." Cronin led Columbo to a booth far enough from the stage that they could hear each other under the sound of the music. He gave a waitress their order.

"This comes together," said Cronin. "The show where Bobby Angela accused Virgil Menninger of incest was *The Paul Drury Show*. Drury was dating the kid. She was only eighteen. He was twenty-five years older than she was. I suppose she told him what her father had done, so he set up a show for her and some other girls to talk about that kind of thing. It didn't hurt her career, that tearful appearance on the Drury show. It hurt Virgil, for damned sure, and it may not have been true. He— Well, you can see how he'd act. Drury showed up here to pick up the girl after her show in this lounge, and Virgil made a fuss. That's when Mr. Sclafani told him he'd probably be happier working in some other hotel."

"He threatened Mr. Drury," said Columbo. "You can see why I want to talk to him."

"Sure. Well, you'll find him at the Sands."

The waitress hurried back with two beers. Columbo peered past her, at the singer.

"You like Mar Lou?" asked Cronin. "She's a nice kid. No trouble."

The two men drank their beer in silence while Mar Lou sang "Song on the Sand," then "Best of Times" from *La Cage aux Folles*.

"Well, I suppose I better get over to the Sands and see if I can find our friend," said Columbo.

"If there's anything I can do, Lieutenant . . ."

"Listen, I appreciate it. You've been helpful enough tellin' me where to find Virgil Menninger. That's helpful, and I do appreciate it. And I appreciate the beer."

"Anytime, Lieutenant Columbo. Anytime."

"I guess— Y' know, there is one other little thing I might ask you, seein' as how we're already together and talkin'. I got this obsession with clearin' up little points. Sometimes I work a day tryin' to figure out some little thing that doesn't amount to anything. But I can't help it. I've got this kinda mind that says I gotta get everything straight and can't just forget the inconsequential stuff. My captain really gets upset about the time I waste that way. Anyway . . . There's a story that Mrs. Drury, I mean Alicia Drury, came to Vegas and saw a lot of Mr. Sclafani, the young Mr. Sclafani. Is there any truth in that, Mr. Cronin?"

"Is there any real point in that question?" asked Cronin.

"Not really. I mean, that might have given Mr. Drury a reason to dislike Mr. Sclafani but not the other way around. Right? She's a suspect, naturally. The wife or ex-wife always is. It's just one of those things that's in the file, and I'd like to be able to make a pencil scratch across that page and say to forget it."

"I'll ask Mr. Sclafani about it, and you can check with me later if you want to," said Cronin.

"That'd be very kind of ya. I'd appreciate that. The more sheets in a file you can scratch off with a note sayin' 'Never mind,' the easier the case gets."

At the Sands, Columbo made a direct approach. He walked up to the floor boss in the casino, showed his shield, and asked to see Virgil Menninger. "I'm outside my jurisdiction here, but I'd appreciate any cooperation you might give me."

Ten minutes later he sat down with Menninger in a small office off the casino floor.

Virgil Menninger was six feet four and so skeletal as to suggest that he was heavily addicted to something. He had about him, too, the air of a man who has spent more than a little time in prison: a circumstance that marks a man for life. Columbo guessed that if he rolled back his sleeves he would show red and blue tattoos. His hair was gray, and he wore a white pencil mustache and rimless eyeglasses.

"What's the beef, Lieutenant?"

"No beef, Mr. Menninger. I'm working on the Paul Drury case and—"

"And I threatened to kill him."

"You threatened it, but you didn't do it," said Columbo. "Wednesday night, when he was killed, you were working as house man at a craps table. Right? You can prove it. Right?"

"As a matter of fact, I can."

"Sure. I knew you could. 'Course, it's possible that your daughter killed him—which is what I want to talk to you about."

"Bobby . . . ?"

"Oh, I don't think she killed him," said Columbo, turning up the palms of his hands, shrugging, shaking his head. "But she did have one of those plastic cards you have to have to get into his house, which whoever killed him had to have, and she doesn't have an alibi for Wednesday night, the way you have. And I suppose it wouldn't be too hard to find a motive. Hey. I don't think she killed him, but I would like to clear up a coupla points."

Menninger lit a cigarette. He smoked like a convict, holding the butt between his thumb and first two fingers, so as to take no chance of dropping it and being disciplined for littering, and sucking the smoke deep into his lungs in long pulls that would burn the cigarette away in a minute and a half.

"I didn't do to Bobby what she told on the Drury show. I don't know what made her talk that way. Actually . . . Actually, hell yes, I know! He came between me and her. Bobby and I traveled around. I brought her up, Lieutenant. I taught her to play the guitar and sing. I'd liked to of done that myself for a livin', but I wasn't good enough. She was. I brought her to Nevada when I come. When she was sixteen I named her Bobby Angela and got her a job singin' and playin', in Reno. Then I got a job in Vegas and brought her with me. I got her the job at Piping Rock. Then . . . Drury took her away from me. Permanent. I didn't kill him, Lieutenant Columbo, but I'm glad he's dead. I read about his death and saw about it on TV. I'm only sorry he died so easy. I'd have shot him somewheres else."

Columbo took a fresh cigar from his jacket pocket and reached for the lighter that sat on the desk in this small office. "You get to know the man at all?"

Menninger shook his head. "I saw him around here. We were never formally introduced."

"Y' ever meet his wife?"

Menninger grinned. "Alicia? You bet. She never comes here, to the Sands, but she was at the Piping Rock all the time, as long as I worked there."

"Good friend of the boss?" Columbo asked, lifting his eyebrows and smiling faintly.

Menninger hesitated. "I see what you're drivin' at. But you're on the wrong track, I'd guess. I mean, Phil Sclafani could have any broad in the world. And does. I never saw him with one as old as Alicia Graham . . . Alicia Drury. Bobby would have been more his style."

Columbo drew down the corners of his mouth and tipped his head from side to side. "She and Sclafani were seen together a lot, I hear."

"I noticed. I figure she was into him for some money," said Menninger.

"Come again?"

"Alicia dropped a lotta money at the tables. Look, she walked away from my table one night, down what had to be between fifteen or twenty thousand dollars. I mean, Christ, man, Drury wasn't stakin' her to that kinda dough! I mean, she was obsessed. You see the type all the time, you work around the casinos. A gentleman from Arizona was droppin' more than ten thousand when you got me called away from my table. You know how they figure—they're sure to win if they can just hold out through a little streak of bad luck."

"So Mrs. Drury . . . ?"

"Was into Piping Rock for a lotta money. I figure she was. That would've been what she was talking to Mr. Sclafani about when she was seen with him."

"Would he have been threatening to break her legs?" asked Columbo.

"Naah. I doubt that. They got different ways of collectin' these days. The Sclafanis are clean, man. It's not like it was in the old days. The casino operators are *businessmen.* Well . . . Some of them can get rough if a debt is not paid, but it's not the usual thing. They don't hire legbreakers. Only one kinda guy gets a visit from a legbreaker. Maybe two kinds. Cheaters and guys who just tell them to go to hell, they won't pay. The casinos can get very tough about that."

"Let's suppose Mrs. Drury did owe a lot of money," said Columbo. "What kinda deal would they make?"

"To start with," said Menninger, "a high roller can usually settle for eighty cents on the dollar. Sometimes seventy. They'd rather have the business. They don't want that known, but that's the way it is. They negotiate. They take payments. They also work out business arrangements, if you know what I mean."

"Tell me," said Columbo.

"Some of the high rollers are in a position to take the casino operator in on a good deal. Look— I could get *my* legs broken for talkin' too much, but I want you to lay off Bobby, okay?"

"Okay," said Columbo. It was an easy promise to make, since he had no thought that Bobby Angela had murdered Paul Drury.

"Look. You remember the Wall Street scandals—Ivan Boesky and Michael Milken, using inside information? If you got inside information about somethin' goin' on in a business, you can make a quick fortune trading in the right stock. Suppose a high roller is an officer of some company. He's into a casino for, say, a hundred thousand. He tells the collector, 'Look, man, I can show your boss how to make a million quick.' He does, and the boss makes the million quick. The hundred thousand is forgotten. I mean, guys can do favors for other guys and wipe out debts."

"How do you figure Alicia Drury could wipe out a debt?" Columbo asked.

"I dunno. What's she got to offer? Her tail? Not worth much. Or . . . I guess maybe it might be, to the right guys."

"How'd that work out?" Columbo asked. "I mean, that's a cheap commodity in a town like this."

Menninger smiled and shook his head. "Lemme tell you about Bobby, my daughter," he said. "Phil Sclafani never asked her to sell herself. But he also made it plain to her that she could pick up some very good extra money if she'd— Well, you know what. Guys that saw her sing in the lounge. That made a fantasy for them, if you get me. Look, Lieutenant. The point is this. If a high roller gets a hard-on about a girl he can only find at, say, the Flamingo, he gambles at the Flamingo. It gets bigger than that sometimes. Look . . . There was a very big star–type comedienne worked Piping Rock a month last year. She gambled like Alicia. Man, she was into the casino for a hundred thousand if she was into it for a nickel. She paid off about fifty thousand, which was her salary for her work on the stage. The rest of it they forgave. Why? 'Cause she slept with two or three high rollers they shoved her way. She kept them in the Piping Rock Casino, they lost God knows how much, and Sclafani profited. I don't know if Alicia did anything like that. What's she . . . forty years old? But she's got a name. She did the weather for a year or so, in a miniskirt, and she was a reporter, on camera all the time. She was on the screen every time the Drury show was on. Some guys might—"

"I see what you got in mind," said Columbo, nodding.

"I dunno," said Menninger. "I saw her around the place. She was hand-in-hand with guys I recognized as high rollers. I mean, could . . . Hell, man, I don't know."

"Give me the names of these high rollers."

"Jesus, if—"

"Don't worry about it. I'm a cop, not a squealer."

Menninger glanced around: a self-conscious tic. "There's a guy from LA that flies over here about once a month. His name is Henry Sanders. He was very cozy with Alicia Drury a coupla times. I don't know if they were just a pair of gamblers who got to be friends, or what. Incidentally, he's in town. The Piping Rock lost him. He's staying at Caesars Palace. His is the only name I can think of."

"Describe him."

"Short, fat guy. Bald. Always wears black three-piece suits. It won't be difficult to spot him if you see him around the casinos. There aren't many of his type in Vegas."

"This has been very helpful," said Columbo. "I'll let ya get back to your work."

ELEVEN

When the cab dropped him at his motel, Columbo realized he was tired. As he often told people, he really needed his eight hours' sleep every night; it was something about his metabolism; and he wasn't much good after eleven o'clock. It was almost midnight now, and he was ready to go to bed. He decided he would not even call home until morning.

"Lieutenant." Cronin. It was Cronin, the security man from the Piping Rock Hotel, rising from the lobby couch where he had been sitting and smoking a cigarette. It wasn't coincidence, that was for sure. If Cronin was here waiting for him, something was up.

"Did you find Virgil Menninger, Lieutenant?"

"Yeah, as a matter of fact, I did. You put me on the right track for that one."

"Hope he was helpful."

"Well . . . you know. Guy like that. You can never really tell if he knows anything or not."

Cronin grinned. "Wanta know why I'm here?"

"I was wonderin'. Looks like you been waitin' for me."

"Mr. Sclafani would like you to join him in the penthouse for a late supper."

"Well, that sure is nice of Mr. Sclafani. I usually get to bed before this, but I wouldn't wanta pass up an invitation to supper with Mr. Sclafani."

Philip Sclafani was a tall, swarthy man, well put together, with a flat belly, wearing a silvery-gray suit that fit him perfectly. His iron-gray hair was brushed back and held in place, obviously, by a nonoily hair dressing. He wore aviator-shape eyeglasses in silver frames.

"Paesano," he said as he extended his hand to Columbo.

"Sono molto lieto di fare la sua conoscenza," said Columbo. *"Come sta?"*

Sclafani grinned. "You got me, Lieutenant," he said. "It doesn't take much to run me through what little Italian I ever learned. But I am a *paesano.*"

"We spoke it at home," said Columbo.

"My father speaks it," said Sclafani. "He came to this country from Sicily, when he was a boy. He's eighty-five now, but he hasn't forgotten."

"When I was a boy," said Columbo, "I knew his name. Giuseppe Sclafani. We knew the name."

"Different days," said Philip Sclafani. "My father was at the Apalachin meet. I'm sure you know what that was."

Columbo nodded. "This is a beautiful place ya got here," he said. "My—"

"The penthouse is my father's," said Sclafani. "I live down two floors."

The penthouse was sumptuously furnished, though Columbo was at a loss to guess what word to use to name its style. It was luxurious without the elegance of, say, the Paul Drury offices in Los Angeles. On the wall behind the bar in the living room, a nude reclined languorously on rumpled sheets, painted with complete realism on black velvet. The bar glasses sat on lighted shelves before mirrors, so it looked as if there were twice as many of them as there really were. The furniture was expensive, but it gave the penthouse the air of a hotel suite, not a home.

Sclafani led Columbo to the bar and pointed at the stainless-steel stools upholstered in tan leather. He sat on one, and Columbo sat on another. "What can I offer you to drink?" he asked. "Scotch? Martini? Vodka?"

"Well, sir, at this time of night I oughta stay away from the hard stuff. A beer. Or a glass of red wine."

"Open a bottle of the Chianti Classico," Sclafani said to Cronin. "Well, Lieutenant Columbo, I guess I know what brings you to Las Vegas. I assume that the fact you are here means you don't really have any suspects in the Paul Drury murder."

"The fact is, what I've got is too many suspects," said Columbo. "What I'm workin' on is trying to get some of them off my list. You know how that is. Of course the ex-wife is always a suspect. Just like the wife always is—unless they got some ironclad alibi."

"And Alicia Drury doesn't have an alibi?"

"Well . . . I'd say she's got a pretty good alibi," said Columbo. "But it's not perfect."

"And you want to know what is my relationship with her?"

Columbo turned up his hands. "If you wanta talk about it, sir. I don't mean to get too personal."

"If, Lieutenant, the question is whether or not I slept with Alicia Drury, the answer is no."

"I'm glad to hear it, Mr. Sclafani. I don't like to have to get into those personal things."

Sclafani lifted the bottle of wine and stared at it critically for a moment. He sniffed the cork. Then he poured a swallow into a glass and tasted it. Finally he poured a glass for Columbo and one for himself.

Columbo didn't perform the wine ritual. He just sipped the wine and said, "My, that is good! Chianti. My favorite."

"My relationship with Alicia Drury was entirely simple," said Sclafani. He paused to salute with the wine. "She gambled heavily here and lost a lot of money. The question was, how was she going to pay? I suppose she met with me a dozen times, proposing a payment schedule, trying to get me to omit interest, and so on."

"Was it a really big amount of money, sir?" asked Columbo.

"Let's say it was a *very* substantial amount of money," said Sclafani. "Look . . . I'll give you an idea of how she tried to pay what she owed. She gave me a stock tip. She tried to get me to buy a short position in an oil company called Orange International. If I'd done it and credited the profit to her, I'd have made enough to retire her debt. The problem was, she was offering me insider information picked up by researchers for the Drury show. If the SEC had figured out the connection . . ."

"I get ya."

"The woman is no innocent, Lieutenant. I can't believe she killed Paul Drury, if that's what you've got in mind, but she's no innocent."

"Docs she still owe you money, sir?"

"No. She paid off. That was . . . about four or five months ago. In full."

"Was that in cash?"

Sclafani nodded. "In cash."

"All at once . . ." said Columbo, shaking his head in apparent amazement.

"All at once."

"Isn't that interestin'? She comes up with it all of a sudden, huh?"

"I'm like you. I wonder where she got it. Maybe she got some more insider information. But to make money off insider information, she'd have had to have money to invest. Anyway, she paid. I figured she'd found a man who'd pay it for her."

"This is excellent wine, Mr. Sclafani. I really appreciate your openin' a bottle like this."

"The hotel is bringing up some roast beef in a little while," said Sclafani. "The wine will go well with roast beef. Let me pour you some more."

"Very kind of ya," said Columbo, watching with satisfaction as Sclafani poured.

"Philip . . ." The name had been spoken in a cracked, weak voice, by an elderly man who had just entered the room.

"My father," said Sclafani quietly. "He's eighty-five."

The elderly man walked slowly toward the bar, not shuffling, yet not lifting his feet more than an inch or so off the floor. His chin was high, and he held his body straight, even though it was obviously fragile and slow to respond to the commands of his brain. His yellowish-white hair was thick across the top of his head. He wore round horn-rimmed eyeglasses. A big cigar, unlighted, hung limply in the fingers of his left hand. He wore a blue blazer with the crest of the hotel on the pocket, white shirt, striped necktie, gray flannel slacks, and polished black Gucci loafers.

"Papa, this is Lieutenant Columbo of the homicide squad, Los Angeles Police."

"Ahh . . ." said Giuseppe Sclafani, using his tongue to shove his dentures back into place as he spoke. His voice was raspy, but his words were fully intelligible. "A homicide detective. Pour me some wine, Philip. Well, Lieutenant Columbo . . . Am I glad to see you? Or am I not glad to see you?"

"I hope you're glad to see me, sir," said Columbo. "I'm just here askin' a few routine questions. Nothin' special. Nothin' to worry about."

The old man sampled the wine, then nodded emphatically—whether to approve the wine or to agree with Columbo was not evident. "Detectives investigating murders," he said, "never play games. They are always the finest sort of fellows. The others— Well. You know how it can be." He shrugged.

"I'm from New York, Mr. Sclafani," said Columbo. "When I was a boy, I already knew your name."

"When I was a boy, I knew the name of Julius Caesar," rasped Giuseppe Sclafani.

His son laughed. Columbo joined in.

"You ever hear of the Castellammarese connection?" the old man asked Columbo.

"Yes, sir. I've heard of it."

"Salvatore Maranzano . . . He brought me to America,

from Sicily. Paid my passage. Later he was murdered. That's how things were in the old days. He was murdered."

Giuseppe Sclafani spoke with a faint accent. He put the unlighted cigar between his lips from time to time but quickly took it out, as if he found no satisfaction in it and longed to strike a match and light it.

"That's how things were in the old days. If a man offended you—"

"*Papa.*"

"Well. It is so. These things are history today. Except in Sicily, where they still do it."

"Except back home in New York, where they still do it," said Columbo.

"No," said Giuseppe Sclafani, turning down the corners of his mouth. "Hoodlums. Hoodlums killing hoodlums. In the old days, it was business. Strictly business. No one died unless he had given offense. Major offense. Major offense, giving honest men reason to put him aside. No . . . All that is gone. Lieutenant— I have never been in prison. Not a single day. If what some say about me were true, would I not have been in prison? Even Meyer Lansky served six months in jail. My son is timid." The old man paused and smiled. "Maybe that is why I live in comfort today. But . . . Forgotten. You know, I haven't been out of the hotel in two or three years, not even downstairs for . . . What, Phil? Two years?"

"You came down for the staff Christmas party in 1991, Papa. But you know you don't have to stay up here. You can go anywhere you want, anytime. We can arrange a flight back to Sicily if you want to go."

"Thank you, but I don't think I'd like what I'd see there."

The old man turned to Columbo. "My health isn't too bad for a man my age. I'll leave it to you to judge if I've lost my mind or not. I listen to music, watch television, read. Once in a while I have a showgirl come up and eat dinner with me, just so I can look at her, just so I can hear a young voice and hear how much they haven't learned. I don't have any reason to leave the penthouse. The first time I think of a reason, I'll go. Anyway, for me it's a good idea to be forgotten."

"I haven't forgotten you, Mr. Sclafani," said Columbo.

"Nor has the FBI," said the old man. "If we open the door, maybe we find one of those scumbags listening. Maybe the apartment is bugged. So okay. *'J. Edgar Hoover was a faggot!'* Get that on your tapes, smart FBI men!"

"Papa . . . We're going to have a supper."

"And I'm going to light my cigar," said Giuseppe Sclafani defiantly.

"I'll join ya in that, sir," said Columbo.

"No. You have one of mine. From the humidor, Cronin. A cigar for Lieutenant Columbo!"

"Oh my!" said Columbo as he accepted the cigar and sniffed at it. "I've never smoked one as fine as this. This is real nice of you, Mr. Sclafani."

"Cuban," said the old man. "Not easy to get. I lived in Cuba for a while and acquired the taste for them. Castro smokes Cuban cigars. Can you imagine that? *He* smokes Cuban cigars, but *we* are not supposed to. What case are you working on, Lieutenant? The Drury murder?"

"Yes, sir, that's the one."

"I watched his television show. Not all the time. Sometimes. He was an evil man. You could see why somebody would want to kill him."

Columbo savored the big Cuban cigar. "I get your point," he said.

"What's more, his wife is a hooker."

"Papa!"

"Well, she is. Do you deny it? I do not condemn her, you understand, but I thought I should have seen in her eyes the decent shame a woman should feel when she is a whore. It wasn't there. No such thing. Her eyes are cold as ice, and she stares at you without humility. I—"

"Will you sit down to dinner with us, Papa?" the younger Sclafani interjected forcefully.

"Only if you are having *farsumagru palermitano.*"

"The chef who does that for you doesn't work this late. You can have it for dinner tomorrow night."

Giuseppe Sclafani spoke to Columbo. "My mother made *farsumagru palermitano,*" he said. "Do you know what it is, Lieutenant Columbo?"

"Yes, sir. It's a stuffed beef roll, with veal and prosciutto, tomatoes and onions, and chopped hard-boiled eggs."

"I was not born in Castellammare del Golfo but in San Vito lo Capo. Close enough. When I was last at home, in 1934, my mother spent an entire day making *farsumagru* for the whole family. The tables were set up in the garden in the evening, and we ate under the lanterns."

"What we're having for supper tonight, Papa, is roast beef and a salad."

"Ahh. Well, I am not hungry. When I've finished my cigar, I will go to bed. What could my son know about the Drury murder, Lieutenant?"

"Nothin' about the murder directly, sir. I just wanted to ask him a question or two about a coupla suspects."

"Why Menninger, Lieutenant?" asked Philip Sclafani.

"Because of his daughter. Y' see, she had one of the plastic cards that shut off the alarm system and opened the locks at Drury's house, and Drury was killed by somebody who had a card. What's more, she's got no alibi."

"Why would *she* want Drury dead?"

"That's the point. That's what I wanted to ask you. Can you think of any motive she might have had?"

"Virgil had a motive," said Sclafani. "A grudge. I am sure you know what the grudge is about."

Columbo nodded.

"Alicia . . . I don't know what her motive could have been. Maybe Drury lent her the money to pay her gambling debt and was pressing her for it."

Giuseppe Sclafani put his half-smoked cigar aside in an ashtray. "I am pleased to have met you, Lieutenant," he said, "but I am not interested in this conversation and so am going to bed. Good luck to you."

"Thank you, sir. It's been great meetin' you."

Cronin accompanied the elderly man until he was almost out of the room, at which point another man, apparently a valet, came and offered his arm.

The supper was brought in. It was what Sclafani had said it would be: rare slices of cold roast beef with sliced tomatoes, sliced onions, some relishes and condiments, and bread. It was on a wheeled table, and Columbo and Sclafani sat over it alone.

"My father dislikes Alicia Drury," said Sclafani. "That's why he calls her a hooker. He got it in his head I was sleeping with her and was going to marry her. She's been married and divorced twice, she's not Catholic, and she's not Italian. The idea of my marrying her made him very angry."

Columbo nodded. "I can understand that. Parents usually want their children to—"

"Papa took a strong dislike to Alicia. I've heard him call her worse than hooker."

"Is it possible she *was* a hooker? He's not the first person to suggest it."

Sclafani shrugged. "She didn't give her marker for *all* the money she lost at the tables. Maybe she was picking up a little on the side. I don't know. I didn't want to know. I'd have had to put her out of the hotel if I thought so. The Gaming Commission is strict about letting hookers work the casinos."

"Well . . . cheers, sir," said Columbo, saluting with his wine glass.

They ate sparingly. A postmidnight supper had not been the best of ideas. Columbo was tired and anxious to get back to his motel and to bed. They finished.

"It's been very, very kind of ya," Columbo said as he walked across the foyer to the open and waiting elevator. "Please give your father my best wishes. He's a legend."

"Okay, Lieutenant. If there's anything I can do for you, let me know."

Columbo stepped into the elevator. He grinned and lifted his hand. Then abruptly he frowned and stepped out of the elevator. "Oh, there is one little thing I ought to ask. Little point . . . kinda bothers me. Your father's description of Alicia Drury is awfully definite, sir. Where'd he meet her? You say he hasn't been out of the penthouse since 1991. Does that mean she was up here?"

Sclafani sighed. "Papa has a vivid imagination, Lieutenant. I imagine he read someplace about the woman's cold eyes and how she stares at people, and he incorporated that into his impression of her. He's seen plenty of pictures of her. He's seen her on television a hundred times. If you asked him directly if he'd met her, he might say he has. But I promise you he never did."

"Well, thank ya. That clears up that. Thank ya again for all your kindness, sir. Good night."

Before he left his motel room in the morning, Columbo placed a call home.

"Ah, yeah. It's a great place. We oughta come over here sometime. We oughta come over here and stay a coupla nights in one of the *big* places, see a great show. We can drive. Flyin's too hard on a person. It gave me an upset stomach. I didn't get to bed last night until . . . oh, I guess it was close to two o'clock. An' you know what? Nothin' had slowed down. The streets were full of people. It's like they say: twenty-four hours a day. I was offered a great supper last night, but I couldn't eat too much; I was too beat. Yeah, it's goin' okay. I'll catch a flight sometime later today, I'm pretty sure. Should be home for dinner. If anything gets in the way, I'll call. Hugs for everybody. See ya."

By chance he got the same waitress for breakfast he'd had for his mid-afternoon lunch yesterday. "Hard-boiled eggs? You *live* on hard-boiled eggs?" she asked.

"Well, I like 'em for breakfast," said Columbo. "Yesterday I had them to settle my stomach. And some black coffee strong enough to melt the spoon. 'Kay?"

"Decaf?"

"Any spare caffeine ya got left over from the decaf other people are drinkin', give it to me."

He left the motel a little after nine. He wore his raincoat this morning.

A taxi dropped him at Caesars Palace. As he had told his wife an hour before, time of day meant little or nothing in Las Vegas. Neither did it make any difference that this was Sunday morning. The casino hotel was as active as it had been twelve hours before. He decided not to go to the desk and ask for the room number of Henry Sanders. The desk would not give a guest's room number, maybe not even if he showed identification, and he didn't want to alert anyone to who he was. He walked into the casino. He had come out ten dollars ahead in the casino at Piping Rock, so he went to the cashiers and bought a hundred dollars' worth of five-dollar chips.

This was different. No miniskirted legs were displayed under glass tabletops at Caesars. The amount of money circulating was far greater here than it had been last night at Piping Rock. He went to a blackjack table and began to play. The security men were on the lookout for people who didn't play. They wouldn't interfere with them. They just watched them. By playing he satisfied them, and they would by and large ignore him—to the extent they *could* ignore a tousled man in a rumpled raincoat. For a little while he was able to keep even with the house. Then in a few minutes he was down thirty dollars. Players who were down three hundred or three thousand smiled condescendingly as he walked away from the table.

Okay. It was all right. A short, squat man in a black vested suit walked in, bought chips, and walked toward a craps table.

"Uh, excuse me, sir. Are you Mr. Henry Sanders from Los Angeles?"

"Right. That's me. Why?"

"Lieutenant Columbo, LAPD, Homicide. I wonder if you and I could talk for two or three minutes?"

"What's the problem?"

"Oh, no problem for you, sir. Just tryin' to check out a little detail that's come up in the course of an investigation and thought you might be able to help out. Won't take you five minutes."

Henry Sanders glanced around. "All right. We can sit down over here. What you got in mind?"

Before they could sit down, an officious man, obviously house security, blustered up. "Is this man bothering you, sir?" he asked Sanders.

"No, no. Friend of mine. No problem."

Columbo watched the man retreat, obviously still suspicious. "That's right, sir," he assured Sanders. "No problem."

"Okay. What do you want to talk about, Lieutenant?"

"I'm sure you're aware of the fact, sir, that Mr. Paul Drury was murdered last Wednesday night—"

"Uh-oh. I figured this'd come up."

"Sir?"

"What was my relationship with Alicia Graham—Alicia Drury? When I saw he'd been killed, I figured this question would come up sooner or later."

"All right, sir," said Columbo. "What *was* your relationship with Mrs. Drury?"

Sanders licked his lips. "Wanta drink, Lieutenant? We can pop in the bar."

"A little early for me, sir."

"Well, come on with me. You can have coffee."

They walked into a tiny bar just off the casino, where

gamblers could retire for a few minutes to ponder their strategy. Columbo ordered coffee as Sanders had suggested. The rotund little gambler ordered a Bloody Mary.

"I could, uh . . . I could decline to answer your questions," said Sanders. "You're outside your jurisdiction, Lieutenant. Besides, I could decline to answer *anybody's* questions until I consult with a lawyer."

"All that is very true, sir," said Columbo apologetically. "That's very true. I'm sorry if I'm a nuisance to you. I'm not tryin' to make out you've done anything at all wrong. I'm just a poor workin' detective, tryin' to clear up points in his record."

"To start with, I didn't bring her to Las Vegas, Lieutenant. I *found* her here."

"You talking about the old-fashioned—?"

"Transporting a woman across a state line," said Sanders.

"Oh no, sir. Nobody suggests you transported the lady anywhere."

"Well, I didn't. I was staying at the Piping Rock, gambling there. You see, Lieutenant, I love to gamble. Over the years I may have lost a hundred thousand, maybe two hundred, but if it's a two-hundred-thousand loss, I've had a lot more than two hundred thousand dollars' worth of fun. Some men like to go to Europe and trudge through the art galleries, some to buy expensive treasures. Some will spend ten or twenty thousand a crack for the opportunity to hunt or fish in some spectacular place. I know a man who spent twenty thousand to be allowed to accompany an expedition toward the South Pole—and they didn't make it there. I like to gamble. You know what business I'm in, Lieutenant?"

"No, sir. I don't."

"I sell *wire,* Lieutenant. I guess I'm just about the biggest wholesaler of wire in the country. Electrical wire. Telephone wire. Electronics wire. Hell, I even sell barbed wire for fences. Would you believe I've got an inventory of over a hundred thousand different kinds of wire?"

"That's hard to imagine, sir," said Columbo, frowning and turning down the corners of his mouth as if it really were hard to envision a hundred thousand different types of wire.

"I came back from the war in Korea. They were still selling what was called war surplus then. I bought some stuff, opened a store. And pretty soon I decided the future was in wire. Do you have any idea how many miles of wire are in a space shuttle? The talk is all about chips and circuit boards. Well, it's true we don't hook tubes and resistors and capacitors together with wire, the way we used to do in radio and television sets. But what those chips and boards do still has to be sent out to perform their functions . . . over wire, mostly. I've made ten fortunes in wire."

"That's fascinatin'," said Columbo.

"No, it isn't. It's boring as hell. Like a lot of businessmen, I have to find some way to make life worth living. Alicia. All right. Whatta you figure the relationship was?"

"I'd rather you told me, if you don't mind, sir."

"I bought her services as a prostitute," said Sanders. He drew a breath and blew a sigh. "I couldn't imagine she was one. But she was. And— My God, Lieutenant! My wife had been dead for seven years, and I'd been without a woman in bed since she died. And then suddenly I find out that this . . . *television personality* that I'd seen on TV for years and admired for years was available— But, Jesus Christ, it didn't have anything to do with the death of Paul Drury. In fact, I haven't seen Alicia for six or eight months."

"Would you mind telling me how much you paid for her services, sir?"

"A thousand dollars a night," said Sanders. "Plus dinner and a show, champagne from room service. All that. She wasn't cheap. But—"

"You weren't bored when you were with her," said Columbo, nodding, communicating sympathy and understanding. "And you looked forward to the next time."

"Exactly." .

"How did you find out she was available?"

"She came to me in the casino. It took me a little while to figure out what she was saying."

"How many times were you with her, Mr. Sanders?"

"Six times. Then suddenly, about the first of April, she stopped coming to Las Vegas. I telephoned her at KWLF, and she would not return my calls. I felt like a fool."

"Why did you feel like a fool, sir?"

"Because I *was* a fool. The last time I was with her, I asked her to marry me."

Columbo nodded. "Well, I'm sorry to hear you were embarrassed, sir. Please understand that *I* won't embarrass you. I can't think of any reason to bother you again."

"You are a gentleman, Lieutenant."

"I try to be, sir. It isn't always easy in my business."

Sanders swallowed the last of his Bloody Mary. They got up from the table.

"I guess there's one other thing I oughta ask you, sir," said Columbo. "I notice you're here, not at the Piping Rock. Is there any particular reason for that?"

Sanders scowled. "I never saw her anywhere but at the Piping Rock," he said. "I don't want to run into her accidentally. Besides—I can be a bitter and suspicious man, Lieutenant. I began to wonder if she hadn't been a shill for the Sclafanis. The casinos use women that way, you know."

Lieutenant Bud Murphy of the LVPD had offered to drive Columbo to the airport.

"It's possible," he said in the car. "She wouldn't be the first woman who signed on to pay off a gambling debt by selling herself. Alicia Graham . . . Alicia Drury. Sure, she'd be worth a thousand a night in this market. A celebrity woman is worth as much as her celebrity, to some of the high rollers."

"The question is," said Columbo, "do the casinos use them to keep the high rollers in the house?"

"It's not unheard of," said Murphy. "The penalties for doing it are severe, but how are you going to prove it? Alicia Graham Drury would be small peanuts in this market. She'd be worth a lot more than a showgirl, not worth anything like a featured performer on one of the big stages. I suppose she'd be worth her thou. Yeah, I suppose she would at that. Easy."

"It'd take a long time to work off a big debt at a thousand a night," said Columbo. "Particularly when she was only in Vegas on weekends."

"It doesn't make much sense, does it?" asked Murphy. "But I've seen worse."

TWELVE

Columbo stopped at his office on Monday morning.

On his desk he found a telephone message from Karen Bergman. He called her, and she said she would like to see him. She didn't want to talk on the telephone. He met her in a drugstore on La Cienega Boulevard, where she waited for him at the lunch counter, drinking a cup of coffee and munching on a cheese Danish. Once again she was wearing the white blouse and tight, short black skirt that identified her.

"I appreciate your coming, Lieutenant," she said when he sat down beside her. "I don't trust the office telephones anymore. In fact, you never could be sure who was listening. Even Paul himself sometimes listened in on the lines."

"Was that the way it was?"

"It was never a friendly little office," she said. "Coffee? There was always a certain degree of hostility, always a certain amount of suspicion."

"Yeah, coffee," he said to the counter girl. "I wondered about that. Hostility. What, jealousy?"

"I don't know, exactly. Tension. It had nothing to do with the divorce. Or at least I don't think it did."

"No?"

"No. Alicia didn't care what Paul did. And I don't think he cared what she did. The thing is, you know, Tim fell madly in love with her. I suppose he was before she and Paul were divorced. Anyway, the man is one hundred percent totally mad about her. And she is a manipulative woman. She plays Tim like a puppet on a string. Paul frustrated her. She couldn't manipulate him."

"Tim . . . ?"

"Tim could have killed Paul. He hated him."

"Why?"

"Business reasons, partly. Mostly because he thought Paul had abused Alicia: dumped her."

"Miss Bergman . . . I don't think you called me to tell me stuff like this."

"No. I found out something. Bill McCrory asked me to go through Paul's bills, checkbook, and credit-card accounts, to try to get some idea of what he owed, what bills have to be paid somehow. He kept most of that stuff in the office, not at home, so it wasn't hard to get a rough idea. I was scanning his VISA account and came across something interesting. Last month he bought four boxes of three-and-a-half-inch microdiskettes. Floppies . . . y' know? That's forty diskettes. Looking around the office, I couldn't find forty diskettes. I found about six. I ran back through his bills for the past two years and found that he'd bought more than two hundred microdiskettes since 1991. That's an awful lot of diskettes, and there are only like six in the office."

"Does that mean he kept copies of what was on the computer hard disks?" asked Columbo. "Does that mean that wipedisk deal didn't really destroy his archives?"

"That's a real possibility. It means he wasn't as big a fool as we thought he was," she said. "Isn't that what we thought, Lieutenant? That he was a fool to have kept everything on those hard disks, even if he did have two and so had redundancy."

"Well now, ma'am, I never said Mr. Drury was a fool. I did think it was strange he kept all that information in one place that way. That didn't seem to make sense, no matter how people explained it."

"Let's talk about something else, Lieutenant. Ordinarily, computer supplies were bought through the office accounts, not on Paul's personal credit cards. Why would he buy them that way? The only reason I can think of is that he didn't want the whole office to know he was buying them. Maybe no one knew there were other copies."

"The big question, ma'am, is, where are those diskettes? Could they be why somebody went through his home desk?"

"Could be," she said. "But think of something. We're talking about— The actual number is two hundred forty diskettes. That number would pack a desk drawer totally full. And what advantage would there be in trying to save the data by taking it home? If someone were smart enough and desperate enough to wipe his main disks, why wouldn't they steal or destroy the copies he kept in his desk at home? No, Lieutenant. I don't think they knew he had them."

"Okay, suppose he did, ma'am. Where are they?"

"The same place the pictures are," she said. "We know he had pictures. Where are *they?*"

The counter girl put Columbo's coffee down in front of him. He took up the cup and sipped. "Have you told anyone else about the twenty-some boxes of diskettes?"

"No. Not even Mr. McCrory."

"Let's don't," said Columbo.

"I went through his checks, looking for a safe-deposit-box rental. I haven't found a check that looks like rent on a box."

"Keep looking," he said. "Make a list of any checks you can't understand."

"Alicia doesn't like it. She doesn't like it that Mr. McCrory asked me to go through Paul's records. Next thing I know, I'm going to be locked out of the office."

Columbo shook his head. "Naah. They won't do that."

From a telephone booth in the front of the drugstore, after Karen Bergman left, Columbo telephoned Assistant District Attorney Jonathan Lugar.

"Listen, I appreciate your cooperation. Didn't find a deposit box in the name of Paul Drury, huh? Lemme give ya some more information. It would hafta be a *big* box. Bigger'n a desk drawer. That could hold more than two hundred computer disks. Plus probably some photographs. Maybe not at a bank. Maybe one of those vault companies. And, what's more, it probably wasn't in his name. Maybe he paid the rent with cash."

Columbo puffed on a cigar as he listened to the assistant DA explain that he'd faxed a request to every bank and vault company in Los Angeles.

"Would ya extend that out to the county, sir? Oh, ya

already did. Well, that's first-class. I appreciate that. So there's one more thing, Mr. Lugar. You know we sealed the house. Now I think we oughta seal the offices. I think you'll find the late Mr. Drury's lawyer will cooperate a hundred percent on that. There's some important records missing. On computer disks. When we find those records we'll know why Mr. Drury was killed. Oh no, sir. I got a pretty good idea who did it. But I can't make the case till I get the *why* of it straight. Yes sir, you're right. We shoulda sealed the office last week. But last week we didn't know what we know now. Yes, sir. That's right, and I sure do appreciate your cooperation."

Martha Zimmer entered Burt's a little hesitantly. She did not feel menaced by the place; it was just a greasy spoon with a couple of pool tables in the back. It was smoky. It was shabby. But it was one of Columbo's favorite places, because it offered two of his favorite things: a friendly game of pool during the lunch hour and deep heavy white bowls of fiery chili.

"I thought I'd find you here."

Columbo raised his eyes and looked beyond the end of his cue, beyond the colored balls on green cloth, up at the figure of Martha Zimmer. His raincoat was smeared with blue chalk and talcum powder. His cigar burned on the edge of the table.

"Martha," he said. "Gimme a minute. I'm shootin' at the nine ball."

Fixing his attention once again on his shot, he slipped the cue back and forth between his fingers, adjusting his aim.

He shot. The white cue ball went almost the whole length of the table, struck the white-and-yellow nine ball, and propelled it toward the right-hand corner pocket. It sped between the corners without touching, slammed into the rear of the pocket, and dropped out of sight. The cue ball came to a rest on the bottom rail.

"Aw-*right!*"

Columbo gathered up three one-dollar bills, his own and the two bet by his friends. He walked to a tall stool away from the table and picked up his bowl of chili, which sat on a railing behind the stools. "Sorry, fellas," he said. "She's a detective. Duty calls. Hey, Martha, you wanna bowl of some of the best chili this town has to offer?"

"I've already eaten," she said, eyeing with conspicuous skepticism the half-eaten bowl of chili, in which soggy crackers lay in a stratum that almost hid the concoction below.

"Aww . . . Too bad. Burt's has some of the best chili in Los Angeles. And you're talking with a connoisseur. So, anyway, what can I do for ya?"

"Coupla things. Captain Sczciegel says you're to report to the pistol range and requalify *today.*"

"Yeah. Well . . ."

"How a man who can cut a nine ball like that can't hit a target with a pistol is beyond me."

"Well . . . the pool balls don't make so much noise. What's the other thing?"

"You wanta see people mad? I got the great assignment of goin' over to La Cienega at the head of the squad that sealed the Paul Drury offices. They're gonna get lawyers. All that. And they wanta see you, toot dee sweet."

"Lessee. That'd be Mrs. Drury, Tim Edmonds, and . . . Bell."

"Bell wasn't there. The other two were furious. They're gonna call the chief."

Columbo shrugged.

Charles Bell swung his glass around in a circle, setting the ice in his drink in motion, staring over it at Alicia and Tim. He had not been at the office this morning and was dressed in the yellow slacks and pale blue shirt he invariably wore at the Topanga Beach Club. "What could they find?" he asked. He answered his own question. "Nothing. They sealed the house and searched it with metal detectors, and they didn't find anything. What are they going to find in the offices? Nothing. And I'll tell you why nothing. Unless one of you made some stupid mistake, there's nothing *to* find. The pistol . . . . It's gone. The laptop. It's gone. Sure, they suspect you. That's routine. But even if Columbo breaks your alibi, he can't prove you killed Paul—and prove it is what he has to do. Cool it."

Alicia stared at the swimming pool. "He went to see Phil," she said.

"And what'd Phil tell him? Nothing. The *omertà.* The *omertà.* Phil wouldn't talk to save *himself.* The only people who could talk and foul you up would be Phil . . . or *me.* And you know *damned well* that isn't going to happen."

"He'll never make the connection," said Alicia grimly. "Tim and I are his chief suspects. But he'll never make the connection. He can't make a case until he figures out a motive, and that he'll never do. Like I said before, why would any of us want to kill Paul? We had no reason—no reason Columbo will ever discover, no matter how smart he is."

"I'm losing a lot of money on this deal," said Tim. "I've got to find new office space, get a new show—"

Alicia put her hand on his. "Concentrate on your sports stuff for a while," she said. "Maybe in time we'll find some way to cash in on the notoriety of Paul's death. I'm the one who's gotta come up with a way to make a living. I'm wondering if I could do a book."

"You don't have to make a living," said Tim, turning his hand over and closing it on hers. "When we're married—"

"You two are grown-up, self-sufficient people," said Bell. "Maybe it won't be impossible to do the Drury show without Paul Drury. I—"

The maitre d' approached their table. "There is a telephone call for Mrs. Drury," he said.

Alicia left the table and went to the telephone in the foyer. "Hello."

"Alicia. Thought I might catch you there. This is Phil. The cops are answering your office phones."

"The brilliant Lieutenant Columbo had the offices sealed this morning," she said.

"That's what I need to talk to you about: Columbo. You know he spent the weekend here. He talked to several people and asked a lot of questions. I had him up to the penthouse, and he had quite a chat with Papa."

"Charles says we can rely on the *omertà*. Is that true? You and your father—"

"Charles shouldn't talk about things he knows nothing about," said Sclafani curtly. "Anyway, your man Columbo is too smart by half. I had him tailed. He didn't talk to anybody who knew anything. Except one. I can't figure out where he got the name or how he located him, but he talked to Henry Sanders."

"Jesus Christ!"

"I doubt Sanders told him anything," said Sclafani, "but I don't like it that he had the name."

"He couldn't have got a worse one."

"Why?"

"Because Sanders asked me to marry him. He tried to call me at the station, and I wouldn't take his calls. He may be in a mood to get back at me, and he might figure telling Columbo some ugly things is a good way to do it."

"When did he ask you? Was this before or after our deal?" asked Sclafani.

"Well, of course I never saw him again after we made our deal. When he was trying to call me it was after our deal, after I quit coming to Vegas."

"Damn!"

"What can we do, Phil?"

"Play it cool, that's what you do—like the word you sent me. Even if he finds out you worked for me last year, that doesn't prove anything. And listen. Don't tell Tim or Charles about this. You have cooler nerves than either of them. Frankly, I'm not gonna tell Papa. He might get Sicilian ideas."

"Okay. I'm glad you called me here. This line is safe. I'll have lunch here every day for a few days. You can call me here if you want to talk to me."

"Got it. Hang in there, kid. This kind of business takes a little nerve, but if you've got it everything comes out okay."

"I met Joe Sclafani," said Columbo to Ben Palermo. "Giuseppe Sclafani. Ya ever meet the man personally?"

They sat together in Palermo's office in FBI headquarters, Los Angeles. Palermo shook his head.

"It's like meeting somebody out of history. It's like if Al Capone suddenly walked up and shook hands."

"I once met Meyer Lansky," said Palermo.

"That must have been somethin'," said Columbo. "But I don't wanta take too much of your time. I found out something troubling about Mrs. Drury. I was wonderin'—"

"I'm way ahead of you," said Palermo. "I could see which way your inquiry was going, so I ordered some information from Las Vegas. Here is a copy of a report one of our agents made on her. Notice the date."

Confidential File Memorandum
Subject: Alicia Graham Drury
Date: 12/17/92

Inquiry has been made about the current activities of the above Subject, who is apparently closely associated with Giuseppe and Philip Sclafani. Background information will be found in other reports already filed.

Specifically, inquiry has been made as to whether the Subject is currently working as a prostitute in Las Vegas. While the information accumulated is not conclusive, it seems highly probable that the Subject is in fact a prostitute, working in the Piping Rock casino and hotel owned by the Sclafanis. Information in support of that conclusion is as follows:

Columbo: The Grassy Knoll

(1) Subject has been observed to have lost a very substantial amount of money gambling at the Piping Rock Hotel and Casino. Inquiry by the Los Angeles office has discovered no assets from which a large gambling debt could be paid.

(2) Subject has been observed in very intimate conversation over dinner tables with a number of male subjects known to consort with prostitutes. Telephone calls to her room in the early hours of the morning have not been answered, leading to the conclusion that the Subject was not spending the night in her room and the tentative conclusion that she was instead spending the night in the room of the male subject with whom she was earlier seen. (The Subject has not been followed, nor have listening devices been installed in the rooms where she apparently spent nights.)

(3) Male subjects with whom Subject has been observed include:

(a) Charles Duro (54), San Francisco, who was the subject of a complaint by a San Francisco bar owner that he repeatedly offered money to waitresses to accompany him to a motel room. Matter disposed of by a warning issued by San Francisco Police. The Subject was observed three times in the company of Duro.

(b) Emilio Contadora (61), San Diego, who in 1990 filed a complaint with San Diego police that he had been robbed by a prostitute. The Subject was observed four times in the company of Contadora.

(c) Henry Sanders (61), Los Angeles, arrested LAPD 1987 for having solicited sex for pay with a woman vice squad detective. Case disposed of on receipt of written promise not to repeat conduct. The Subject was observed six times in the company of Sanders.

(d) Richard Bernardin (58), Greenwich, Connecticut,

arrested White Plains, New York, 1985, on charge of having beaten a prostitute in dispute over payment. Served ten days in jail, fined, and placed on probation. The Subject was observed twice in the company of Bernardin.

These subjects were identified by taking fingerprints from glasses or utensils used by them. Other male subjects have not been identified because no fingerprints were on file for them.

It should be noted that all these male subjects have been observed to be heavy gamblers at the Piping Rock Hotel Casino.

More intense surveillance of the Subject will be required if more definite information is desired.

Addendum to Above File Memorandum
Date: April 16, 1993
The above Subject, Alicia Graham Drury, has not been seen in the Piping Rock Hotel and Casino for several weeks. Nor has she been seen in any other hotel or casino.

"I don't see the connection, do you?" Columbo asked. "What has this got to do with the fact that possibly she murdered her ex-husband? That's a mystery. Y' know, I enjoy mysteries. That is to say, I like to read 'em. But I never can figure them out. Maybe that's more in *your* line. My line is just to keep accumulatin' information, till finally it's all very clear. But if it's a mystery, where you got to hook information together in funny ways, that's not my line."

Palermo grinned. "My line and yours are just the same, Columbo."

"Sherlock Holmes, Ben. Think about Sherlock Holmes.

That's how he solved mysteries. I mean, our way: by puttin' together evidence, includin' information Scotland Yard overlooked. It wasn't great insights that made his successes possible; it was plugging away and gettin' more and more information."

"Alicia Drury must be quite a woman," said Palermo. "Quite a career."

"Yeah. Yeah, she's quite a woman, all right. It's too bad, this here," said Columbo, tapping the memorandum that lay on the agent's desk. "I feel sorry for her. I bet she was *abused.*"

"Don't get too sympathetic," said Palermo.

"Yeah. I bet I'm gonna get less sympathetic this evening. I gotta meet her, she and her friends, and I bet they're gonna raise hell with me. Y' know?" He shrugged. "What can I do? It's an obsession of mine to find out things—even when it makes me wish I didn't know what I know."

THIRTEEN

Columbo reached Alicia Drury's house before six that evening. To his surprise, he found that she was alone. He had supposed he could not see her outside the presence of Tim Edmonds and Charles Bell, but the contrary proved true. She met him at the door, wearing a beach coat over a swimsuit, and invited him in.

"I'm trying to get a little sun on the lanai," she said. "If you don't mind, could we sit out there? Scotch? I've also got beer, bourbon, gin, and so on."

"The Scotch, thank ya kindly, ma'am," he said. "Just a light one."

Her house was modest by the standards of Paul Drury's home on Hollyridge Drive. Besides being far smaller, it sat on a heavily trafficked street of modest homes and was in a state of some disrepair. The stucco having fallen off in two big patches, exposing concrete block, and a part of the roof had been replaced with roofing that did not match the rest of it. In back, she had the lanai, a small pool, and a small green lawn, all shielded from her neighbors' sight by a high, stucco-covered concrete-block wall. A low, round redwood table sat by a wheeled redwood chaise longue.

"Make yourself comfortable," she said, pointing to another chaise. "And . . . You know, you'll never get a suntan if you won't take off that raincoat."

"No, ma'am. I guess I won't. I guess I'm not the type who can get much interested in a suntan. I did get interested one summer and went to the beach every chance I got. Guess what happened. I just burned."

She tossed her white terry-cloth beach coat aside. Her swimsuit was a black bikini: neither prudishly modest nor extravagantly revealing. He renewed his judgment that Alicia Drury was a strikingly handsome woman: distinctive in her bearing and self-confidence. "Now that I've been thrown out of my office, I have nothing better to do than work on a tan," she said.

"I'm sorry about that, ma'am. We won't keep it sealed too much longer."

"I'm told you found out some interesting things about me during your weekend in Las Vegas."

Columbo sipped Scotch. "I hate ever to have to look into personal things, Mrs. Drury," he said.

"Lieutenant Columbo, have you ever seen the original Dracula movie, starring Bela Lugosi?"

"Ah, I sure have. Six or eight times."

"Dracula was given a line in that film," she said. "He was confronting Dr. Van Helsing, who had just ascertained that the count was a vampire. And Dracula said something like this: 'Now dat you know . . . vat you know . . . vat do you plan to do, Dr. Van Helsing?' Do you see my point? What are you going to do to me, Columbo, now that you know what you know?"

"Oh ma'am, what I found out—supposing it's true—doesn't seem to have much to do with the death of Mr.

Drury. I didn't go to Las Vegas to look into your personal life. I found that out sorta by accident. To tell ya the truth, ma'am, I'm sorry I heard about it. I'd rather not know."

"What you found out could hurt me very much if it got widely known."

Columbo nodded. "Oh, yeah. I wouldn't want that to happen. It's not information that's useful to me."

"Do you want an explanation?"

"Ma'am, you don't have to give me one."

"I want you to know. I trust you, Lieutenant Columbo."

"Ma'am— Maybe you shouldn't. I am after all the police detective investigatin' the murder of your former husband. I can't say to you that the thought hasn't crossed my mind that you might have somethin' to do with it."

"Of course. You've said all along he had to have been killed by someone close to him, someone who had a card, someone who knew the house. I have to be on your short list. So, listen. Let me tell you something about me. You see, I am a compulsive gambler. I don't have to explain what that is. I've always gambled, since I was a teenager. When I came to LA I started going to Vegas. I settled on the Piping Rock after a while and started to do all my gambling there. Lieutenant . . . I *loved* it! I *do* love it! I'd give anything, almost, to be at a blackjack or craps table in Las Vegas. I've won. I've lost. Of course, in the long run most of us lose. I lost more than I could afford, and the house began to take my markers. After a few months, Philip Sclafani called me into his office and showed me all my markers. Lieutenant, I owed the house over sixty thousand dollars!"

"That's a lot of money, ma'am."

"The chief problem for Mr. Sclafani was that I was recently divorced. He'd authorized that much credit, supposing Paul would make good if he had to. Lieutenant Columbo . . . Paul didn't even know about it! When we were divorced, I got a nice settlement, including this house which— Frankly, it was a house he bought to keep a girlfriend in, before he married me, and he'd kept it for a love nest. Anyway, I paid Mr. Sclafani half what I owed. He was nice about it, but he said I had to pay, that debts like that couldn't be allowed to stand; people would get the idea they could tell the casinos to go to hell. He suggested I borrow from Paul. I couldn't. Paul would have scorned me, might even have fired me. Well, he said, think about it. Let me know what you decide you can do." She stopped.

"I see," said Columbo.

"Out of my salary I could pay him five or six hundred a month. He said he'd accept that temporarily, but I'd have to do better. Lieutenant, he wasn't even charging me interest, and even so it would have taken me five years to pay off at that rate. Well . . . if I'd been propositioned at the tables once, I'd been propositioned a hundred times. The next time a nice-looking older man propositioned me I negotiated a deal."

"I'm sorry to hear about this," said Columbo. "You don't have to go into details."

"I won't. I handed the money over to Mr. Sclafani, didn't tell him where I got it. I did it again. And again. By about February of this year I had paid my debt down to something like fifteen thousand. I'd surrendered every shred of dignity I ever had, but I was working my way out of the mess. By this time Tim was in love with me and had started to talk about marriage. He didn't know what I was doing, of course. Didn't guess. I couldn't go on—I guess the term is 'turning tricks'—and seeing Tim. I told Tim I owed Mr. Sclafani fifteen thousand. I told him why. He made me a loan of that much, provided I never go back to Las Vegas. I paid off Mr. Sclafani, and I've never been back to Las Vegas since."

Columbo nodded. A faint smile appeared. "All of this," he said, "has got nothin' to do with the death of Mr. Drury. And I'm glad to know it, ma'am. 'Cause I sure wouldn't want to have all this come out in the news."

"I wouldn't want the man I'm going to marry to know about it," she said.

"It was a terrible thing you had to do," said Columbo.

"I appreciate your understanding."

"Did you think the Sclafanis would have got rough?"

"Probably only in the sense of making my indiscretions public—which is the worst thing they could do to me."

"I can understand that."

"Tim is very angry about the office being sealed. So is Charles Bell."

"Yeah," said Columbo. "I can understand how they would be. So, uh . . . I expect I'd better be gettin' on." He stood. "Mrs. Columbo is makin' spaghetti carbonara tonight. She can get upset if I don't show up on time for somethin' like that. You don't need to get up. I know the way out. I'll just leave my glass in the kitchen. And, uh, you don't need to worry about me tellin' the story. I'm just sorry it all had to happen."

Alicia swung her feet around and sat up, but she did not rise from the chaise. "It's been a rough couple of years," she said.

"Yeah. You have my sympathy."

"I thought I'd be married to Paul Drury for the rest of my life, then—"

"Oh yeah. That's awful rough. And I bet ya still cared for the guy."

"Yes, sure. So— Well, good luck, Lieutenant. I hope you get it all straightened out soon."

"So do I," said Columbo as he walked toward the back door of the house. "Uh . . . Oh, say," he said, turning. She had just turned to stretch out again on the chaise. "Maybe you can clear up a point for me. Little things, little details, get stuck in my head, and I have a hard time keeping my attention on the big issues. I'm sure it doesn't make any difference, but—"

"What?"

"Well, ma'am, Mr. Giuseppe Sclafani, the old gentleman, talked about how he met you and what your eyes look like and so on. He also said he hadn't been down from the penthouse since 1991. So, did you meet him up there, in the penthouse?"

"Are you asking me if I had a relationship with that old man?" Alicia asked sharply.

"Oh no, not at all, ma'am! No idea like that ever crossed my mind."

"The hell it didn't," she said. "Well, the answer is no. Hell no. I met with Philip Sclafani up there. Twice. I met the old man. Twice. Frankly, he wasn't very cordial."

Columbo grinned. "He thought you wanted to marry his son."

Alicia softened and grinned. "He's senile," she said. "But I bet he was tough when he had all his brains."

"I bet he was. Well, thank you again. Thanks for the Scotch."

As Columbo left the house, he met Tim Edmonds coming up the walk.

"Good evening, sir."

Tim shook his head. "Lieutenant," he said. "How long is this going on? When do I get my office back? Frankly, I think your investigation is foundering, and you're foundering."

Columbo tipped his head to one side. "I'm sorry you feel that way, Mr. Edmonds. It's in the nature of the job. I just can't do it so as to please everybody. I wish I could, sir. I don't like to inconvenience people."

"You're inconveniencing me very seriously."

"Well, I'll expedite the examination of the office, so you can get back in as soon as possible."

"I would appreciate that," said Tim, and he turned and strode toward the house.

Martha Zimmer was temporarily in charge of the Paul Drury Productions office. Columbo had told her to admit Karen Bergman and Leslie Whistler, Drury's secretary, to the office. The three women were there when he arrived the next morning. They had made a pot of coffee.

"I've come across something interesting," said Karen Bergman. "In the company records. It was Paul's practice to pay travel expenses for some of the people who appeared on the show, but he only rarely paid an appearance fee. Even so, he was paying Professor John Trabue two thousand dollars a month. He began paying him in February. The checks are listed as being for consulting services. Also, there is one more. In March he sent Professor Trabue a check for one hundred eighty-five dollars. It's marked 'Expenses.' It's not travel expense. You can't fly from Texas to California and back for one hundred eighty-five dollars. Besides, Professor Trabue was already a visiting professor here in Los Angeles in March. There's no suggestion about what it was."

"There's one sure way to find out," said Columbo. "Ask Professor Trabue."

He met with the professor in a small office just off a classroom. The old oak desk was scarred with cigarette burns and scratches, as were the three wooden armchairs. Shelves were crammed with books and files and loose papers. The professor sat comfortably behind his desk, not wearing academic tweed but a light brown suit. His eyeglasses were lightly tinted, green. He was not condescending to the rumpled detective who sat across his desk and was fumbling in the pockets of a wrinkled old raincoat, but he was plainly intensely interested in him.

"Since you're smokin' a pipe, sir, maybe you won't mind if I smoke a cigar."

The diminutive professor's fixed smile broadened slightly, and he said, "Not at all, Lieutenant. I hope it's a cheap cigar. My pipe tobacco is cheap, and I'm told it stinks."

"Y' know," said Columbo, "I've always been sorry this is a part of life that I missed. I mean, college. Mrs. Columbo, she takes courses at night, and I think she's goin' to get a degree sometime. Two of my kids graduated from college. But me, I went from high school to Korea and came back and joined the New York Police Department. All this kinda thing . . . the campus, the classrooms, the offices, is very interestin' to me. Gotta match?"

Professor Trabue shoved a package of paper matches across the desk. "It's never too late, Lieutenant Columbo," he said. "You could take classes, too."

"Well . . . I live with an odd schedule, y' know. I never know where I'm gonna be when."

"On the other hand," said the professor, "there is nothing magic about a college degree. Abraham Lincoln didn't have one. Neither did Harry Truman."

"And neither did Sherlock Holmes," said Columbo as he lit his cigar.

"Good!" The professor laughed. "Well . . . Lieutenant, if you hadn't called this morning, I would have called you. I assumed you would be hard-pressed and would in your own good time inquire about what little I might be able to contribute to your investigation of the death of Paul Drury."

"What *can* you contribute, Professor?"

"Very little, I'm afraid. But since you've come to see me, you must have something in mind."

"Well, goin' through the corporate records we've come across some checks written to you."

"Exactly. I thought you'd ask about that. I was acting as a consultant to Paul Drury Productions. He had me on what lawyers call a retainer."

"Meanin'—?"

Professor Trabue grinned. "Meaning he paid me whether

I did any work or not. Actually, I was doing some work for him. You know, he was preparing a special show for the thirtieth anniversary of the assassination of President Kennedy."

"So I understood."

"My job was to prove he was wrong in what he was planning to broadcast," said the professor.

"And what was that, sir?"

"Frankly, it's another Grassy Knoll theory. Paul had photographs showing two men on the Grassy Knoll, one of them holding a rifle. He had the pictures computer enhanced. Do you know what that is, Lieutenant?"

"I have heard of it, yes, but suppose you explain it to me, Professor."

"I don't understand it exactly myself," said Professor Trabue, "but I've seen a wonderful demonstration of the technique. There are photographs of Abraham Lincoln delivering his second inaugural address. Those pictures were taken from a distance. You can see which figure is the President, but you couldn't recognize him. Computer enhancement of those photographs produce portraits of Lincoln as he looked that day. They also produce a portrait of John Wilkes Booth, standing not far from him."

"Let's see," said Columbo. "If I remember, it's got to do with the laws of probability."

"That's right. Like this—" The professor took a pencil and began to make dots on a sheet of paper. "Suppose each dot represents a grain of silver on a photographic negative, enlarged as far as optical enlarging can go: thousands of times. Suppose they look like this—"

He pointed at his line of dots:

. .   . .

"It's fair to suppose, by the mathematical laws of probability, that with the missing information the line of dots would look like this—"

. . . .

"And that," he concluded, "is the photographic representation of a line like this—"

_____

"Dots like this—"

.

.   .

.

.   .

.

.

"—almost certainly represent an egg shape, roughly. The technique was developed for the enhancement of aerial reconnaissance photographs."

"And Mr. Drury—?"

"Had a computer lab apply the technique to some photographs taken on Dealey Plaza on the day of the assassination. The enhanced photographs show two men standing on the Grassy Knoll. One has a rifle."

"Where'd he get these pictures?"

"Because he was a popular television personality, people sent him pictures, letters, notes, and so on, that they had never shown to the police or FBI. Very few of the items he received were of any value, but he did have these two photographs of the Grassy Knoll, and he had them computer enhanced."

"Where are those pictures, sir?" asked Columbo.

"Locked up in a vault," said Professor Trabue. "Paul kept the most important of his Kennedy materials in a vault. He'd come to the conclusion that they were dangerous. I mean—"

"Are you sayin', sir, that somebody might have killed him to prevent his runnin' the thirtieth-anniversary show and broadcasting TV images of those photos?"

"I imagine you have a better theory than that, Lieutenant. It's just an idea."

"You know somebody erased his disks. All his information is gone."

"Not the Kennedy stuff," said the professor. "It's in the vault with the pictures. He told me that was where it was."

"Diskettes?"

"That's right. He ran some of them for me, right here in this office, on his laptop computer."

"What about a script for the show? Did he have a script on the computer?"

"It would have been a little premature for that. We had working notes."

"Do you have a copy of those notes, Professor?"

"No. Only *my* notes, not his."

"Well, okay. These two men in the enhanced photo. Who are they, do you know?"

"No. Maybe we could find out by going through his data base. We'll need the diskettes."

"Which are in a vault."

Professor Trabue nodded.

Columbo shrugged and stood. "Well, okay, sir. I guess I know what we have to do. I won't take any more of your time. I may call on you again, though. You've been more than helpful."

Professor Trabue stood and reached to shake hands with the detective. He looked a little confused.

"Oh. There is one other thing, sir," said Columbo, pausing in the door. "Your checks from Paul Drury Productions were for two thousand apiece. Except one. It was for one hundred eighty-five dollars. What was that for, sir? Can ya tell me?"

The professor nodded. "A year's rental of the vault," he said. "I rented it in *my* name, as Paul asked me to do. He thought it would be more secure if it were not in his name."

Columbo ran his hand across his tousled hair. He pulled out his cigar and all but crushed it in his hand. "You rented the vault? In your name? So you know where it is?"

"Exactly. I wondered if you wouldn't ask."

"Mustard and relish," said Columbo to Martha Zimmer and Geraldo Anselmo, the computer technician. "Mort knows how to do 'em. There aren't that many hotdog vendors in town that know how to do it right. Look at that! Just look at that." Martha and Geraldo looked at Columbo's hotdogs and at theirs. His were burned. Much of the skin was black. "Some of these guys actually *boil* their hotdogs, can ya believe it? Ya never get as good as Coney Island hots, not anywhere but Coney Island, but Mort does come close. And look at this mustard! Yellow. Not that awful brown stuff. Oh, well . . . The brown stuff is good on salami and stuff like that, but for hotdogs— Hey! Those people bought me country-club lunches lately, but nothin' was as good as this."

They were in Pershing Square, where Martha had sat on a bench and held places for them while the two men bought hotdogs, chips, and orange soda from Mort. A little way from them a ragged zealot was haranguing the crowd about something or other: no one could really tell; certainly no one cared.

"Geraldo, I need to talk with ya about those two computers in Mr. Drury's office."

"Yes, sir," said Geraldo apprehensively.

"Okay. Now. What I need to know is, are the machines damaged? I mean, like tryin' to bring Frankenstein back to life, can they be made to work again?"

"I don't see why not," said Geraldo.

"That virus that screwed 'em up. Is it still in there?"

"I don't think so. I worked with them until the police closed the office yesterday. Looks like they're all right. The hardware's okay. All that happened was, the disks were erased. I tried a piece of software that sometimes can bring the lost data back, but these disks were too much erased. Wiped."

"So you think you can make those two computers do what they did before?"

"I think so."

"Okay. We'll let you back in the office. Put 'em back together, so they can do what they used to do."

"I can reinstall the programs. In fact, I've already re-installed the word processor. What's lost is the data."

"Suppose I had some new data for them to work with. Can they do it?"

"Sure."

"Okay. Tell me how to protect that data, so it won't be erased the way Mr. Drury's original data was."

"Is this data on diskettes?"

"So I'm told."

"You copy those," said Geraldo urgently. "Make backup disks. Don't bring the only copy. Make two backups. Don't take chances."

Columbo turned to Martha Zimmer. "The police computer center can do that, right?"

She nodded.

"Now, Geraldo. Where did the virus come from, do you think?"

"In on the telephone line, I think."

"Can ya cut that line off?"

"You bet, Lieutenant. Pull the telephone plug."

Columbo nodded and smiled. "Well . . ." he said. "We may be gettin' somewhere with this thing. As soon as the professor's classes are over, we're going to open that vault."

"Don't you need a court order?" Martha asked.

"What for? It's the *professor's* vault. He's got the key. I want you with me on this, Martha. I might need an officer with a sidearm."

FOURTEEN

Professor Trabue admired the Peugeot. He called it a classic car and said he wished he owned it.

"It gets a lot of attention," said Columbo. "I've had it a lotta years, and it's got a lotta miles on it. I always say, if you take good care of somethin', it'll take good care of you."

"Like your service revolver," said Martha sarcastically from the back seat.

The Innes Vault Company occupied a one-story steel-and-glass building that sat behind four tall, well-tended palms. A small fountain played in the lawn between the parking lot and the building. Someone had dumped in a box of detergent, and foam skittered across the parking lot and into the street, on gusts of wind.

Going inside, Columbo and the professor carried leather satchels.

Inside, the building was all brushed aluminum and polished wood, fluorescent light and marble floors. A glass wall separated the reception area from the vaults and the cubicles where people could open their boxes.

Professor Trabue identified himself to the receptionist by showing his key. He signed a card, and she compared his signature on that card to the signatures on a second card. Columbo noticed two signatures on the second card: the professor's and that of Paul Drury. Seeing Drury's name, the receptionist picked up her telephone and called the manager. He came out through a glass door in the glass wall.

"Ordinarily, when a box was rented in the name of a deceased—" he started to say, but Professor Trabue interrupted him curtly.

"The box was rented in *my* name. I pay the rent. I allowed Mr. Drury access to it because I wanted him to have access to certain research materials I have stored here, but this deposit box is mine, not his."

"And these two people are—?"

"Lieutenant Columbo, sir. Los Angeles Police, homicide squad," said Columbo, showing his shield. "And this is Detective Martha Zimmer."

The manager escorted the three of them through the glass door, which was unlocked by electric signal from inside a cage somewhere in the building, and led them to a tiny office. After a minute or so, the manager pushed a wheeled cart into the office. He inserted his key into one of the two slots in the box, and the professor used his key in the other. The manager withdrew and closed the door.

The box sitting on the cart was as big as a side drawer on a desk. The professor lifted the lid. Inside were stacked rank after rank of computer diskettes. On top of those stacks were manila envelopes, fat with their contents.

"Treasure of the Sierra Madre!" Martha whispered.

"An excellent simile," said the professor. "Like the gold dust, it could all blow away in the wind." He ran his hand over the stack of diskettes. "Recovering information from these requires technological expertise."

"We got that," said Columbo. "Let's look at the pictures."

The manila envelopes contained maybe fifty photographs. About twenty of them had to do with the Kennedy assassination. The others were graphic pictures of the victims of diseases and accidents, some of them of bodies on the autopsy table, pictures of lungs ravaged by tobacco smoke, pictures of prominent politicians conspicuously in their cups, pictures of two others in flagrante delicto, pictures that were unidentifiable without information from the diskettes, and so on. One photograph was a nude of a prominent female member of Congress, taken apparently with a long telephoto lens. Another was a sexually explicit photo of a pair of famous popular singers, both male.

"These pictures were entrusted into my custody," said Professor Trabue of the sexually scandalous pictures. "And I propose to burn them."

"Martha and I couldn't say if you did or didn't, sir," said Columbo. "We were looking at somethin' else when you showed those pictures."

"Here are the Dallas photographs Drury was so fascinated with," said the professor. "Both the originals and the computer-enhanced versions."

The original photographs were unremarkable. They had been enlarged from 35mm negatives probably and were grainy and not perfectly focused. They showed, chiefly, a crowd on a sloping lawn, some in the shade of trees, others in the sunlight. The photos had been taken from such a distance that it was impossible to tell if the people in the crowd were smiling or scowling. Some seemed to be in white shirtsleeves. Others were in dark clothes. To anyone but cognoscenti of the whole drama of the Kennedy assassination, it was just a crowd on a slope, watching the street between them and the camera. To someone very familiar with the assassination scene, it was apparent that the two pictures had been taken from the triangular park between Elm and Main streets and that the sloping lawn was what would become known to history as the Grassy Knoll.

Motorcycles were on the street in the first picture. In the second, an old open Cadillac was passing by, men riding on the running boards. In some odd way the crowd looked different, though the figures were so small and indistinct it was impossible to tell exactly what the difference was.

"Didn't the guy take a picture of the presidential limousine?" Columbo asked.

"Maybe what the man saw was so shocking that for a moment he couldn't take a picture," suggested Professor Trabue. "Maybe he was winding his film. Anyway, people sent Drury all kinds of pictures, their snapshots from that day. The ones showing the President had probably been turned over to the authorities a long time ago. These pictures were the leftovers, sent along to Drury maybe in the hope of getting his autograph on a thank-you letter."

"Did Mr. Drury work his computer thing on all of them?" asked Columbo.

"No. But he had studied enough to know that this was the crowd on the Grassy Knoll. A lot of witnesses said they heard shots fired from the Grassy Knoll. That's why he had these enhanced."

"Okay. I'd like a look at the computer-enhanced versions," said Martha.

The professor handed over two glossy eight-by-ten prints,

each representing a postage-stamp-size segment of the original prints. These were strange. They had an odd look, as if they were photographs heavily retouched by an artist. The explanation of computer enhancement was dramatically displayed in these pictures. The computer had located the dots representing each grain of silver left on the negative by the developing process—that is to say, grains changed by the impact of light from the camera lens—and it had applied laws of mathematical probability to put additional grains where none actually existed. The process had changed a few of the tiny, vague, anonymous people on the film to real people with features and expressions, postures, clothes . . . and reality.

"Could this thing work wrong?" Columbo asked. "I mean, could this process make somebody look like somebody he wasn't?"

"The process depends on probability and isn't perfect," said the professor. "But the answer to your question is no. The process could not create a false image. When it fails, it creates a vague image. These two men in the enhanced picture must have looked very much the way they are shown."

"Fascinatin' . . ." muttered Columbo.

The first computer-enhanced photograph portrayed two men standing near a tree on the Grassy Knoll. Both looked young. They wore white shirts, one with his shirtsleeves rolled back. That they were together was evidenced by the fact that one stood with his arm over the other's shoulder. The one seemed to be speaking to the other, quietly into his ear. Between them, held by the man who was listening, was a rifle: an object clearly identifiable as a rifle. They stood close together, so close that maybe they were shielding the rifle from the people standing around them. It looked as though that would not have been difficult. The crowd's attention was intently focused on whatever was in front of them: in this case, clearly the motorcade carrying not just the President of the United States but also his fascinating wife.

The second photograph was different. The people in the enhanced fragment were obviously mesmerized by something. All their heads were turned to their right, staring toward the Triple Underpass where Elm Street passed under the railroad tracks. In their conspicuous agitation, none of them seemed to notice that the man with the rifle was striding up the slope toward the picket fence. The rifle was clutched close to his side, the muzzle pointing at the ground.

The man who had stood beside him in the first picture did not appear in this one.

"So much for Lee Harvey Oswald," said Martha.

"No," said the professor. "The shots that killed the President were almost certainly fired by Oswald. At least one of them was. The Grassy Knoll is at the wrong angle. But if there were other shots fired, maybe from the Grassy Knoll, as some witnesses insist, there you see two men with a rifle."

"Two men in the first picture," said Columbo. "What happened to the other man between the time the first and second pictures were taken?"

Professor Trabue shook his head. "Every square centimeter of that photograph was computer enhanced. He was not on the knoll when the second picture was taken. In other words, between the time when the motorcycles went by and the time when the limousine carrying the wounded President went by, the second man left the scene. A matter of half a minute maybe."

"Could he have been behind one of those trees?" Martha asked, looking at the original, non-enhanced picture.

The professor shrugged. "I suppose. But clearly the other man is scramming, carrying his rifle."

"No way to tell if he actually fired a shot," said Martha.

Professor Trabue shook his head. "I'll tell you what makes me think he didn't. If he had, wouldn't *someone* have been looking toward him? Wouldn't someone have heard the shot and turned to look at him?"

"Well, there was a lotta confusion there," said Columbo. "Noise. I read somewhere that the motorcycles were back-firing. A rifle makes less noise than a revolver . . . It coulda been one way or the other."

"Do you have any idea who the two men are, Professor?" Martha asked.

"No."

"Do you think Mr. Drury knew?"

"If he did, he didn't tell me."

"Well . . . This stuff should be taken out of here and hauled to headquarters," said Columbo.

"Everything should be copied," said Professor Trabue.

"That's exactly what we got in mind. I hope the satchels are big enough for everything. I guess if we got diskettes left over, I can get some of 'em in my raincoat pockets."

"What you got in the satchels, Columbo?" asked Captain Sczciegel.

Columbo was glad for the opportunity to put down the

two heavy satchels. He had played the gallant and insisted he would carry both, so Martha, the new mother, would not have to carry heavy weight; and as they walked through the halls at headquarters he was flushed and breathing heavily.

"That's evidence, sir," he said. "Evidence. It's got to be duplicated, then locked up."

"In the Drury case?"

"Yes, sir. In the Drury case."

"Lieutenant, let the uniformed boys take care of that." The captain took the time to glance at his watch. "There's time for you to get out to the pistol range and requalify. I want you to do it! That's an order."

"Sir, I . . . uh, I'd have to go home and get my revolver. I . . . uh, wouldn't want to try to qualify with a strange pistol."

"Lieutenant Columbo, I will pretend I didn't hear you say your service revolver is at home. I— You *did* find it, didn't you? The last time we spoke on this subject you said you weren't sure where it was. You're supposed to *carry it,* Columbo!"

"Well, uh . . . The fact is, sir, I'm always afraid I'll lose it. I got a certain . . . what my wife calls *untidiness* about me."

"Columbo. Now. They have plenty of perfectly good pistols at the range. Just go out there and requalify. I'm gettin' flak about this. Go *qualify,* Columbo! Martha. You go with him. Don't let him find any excuses."

Columbo glanced around. This was going to be worse, much worse, than firing across a creek at some tin cans.

This was a regular range, with lines of targets at twenty-five feet, fifty feet, and fifty yards. You had to qualify by shooting at man-size silhouettes at fifty feet. He figured he'd be lucky if he could hit the hillside behind the targets, much less the targets.

"Lieutenant, uh . . . Columbo. Yes, sir. All right, sir. Whenever you're ready. Just step up there and punch a few holes in the target, and it's done. I'll sign off on you and send the paper downtown."

Sergeant Brittigan was a big, ruddy-faced man in the image of the old-time Irish cop. The fact was, he had been severely wounded in the line of duty and was serving as sergeant of the pistol range until he could retire on full pension. He carried himself with a stiff military bearing, and his uniform had been retailored to fit him like the uniform of a Marine drill sergeant—which in fact he had once been.

Columbo puffed on a cigar. The wind whipped his raincoat around him. "Problem is, Sergeant, I don't have my service revolver with me. It's, uh . . . Well, it looked like a crack had developed in the cylinder. I'm gonna have to send that gun back to Colt to have the cylinder replaced."

"No problem, Lieutenant. We've got all kinds of fine weapons available here."

"I thought there was some kinda rule that a man had to qualify with his own sidearm."

"Lieutenant Columbo, you can qualify with any weapon you want to fire."

Columbo looked out across the range. Half a dozen uniformed officers, wearing big earmuffs, were firing at targets fifty feet away. Splinters flew from one of the target frames: dramatic evidence that the officer had missed wildly.

"Well, I figure I oughta qualify with my own revolver. Maybe I should just wait till it's available."

Sergeant Brittigan shrugged. "Up to you, sir," he said.

"No, it's not up to him," Martha interjected. "The captain ordered him to qualify today."

"In that case—"

"Captain won't mind if—"

"*Columbo.*"

"Not havin' the revolver I'm used to—"

"We can make an allowance for that, Lieutenant," said the range sergeant.

"Y' can?"

"Oh, sure. Look, sir, take a look at this."

Sergeant Brittigan snapped loose the strap that held his own sidearm in his holster and handed Columbo a gray steel automatic.

"What's this?"

"That's a Beretta, sir. Standard U.S. military issue these days. Replaces the old Colt .45. Very accurate. Easy to hit your target with that. Look, just let me put some earmuffs on you, and you fire five rounds through that. Just for practice. Let me show you. Here's the safety—"

Sergeant Brittigan and Martha stood back and watched Columbo take a stance and aim the Beretta. His cigar smoke drifted away on puffs of wind. He fired, squinted at the target, and took aim again.

"You know who he is, Sarge?" Martha asked Sergeant Brittigan.

"Columbo . . . I've heard his name."

"Do you remember the Morrow case?" she asked. "Child

stabbed. Mama insisted it had been done by a man who'd broken into the home, tried to rape her, then killed the child in a fit of rage. Do you remember who broke that case?"

"Columbo?"

"Columbo. And do you remember when Officer McCarthy was killed when he responded to a call for help from a man dying from a heart attack? The man died all right, but the officer was bludgeoned to death, and—"

"Columbo?"

"Columbo. But he can't shoot worth a damn."

Sergeant Brittigan glanced at Columbo, who was now firing his fourth shot. "The problem is, I'm not supposed to find they're crack shots; I'm supposed to make sure they are good enough they won't send stray shots at innocent people."

"Couldn't happen with Columbo," she said. "He doesn't *carry* his service revolver. He's one of the finest detectives on the force, but he doesn't carry his service revolver, and he can't swim."

The sergeant watched Columbo fire his fifth shot, then picked up his spotting scope and studied the target. He glanced at Martha, frowning. "Now that I think of it," he said, "there is some kind of rule that an officer is entitled to requalify with his own personal sidearm."

"That bad, huh?" Columbo asked, squinting toward the target.

"Well, let's say that you need practice with the Beretta. All your practice has been with your Colt, huh?"

"Yeah. Right. All the practice I've had was with the Colt."

Sergeant Brittigan looked at the report form for a moment, then began to scribble. "What I'm writing here,

Lieutenant, is— 'Lieutenant Columbo was unable to fire his qualifying rounds with his personal sidearm, since it appears to have a cracked cylinder. Firing a 9mm Beretta, which he had never fired before, he nearly qualified. When his own sidearm is repaired he can fire qualifying rounds again.' I'll sign that, and you can hand it over to Captain Sczciegel."

"Well, thank ya, Sergeant. Thank you very much. Uh . . . 'Nearly qualified.' I imagine that means I didn't shoot myself in the foot."

Brittigan grinned. "Something like that. Come back and practice, Lieutenant. I'll work with you. You'll requalify. I promise you will."

Columbo took the sergeant's hand and shook it. "I'll do that. I'll be back first chance I get."

"Let's stop by the house on Hollyridge Road for a minute on the way back," said Martha. "I came across something interesting yesterday."

A uniformed officer continued to guard the house, six days after the murder of Paul Drury. In only that many days the place had taken on an odor of abandonment. The rooms somehow seemed not just rooms in a house temporarily deserted by an owner who would return but subtly yet distinctly those of a house permanently abandoned. Columbo would have sworn it would be noticed even by someone who did not know the owner was dead.

He remembered the same thing of his parents' home. Returning after both of them were gone, he had entered rooms where silence seemed normal, where the air had not moved for days: rooms heavy with death.

Martha sensed the impact the place had on Columbo, and for several minutes she maintained a studied silence while she waited for him to speak.

"Whatta ya wanta show me, Martha?"

In the living room, she went to a bookshelf and pulled down a volume—

AN AMERICAN LIFE: BIOGRAPHY OF A PATRIOT
THE LIFE AND TIMES OF AUSTIN BELL
By Foster Cummings,
Historian

The book had not been published. It had been printed by a Dallas printer and bound by a Dallas binder.

Inside the front cover, it was inscribed—"Paul. May this biography of my late father be an inspiration to you as it has been to me. A man is fortunate if he is loved by his father. If his father was a great man, he is triply fortunate. Charles Bell."

Columbo flipped through the pages. The book had been written when its subject was still alive. In fact, it contained a foreword in which Austin Bell thanked the author for his honesty and accuracy.

"Look at his affiliations," said Martha.

In the beginning of the book there was a list of the organizations to which Austin Bell belonged, together with a list of causes to which he claimed he had been a major contributor. The organizations included the John Birch Society and the Minutemen. He claimed to have been a major contributor to the Campus Crusade for Christ, Young Americans for Freedom, and the Oliver North Defense Fund.

"Go to page 185," said Martha.

Columbo did and read—

On November 17, 1963, Austin Bell sent the following telegram to the White House:

URGE THAT THE PRESIDENT OMIT
DALLAS FROM HIS TEXAS ITINER-
ARY. MANY IN DALLAS BELIEVE
PRESIDENT KENNEDY A TRAITOR
AND COMMUNIST. HIS VISIT HERE
MAY RESULT IN VIOLENCE. RIOTS
ETC. WOULD BE EMBARRASSMENT
TO HIM, TO STATE, AND CITY. TRUE
AMERICANS IN THIS CITY DO NOT
WANT HIM.

AUSTIN BELL,
PRESIDENT
BELL EXPLORATIONS

If President Kennedy and/or his staff had heeded the patriotic warning of Austin Bell, the tragedy that followed less than a week later could have been avoided. The arrogance of the Kennedy Administration in sending their leader into Dallas that November was the immediate cause of the death of the President. The record demonstrates that Austin Bell did all he could to protect the President but was ignored.

"The whole book may be worth reading," said Martha. "I skimmed through and came up with that."

"Worth reading if we think Mr. Drury was killed because of something he was going to broadcast in November. Meaning something he was going to broadcast about the Kennedy assassination. Also, are you suggesting that this man Bell—?"

"I'm not suggesting anything, Columbo. You might draw some sort of inference from that book, and you might not."

"I'll take it home for tonight," said Columbo.

Van Nuys Airport has two parallel runways, one of them eight thousand feet long and so suitable for landings by jet aircraft. As the sun set on Tuesday evening, a Falcon jet settled down through an overcast that had developed late in the afternoon and touched wheels to the longer runway. Charles Bell waited in his Cadillac convertible, and when the small jet came to a stop on the ramp not far from where he was parked, he hurried out of the car and strode to the Falcon. The steps were let down, and Bell climbed into the jet.

"Compagno," said Phil Sclafani, extending his hand.

Bell didn't know what *compagno* meant but guessed it meant friend or partner, and he shook hands.

The copilot came from the front of the plane, carrying a tray of hors d'oeuvres covered with Saran Wrap. He asked what the gentlemen would like to drink.

"Why don't you and Bill take a walk around the airport and stretch your legs," said Sclafani. "The gentleman and I have a couple things to talk about."

The copilot nodded, and shortly he and the pilot left the Falcon. Sclafani opened the bar that was located under one of the front seats and pulled out bottles, glasses, and ice. He mixed martinis.

"So what's the problem?" Sclafani asked.

"This," said Bell. He reached into the pocket of his light-blue sports jacket and pulled out a newspaper clipping. "I thought we agreed—"

"Papa didn't agree," said Sclafani. "Papa doesn't like to take chances."

Bell scowled over the clipping. It was from the *Los Angeles Times* and told that the body of a German immigrant named Klaus Hunzeicker, twenty-two years old, had washed ashore in Malaga Cove. An autopsy on the body, which had been nibbled on by fish, had discovered a gunshot wound at the base of the skull. The German had been murdered.

"No one would ever have made the connection," said Bell.

"No one will now," said Sclafani. "You can be sure of it. No one will ever make a connection."

The newspaper story went on to say that Hunzeicker, who had come to California from Leipzig only a year ago, had been a computer systems analyst and programmer.

"The kid didn't even know—"

"What'd you do with his virus?"

Bell hesitated for a moment, then said, "I've got it. Securely hidden. A thing like that is damned valuable."

"So. We're even. I said we wouldn't get rid of him, and you said you'd destroy his program. Now . . . I want you to make us uneven again."

"You mean destroy the virus," said Bell. "Dammit. It's worth— It's a technological masterpiece."

"You're not dealing with fools!" snarled Sclafani. "That LAPD detective—"

"All right. I'll destroy it," Bell conceded grudgingly.

"For sure. For damned sure."

Bell nodded.

"Yeah. The next question is—"

"No!"

"Maybe. *If she talks . . .*"

"She wouldn't dare! After all, she's the one who pulled the trigger."

"Papa doesn't like the idea that we spend the rest of our lives wondering if she keeps quiet. If Columbo hadn't got so close it might have been something else, but—"

"He's not so close."

"He's closer than you think. He's got her fingered as a hooker. He wants to know why she was a hooker. If he decides to blow the story, let it go in the papers that she was a hooker— She'll be a psycho case."

"Phil! *What the hell you talkin' about?*"

"Suppose she had an accident," said Sclafani.

FIFTEEN

"I've got it in my head," Columbo said to Martha as he watched her make coffee in the Paul Drury Productions offices on Wednesday morning, "that Drury's murder has somethin' to do with the murder of President Kennedy."

"To prevent him from broadcasting the thirtieth-anniversary show," she said.

"Right. What's the significance of those two pictures he went to the trouble of having computer enlarged? Who were the two guys on the knoll? I got the idea that Drury knew who they were and was gonna reveal it on the November show."

"I'm sorry to have to tell you this," said Martha, "but I wasn't born when Kennedy was assassinated."

"I was. I remember that day. I remember just where I was and what I was doin' when I heard about it. There are three things I can remember where I was and what I was doin' when I heard about them. One was Pearl Harbor. Then there was the death of President Roosevelt. Then the assassination of President Kennedy. Anyway . . . Tell ya somethin' else. We were members of the Book-of-the-Month Club, and Mrs. Columbo ordered a copy of the Warren

Commission Report. I got it out last night and kinda sketched a simplified map of the place where it happened. Here."

Martha stared at Columbo's rough sketch map of Dealey Plaza. She remembered now that she had seen maps of the place before, also an aerial photo, but Columbo had sketched in the essentials.

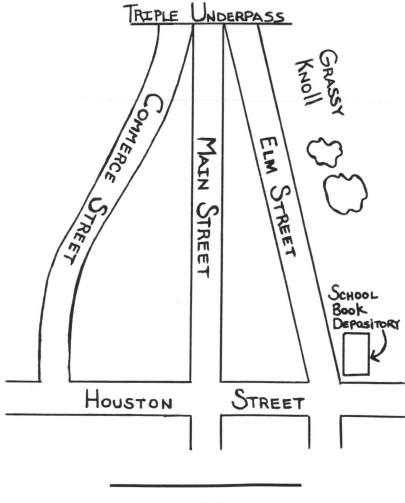

"That map is laid out with directions normal," he said. "In other words, north is up at the top, south is down at the bottom, west at the left, and east at the right. The motorcade came west on Main Street. Main is the traditional parade street in Dallas because it's got tall buildings and more people can see the parade, from the windows. It's the street they used for President Roosevelt's motorcade through Dallas in 1936. It seemed like a nice bow to tradition, to follow the route President Roosevelt had used. So, anyway, the motorcade came west on Main, then turned north onto Houston Street and made a sharp left turn into Elm Street."

"Why didn't they just keep going west on Main Street?" Martha asked. "It looks like the most direct way."

Columbo traced her suggested route on the map with his finger. "Because after they went under the underpass— here—they had to get on the ramp to the northbound lanes of the Stemmons Freeway, which is a right turn off Elm. And you can't do that from Main Street. There's a concrete barrier that prevents it. Right there. See?"

"Why?" she asked.

"Off Main Street, that'd be a right turn across the Elm Street traffic. See? Right there. They don't allow that. It'd be dangerous. Traffic headed for the Stemmons Freeway has to come down Elm. Not just the presidential motorcade. All traffic."

"A person with a camera, standing in the triangular park between Elm and Main—" She tapped the triangle with one finger. "And—"

"And trying to take pictures of the motorcade," Columbo interrupted, "would have been takin' pictures of the Grassy Knoll in the background—unconsciously, not interested in the background, but gettin' it in the pictures anyway. The pictures this photographer took didn't look like much. They were probably just snapshot-size prints. Even enlarging them didn't show the rifle. It took the computer enhancement to do that."

"A stroke of luck that they got them enhanced," said Martha.

"A stroke of luck that the photographer sent them to Drury," said Columbo. "Not just luck that Drury had them enhanced. He'd have recognized that if there really was firing from the Grassy Knoll, these pictures might include some evidence of it."

"Geraldo has the computers up and running. I brought copies of the diskettes, also copies of the enhanced photographs."

"Is he copying the diskettes onto the hard disks?"

"Yes. He says it will take all morning."

"In that case, I've got some other things to do. I'll be calling on Jessica O'Neil again."

"I hope I'm not makin' a nuisance of myself, ma'am," said Columbo.

"Not at all, Lieutenant," said Jessica O'Neil. "Not at all. What can I do for you?"

"Well, I'd like to show you a coupla pictures."

"I'm sitting on the deck again. Come on back. Actually, now that I think of it— You're not a nuisance at all, but if you want to compensate, how about doing something for me?"

"What can I do for you, ma'am?"

"To start with, call me Jessie. Being called 'ma'am' makes me feel like the proprietor of the Long Branch Saloon. But besides that, let me sketch you while we talk. You have an interesting face, Lieutenant. I might want to try a painting of you."

"Well, that's very flatterin', ma'am . . . uh, Jessie. Sure. Sketch away."

She picked up a sketch pad and a bundle of pencils as they walked through the house. The morning smog blocked the view from her deck. It was not a heavy, irritating smog, but it was enough that they could not see the beaches. Columbo sat down, and she stared at him for a moment and began to sketch.

He took a moment to reappraise her, before he began to talk. He confirmed the judgment he had made before: that though she was no *great* beauty, she was a *natural* beauty, not one contrived by a cosmetologist. She was the kind of woman he most appreciated. Like most California women, she was enthralled with the effect of the sun on her skin, and she was wearing a flower-patterned bikini.

"I'd appreciate it if you'd look at two photos I got and tell me if they're the ones Mr. Drury showed you."

She took from his hand the envelope containing copies of the two computer-enhanced prints. She studied them for a moment, then said, "He only showed me one. I'm reasonably sure this is the one. As for the other, I never saw it before."

"And he told you that was the solution to the mystery of the Kennedy assassination."

"Well . . . He said these two men, with that rifle, *could* have killed Kennedy."

Columbo: The Grassy Knoll

"The important question is, who were those two men? Did he give you any idea who they were?"

Jessica O'Neil shook her head. "I got the impression he didn't know, that he figured when he broadcast the pictures on his show someone would come forth with the identification. That was the whole point, that millions of people would see the pictures and someone would know."

The maid came out from the kitchen, bringing Bloody Marys with celery sticks. Jessica O'Neil hadn't asked if he wanted one. She assumed. It was mid-morning and time for a light drink, if you were a person who drank all day. The vodka had been poured sparingly, and Columbo sipped twice before he realized he was drinking anything but a glass of tomato juice.

"It's been thirty years since those pictures were taken," he said. "And only one was taken from the front. They're not the world's greatest images anyway. Wasn't he depending on anything else?"

"On his great big computer library," she said.

"Yeah. But if you're going to search in a library, computer or otherwise, ya gotta have a name to start with. That's the start, huh? A name."

"Or a description," she said.

"Right. But look at those two guys. How would you start to describe them that would make them out any different from any other two guys? One is tall and has dark hair. The other is short and has light hair. Big description!"

"Sorry, Lieutenant," said Jessica O'Neil. "I'm afraid I can't be of any more help. It's really outside my field."

"Yeah. Well, ma'— Jessie. I really gotta go. Thank ya for your time and the drink. You have enough time to get any kind of sketch?"

She turned the pad and let him see her sketch. The likeness, in quick, deft lines, was perfect: rumpled hair, smile-wrinkles around his eyes, the smile that somehow managed to be a smile even when the corners of his mouth turned down, the collar and lapels of his raincoat. She smiled modestly, but Columbo grinned.

"My! That's *amazin'!* You got a real talent there. I sure wish Mrs. Columbo could see that."

"After I try doing a painting from it, I'll send it along," said Jessica O'Neil.

"I'll appreciate that."

"I'm sorry I couldn't be more helpful."

"Actually . . . Actually, you've been more help than you know," he said. "You just gave me what may turn out to be a great idea, and I'm obliged."

He met the artist Diana Williams in her studio on the top floor of a big old brick house. A segment of the roof had been replaced by a slanting glass skylight, affording the room the northern sunlight artists say is best for their work. Mrs. Williams was in her fifties. Her hair was steel-gray. The frames of her spectacles were gray. She was a broad-shouldered, strong-looking woman dressed in a white T-shirt and blue jeans. She was barefoot. On a platform directly under the sunlight a teenage girl stood nude. She was the model for a painting on Mrs. Williams's easel, and she held her pose since the artist continued to work.

"Columbo, I'd rather drink Drāno than eat a bowl of that wretched fiery chili you profess to think is delicious. If

LAPD is too cheap to buy a woman a tuna salad sandwich at a lunch counter—"

"Mrs. Williams, *I'll* gladly buy you a tuna sandwich."

"With half a bottle of champagne," she said.

"Well . . ."

Diana Williams slapped Columbo on the arm and laughed. "Whatta ya want for free this time?" she asked.

"Not free exactly," he said. "You'll have a chance to help solve one of the really big crimes of the century."

"If I don't have to be a witness," she said.

"Promise," said Columbo.

"Well, then?"

He pulled from the manila envelope the computer-enhanced photo of the two men on the Grassy Knoll. He handed it to her, and she stared at it for a moment.

"Take a break, Cecilia," said Mrs. Williams. "And don't worry. This guy's not a bum. He's a cop."

The girl stepped down and pulled on a robe. The artist continued to frown over her canvas, making tiny changes. "I suppose the deal is, you want to know what those guys really look like," she said to Columbo.

"More than that," he said. "I want to see what they really looked like when the picture was taken, yeah. But that was thirty years ago. I need to know what they might look like now."

"It'd be a guess," she said.

"It wasn't when you did it for me before. You know all about people's faces, including how they change as the years pass."

Mrs. Williams frowned over the picture. "This guy's got a rifle. Who'd he shoot?"

"Maybe John F. Kennedy," said Columbo.

"You serious?"

He nodded.

"God, I could even eat a bowl of your chili for a chance to talk about this. Cecilia! Let's take a lunch break. See you a little after one, okay?"

"I appreciate your time, Mr. Bell," said Columbo. "I got an idea I'm takin' too much of it."

They were in the parking lot of the Topanga Beach Club. Columbo had telephoned there, on the chance Bell would be there, and he was. He had met Columbo in the parking lot, explaining that he was meeting with some business associates inside and that it would be a little embarrassing for them to realize he was still talking with the detective assigned to the Drury murder.

"You can have my time whenever you want it, Lieutenant Columbo. I hope you understand our meeting out here. I'm trying to encourage some fellows to invest in a little project of mine, and I— Well, they're sort of naïve types and wouldn't understand I'm not under suspicion or something."

"I understand perfectly, sir. I do. Hey, I don't want you to be embarrassed. Uh . . . if anybody asks me, I'll gladly tell 'em you're not a suspect."

"Fine. Why don't we sit in my car? It's got a little more room in it."

"Right. My car's very efficient. Just enough room in it for two people to be comfortable. But I don't put the top down anymore. Too much risk of tearing it. If we sit in your car we can have the sunshine and the breeze."

They walked over to Bell's custom-built silver-gray Cadillac.

"Say, this is a *nice* car. Y' know, I've got real leather upholstery, too. Mrs. Columbo uses saddle soap on it. You ever use saddle soap on yours, sir?"

"I guess maybe they do, where they take care of it. They use some kind of leather cleaner and conditioner."

"Saddle soap is the very best thing, sir. Believe me. I've had my car a long time."

"I'll remember that, Lieutenant. So, anyway, what can I do for you today?"

They sat down in the front seat of the Cadillac. "Gee, I'd probably go to sleep drivin' anything this comfortable. Uh— To get to the point directly, I remember your sayin' you were on Dealey Plaza the day of the assassination. Just where was that, sir? Where were you standing?"

"On Elm Street, the street where the motorcade went by. On the north side of the street."

"Did you see the President shot?"

Bell shook his head. "It happened before the presidential limousine reached the place where I was standing. I wasn't looking at the limousine when it happened. I must have been looking at one of the motorcycles or something. I heard the shots, but I didn't realize what they were. You know . . . motorcycles backfire. When the limousine reached me, I understood with shock and horror that something was very wrong. The President was down. I couldn't see him. Mrs. Kennedy was out on the back of the limousine. I know now what she was doing; she was reaching for a piece of the President's skull. I mean, I was so horrified I couldn't . . . Lieutenant, I couldn't make myself accept what I saw. Then the limousine speeded up and raced for the underpass and went under and out of sight."

"Where were you standing with respect to what they call the Grassy Knoll, sir?"

"It was behind me."

"Did you hear any shots fired from there?"

"No. Absolutely none. I was questioned by the police and the FBI and later by lawyers from the Warren Commission. Other people say they heard shots from back there. Maybe they did, but I didn't hear any."

"I'd like to ask you to look at two pictures, sir," said Columbo, taking another set of copies from their envelope. "Do you understand what those are, Mr. Bell? They're what are called computer-enhanced photographs."

Bell glanced at the pictures. "I've seen these before," he said. "Paul had the computer enhancement done. He felt sure the object the taller man was holding was a rifle. I don't know. I wonder if it could have been an umbrella. Or something. Wouldn't the people standing around have been all excited if somebody had a rifle?"

"But you were standing right in front of where those two men were," said Columbo, "and if that man had fired a shot, you'd have heard it."

"I couldn't have been much more than fifty feet from him," said Bell.

"Yeah. Well, that's interestin'. That's *very* interesting, sir. Is it your understanding that Mr. Drury planned to use these photos on his November show?"

"Yes. Yes, he was," said Bell grimly.

Columbo scratched his head. "They'd have caused some kind of sensation, wouldn't they?"

"For sure. Whether it would have solved the case is

doubtful. Of course, I don't think there's any mystery to solve. I think Lee Harvey Oswald assassinated President Kennedy, plain and simple."

"Yes, sir . . . Well. That's why I called you. I appreciate your time."

"Uh— Let *me* ask a question, if I may. That is, if you don't mind."

"Why sure, sir. I been askin' *you* plenty."

"Where'd you find these pictures? We've been looking all over for them. Tim and Alicia and I are thinking of doing some version of the show Paul planned for November. We wanted to use these pictures. Still do. Were they in the house?"

"As a matter of fact, they weren't, sir. As a matter of fact, Mr. Drury kept them in a safe-deposit vault, together with some other stuff." Columbo opened the door and stepped out into the parking lot. "We found that vault. It took a little doing, but that's police business: findin' stuff."

"My congratulations to you, Lieutenant. That's fine work. Here we were, Paul's friends, trying to find these pictures; and you, who didn't know him, found what we couldn't."

"It's just a matter of persistence," said Columbo. "That and a little luck. Well, sir. I appreciate your time. You probably better get back to your friends."

Bell nodded and sat watching the detective, raincoat flapping in the breeze, walk off toward his car. Then suddenly he stopped and turned.

"Oh, one other little question, sir, if you don't mind," said Columbo. He had put a cigar between his lips and held the envelope between his legs as he tried to light a match in the wind. "Little loose end. Uh— If you and Mrs. Drury and Mr. Edmonds were so interested in findin' these pictures, why didn't you tell us? We could have worked together on findin' 'em."

Bell walked across the blacktop and handed Columbo a lighter. "I'm ashamed to tell you why, Lieutenant," he said.

"Oh, thanks," said Columbo as he used the lighter.

"You have to understand, Lieutenant, that those pictures are worth a fortune as a property for a television show. Now they're in police custody, and you may feel obligated to release them to the news media. That will make them old stuff and of no particular advantage to us for our show. So we— I'm sorry to say it, but we hoped we would find them first. They're not evidence in Paul's murder, of course, so I guess I can confess that we would have continued to hold them in secret."

Columbo frowned over his cigar and handed the lighter back to Charles Bell. "I can understand that," he said, nodding. "And that explains that. So . . . Thanks once more. I hope I won't have to bother you again."

SIXTEEN

Giuseppe Sclafani shoved his chair back from his powerful telescope. He spent hours at it every day, studying the girls around the swimming pool of his own hotel and around those of Caesars Palace and the Flamingo, which were visible from his penthouse.

"You have no courage. That's what's wrong with you. No courage."

"Papa . . . We've been over all this a thousand times. Things are different. This is 1993, not 1933. Things aren't the way they were in the old days."

"Old days! Old days! In what you call 'the old days,' you had courage. You had the courage to try that damned thing. You—"

"Papa. It was a mistake!"

"Mistake! My son . . . My proud son. *Un albergatore!* Yes, sir! At your service, sir! *Un maledetto albergatore!*"

"Your son, who is nothing but a damned innkeeper, earns the living that makes it possible for you to live in this penthouse," growled Philip Sclafani. "Your son, the *maledetto albergatore,* made the business possible!"

The old man spat on the floor. "Penthouse! In a penitentiary I'd have men of honor for company."

"No you wouldn't. They're all dead. Every last one of them. Gambino. Anastasia. Profaci. Charlie Lucky. Frankie Shots. Even the chairman of the board, Meyer Lansky."

Giuseppe Sclafani spat again.

"Courage . . . We did what we had to do, Papa. You want to tell me I didn't have the courage to do what I had to do? How could you say that to me?"

"Some big courage!"

"It was good enough."

"This thing must be done," growled Giuseppe Sclafani.

"Another risk must be taken?"

"You have to weigh the risks," said the old man, holding out his hands and moving them up and down as if they were two pans in a scale. "Which is the greater risk? That is the question."

"The other two will dislike it. Edmonds might crack."

"Edmonds must believe it was an accident."

"It's something I thought you'd want to know, Lieutenant," said Bill McCrory. "Can I offer you a drink? Smoking in the office is bad for the fish. Sipping a Scotch, unless it makes them jealous, seems to do no harm."

"Well, I'm on duty actually," said Columbo. "Another time. Anyway, you were going to tell me about the will."

"At first I was a little annoyed," said McCrory. "I'd been his lawyer and his friend for many years, and I supposed he'd trust me with writing his will. But, having looked at it, I can see why he had another lawyer do it."

"Why is that, sir?"

"Because he left part of his estate to me. If I had written his will, and I inherited from it, it would be contestable. Conflict of interest. Bad ethics."

"I see. Well then . . . what's in that will, sir, that I ought to know?"

"He left me a quarter of a million dollars," said McCrory. "He left a quarter of a million to Karen Bergman. He left a quarter of a million to Professor John Trabue. He left ten thousand dollars apiece to his housekeeper and his secretary. He left the rest of his estate to a Paul Drury Trust, appointing me and the professor and Karen as trustees. What may be interesting is who he didn't leave anything to. Alicia. She's not even mentioned—and she's furious."

"I can understand that," said Columbo.

"What's going to be difficult is what to do about the trust. The will instructs his trustees to use the several million dollars that will be in the trust to preserve the research information in his computer library, to make it available to scholars, and to encourage publication of papers based on what is in there. The problem, of course, is that the computer information was all lost."

"No, sir."

"What?"

"I'd like to speak in confidence, sir. Will you keep a secret for a little while?"

"Yes, of course."

"The computer information was not lost," said Columbo. "We have it in a vault in the police property warehouse:

about two hundred and twenty microdiskettes. Copies of those diskettes have been loaded back into Mr. Drury's two computers. They can be searched again, just like they were before Mr. Drury died."

"Then the murder was for nothing!"

"If Mr. Drury was killed to prevent the disclosure of what's on those disks, somebody made a big mistake," said Columbo. "Mr. Drury kept copies. It looks like it might be copies of everything—not just the Kennedy stuff, but everything."

"I appreciate your taking me into your confidence, Lieutenant."

"You didn't have anything to do with killin' Mr. Drury."

"How do you know that?"

Columbo smiled. "If you'd killed him, you wouldn't have given me that time-stamped telephone tape that was so obviously a fake."

"Fake?"

"Yes, sir. A sound engineer needed less than half an hour to figure that one out. I don't know how he did it exactly. It has to do with slowin' the tape down, looking at the patterns it makes on an oscilloscope, stuff like that. Somebody took a tape they already had of Mr. Drury's voice— probably off *their* telephone recorder—and copied it onto a little player like a Sony Walkman. Then that somebody called your number and played that tape into your machine. It may have sounded okay to them, but under analysis it came out that the sound quality had deteriorated in the business of recordin' from voice to recorder to recorder to recorder. The instruments proved that."

"Who did it, Lieutenant?"

"That's the tough question, sir. When we know that for sure, we'll know for sure who murdered Mr. Drury."

Karen Bergman was waiting for him when Columbo arrived at the offices of Paul Drury Productions.

"Congratulations on your good fortune, ma'am," he said. "I was at Mr. McCrory's office, and he told me about the will."

"Besides that," she said, "I've been offered a job. I'm going to be a squealer again, do what I did before I came to work on *The Paul Drury Show.*"

"A what, ma'am?"

"You know. On the morning game shows. The girl who squeals when the contestant wins something. Jumps up and down maybe. I think maybe this time I'll jump up and down."

A week after Paul Drury's death, she still wore what he had prescribed for her—the white blouse and tight black skirt—as if she held him in some kind of veneration. He had looked at her personnel file and knew she was twenty-seven years old. She looked like a girl of twenty-one.

"I asked you to meet me because you know how to run the search programs on Mr. Drury's computers," he said.

She shrugged. "If there was anything left to search," she said.

"Just between us, ma'am, there *is* something left to search. Mr. Drury kept copies of all his stuff. The computers have been reloaded, off diskettes—those two hundred and some diskettes you told me he'd bought."

"My God!"

"Mrs. Drury and Mr. Edmonds are talking about doing the November show after all. I haven't told them yet that the stuff's been saved. Please don't *you* tell 'em. In the first place, we want to be sure everything's really okay. Wouldn't want to tell them it was all saved and then have to disappoint them if we find out it's not so good."

"I understand you perfectly, Lieutenant," she said, arching her eyebrows.

"Yes, ma'am, you prob'ly do. Uh— Let's go in Mr. Drury's office. Geraldo tells me everything's workin' first-class."

Columbo had not ceased to be awed by Drury's office. This time he walked behind the desk, which he had never done before, and watched over Karen Bergman's shoulder as she switched on the monitor on the first computer.

Striking keys, the first thing she did was bring up a menu of what the main memory disk contained. The list meant nothing to Columbo, but she looked up and said, "If all of that is really in here and can be searched, nothing is different."

She pressed more keys, and a different sort of menu, more stylized, came up. "This is a program called Folio Views," she explained. "The first thing I'm going to do is select what is called an infobase, and then I can search in it. For example—"

A line on the screen read "URBANGANGS.NFO." She moved the cursor to that line to select that infobase, and the screen filled with the text of a newspaper story from the *Los Angeles Times*.

"This infobase has about a hundred newspaper and magazine articles in it," she said. "Plus three or four academic papers and two or three book chapters. Let's see if—"

She typed the letters C-O-L-U-M-B-O. In a moment the screen filled with a new body of text. In the center of the screen the name appeared in yellow, to highlight it. The text was an excerpt from a newspaper story and read, in part—

Lieutenant Columbo of the LAPD homicide squad said the killing appeared to be the work of an urban youth gang. He said such killings are becoming more and more frequent, and he confirmed that many of them, including this one, are committed by youths armed with highly sophisticated and expensive weapons.

Columbo shook his head. "That sure is fascinatin'," he said. "It's hard to believe a machine could do that."

She amended the search to use three words: COLUMBO, ASSAULT, RIFLE. A screen of text from a different article appeared, including—

Bates was killed by a shot from an assault rifle, probably of Chinese manufacture, according to Lieutenant Columbo.

"Anything a man ever said can come back to haunt him," said Columbo. "What I'd like to see, if you can find it, ma'am, is a draft of the script for the November show, or any notes for that script. Think you could find that?"

Karen Bergman nodded. "We'll use a different program to look for that," she said.

While she worked to change programs and search for the script or notes, Columbo took his notebook from his raincoat pocket, then fumbled in his pockets for a pencil, and finally used the ballpoint pen from the desk set to write a note.

"I'm looking at his Kennedy assassination files," she said after a while. "There are plenty of scripts, but the dates on them tell us they're the scripts for shows already done. Ninety-five percent of what's in here is source material."

"Ma'am, do you have any idea what Mr. Drury was planning to reveal in November?"

"No. He was pretty closemouthed about what his plans were, particularly if he thought a show was important. I suspect he was afraid somebody would leak information and another show would get in ahead of us."

Columbo walked out from behind the desk and went to one of the couches, where he had placed an envelope containing the enhanced photographs. He brought them to her and asked, "Have you ever seen these before, ma'am?"

"Yes. He thought they were very important. I was afraid they were lost."

"Do you have any idea who those two men there might be?"

She shook her head.

"Do you think *he* knew?"

Karen Bergman drew a deep breath. "I don't think he did. I think he intended to broadcast the enhanced pictures and let the whole country see them, hoping then someone would come forward and identify those two men."

"Miss Bergman, I gotta ask you a favor. Could you come back here this evening? I gotta pick up some other information that might be helpful. Besides, I'd like to have Professor Trabue with us when we do some more searching in those data bases."

"What time?" she asked.

"Say seven. That way you'll have time to have dinner before you come back."

"I thought I had till tomorrow," said Diana Williams.

"Somethin's come up," said Columbo.

"Cecilia, you might as well get dressed. This man has no patience."

While the model dressed and Diana Williams cleaned some brushes, Columbo studied the unfinished painting. He had always admired the woman's work, though in some ways it had always puzzled him. The girl on the model stand had had no greenish and angular shadows, but the girl on the canvas did. Somehow, even so, the odd shadows in the odd color gave the painted image of the girl's body a more three-dimensional character than she had when you looked at her standing there. That was what distinguished an artist, he supposed. In some way, the girl on the canvas was more real than the real girl. He resolved to ask Mrs. Columbo what she thought of that, first chance he had.

Diana Williams stood at a work table, where she had already pinned the enhanced photograph of the two men on the Grassy Knoll. She put a finger on the man with the rifle and began a sketch of the face she saw. It went as Columbo had hoped. With her artist's eye she saw more than he did. She had studied anatomy and knew that one of the lines made by the enhancement was, though logical, impossible; the bone beneath the skin dictated the line, and the one she drew was the possible line.

"I'd guess our rifleman was in his twenties," she said as she sketched. "From the way he stands. I'd also guess he hasn't gained twenty pounds in thirty years. Something about these tall fellows; they tend not to go to flesh."

"How *would* he change?" Columbo asked.

"Well . . . You want him as he is now, not as he was then, I suppose. Okay. Let's suppose he did gain a *little* weight. Likely you'd see some evidence of that along here." She rounded the line under the jaw. "And he'd get some lines around his mouth, like this. With age his eyelids would loosen a bit. So . . . And his hair— That was black, from the look of the photo. It'd be a little lighter by now, and he'd probably wear it very different, not brush-cut. We can assume he didn't lose his hair, but it probably backed up a little. Beginning to look like anybody you know, Columbo?"

"Put a pair of glasses on him, ma'am. Goggle-shaped with silver frames."

"Like so?"

Columbo grinned. "Aw *right*! Mrs. Williams, you are a *wonderful* artist!"

She smiled wryly and shook her head. "Let's see what we can do with your other man," she said. "Much less distinctive, this one. Shorter. A rounder face. Let's suppose *he* was in his twenties. He was a little too round for a man his age, so we have to expect he got rounder yet as the years went by. Probably aged a little less gracefully. I'd guess we'd have now a tubby little fellow. Lots of jowl. Thin hair, probably graying. Kind of a contrast with the other one."

As this sketch developed, Columbo frowned. As she had said, the face was much less distinctive. It would be difficult to match sketch to man. A possibility crossed his mind. He put it away and left it to think about later.

As she stepped back from the two sketches, Diana Williams said, "I guess I've helped you a little."

Columbo nodded. "More than a little," he said. "More than a little."

"Yeah, yeah. Right. I'm glad you got a class tonight, 'cause I'm gonna have a meeting with some people about the Drury case. Oh, sure. I saw the story. If that reporter thinks he can bring a charge that will stick, let him try it. Me? Sure, I gotta pretty good idea. I just don't wanta stick my neck out before I'm sure. Listen, when this is over I'm gonna arrange for you to see how these computers work. I'm afraid you wasted your time learning to write programs in BASIC. Yeah, I know it was required. But nobody uses it anymore. Also, hey, did you pick up those pills for Dog? Well, if you ever go in that vet's office and look at those heartworms in those bottles— I'll get 'em down him. I gotta method. You mold the pill into a ball of cream cheese, and down it goes. Me? I'm gonna have a couple egg rolls and some chicken stirfry. Yeah. Well, you too. I won't be too late. Prob'ly be home before you."

Columbo took a stool at the counter of the Chinese diner. "I'll have a Chinese beer. An' a coupla egg rolls. An' I'll look over the menu."

At seven he arrived at the offices on La Cienega. A

uniformed officer guarded the door and let him in. He had relieved Martha of any duty this evening, so she could be at home with her baby.

Professor Trabue was already there, sitting in the reception room smoking his pipe.

"I bet you been here more times than I have, Professor. Isn't this some place!"

"I'm not sure I'd be comfortable working in a place like this," said the professor.

"I know what ya mean. That office of yours . . . It shows that a man loves his work. A man's awful lucky when he can make his livin' doin' what he loves to do."

"I guess that means you, too, Lieutenant."

"Yeah. I never regretted goin' on the job. Not that I haven't sometimes wondered what it'd be like to do somethin' else."

"Did the diskettes prove to work?" asked Professor Trabue.

Columbo nodded. "Looks like it. Miss Bergman was able to make the computer find the name Columbo in Mr. Drury's computer files. In newspaper stories."

"Miss Bergman . . . ?"

"Mr. Drury's assistant. She'll be here shortly. Incidentally, Professor, did you get your call from Mr. McCrory?"

"Yes. Unbelievable."

"Congratulations, sir."

"I'm not sure how far we will be able to go, spending the trust money to extract historical data out of the Drury files."

"Gotta match?"

Karen Bergman arrived ten minutes late, apologetic for the difficulty she'd had finding a parking place. The three walked into Drury's office. Geraldo was there, working with the second computer. He left the room.

"Before we work with the computers, I'd like to show each of you a drawing done by a fine artist, a friend of mine," said Columbo. "What she did was, she took the enhanced photo of the two men on the Grassy Knoll, and she drew their portraits. Then she worked some more on her drawings to try to get some idea of what those two men would look like today. Here's the first one. That's of the taller, darker man. Did either of you ever see that man?"

Both of them shook their heads.

"Here's the shorter man."

"No."

"No."

"You're sure? About the second man, especially. Never saw him before?"

"The problem with him, Lieutenant, is that he could be anybody," said Professor Trabue. "Thousands of men look like that. That man could even be me."

"Well . . . We don't need to worry about that. It's not you. Miss Bergman?"

"It could be a lot of men, Lieutenant. That's the trouble. The other face is much more distinctive. But I feel sure I've never seen him."

"I'd like to get some information out of those computers, then," said Columbo.

He and Professor Trabue stood behind her as Karen Bergman called up the Folio Views program.

"First question?" she asked.

"Is there anything in there that would tell us if any weapons were found abandoned on the Grassy Knoll?" asked Columbo. "Maybe the professor already knows."

"I don't remember anything of that kind," said Professor Trabue.

"Well . . ." said Karen Bergman. "Paul stored some of the Kennedy information chronologically—that is, by when he got it—and some of it by subject. He must have considered the Grassy Knoll a major topic, because there's a special file for it. What would we be looking for?"

"I'd like to know if that rifle was left behind sooner or later," said Columbo.

She typed in the word "rifle." It generated fifty-eight items. Then she put in "abandoned." She shook her head. "No matches," she said. "A window in this system is defined as about half a typewritten page. This means there is no place in this file where those two words fall within the equivalent of half a typewritten page—say, a hundred fifty words."

"Try 'find' or 'found,'" said the professor.

The same result. No matches.

"Okay," said Columbo. "How 'bout a pistol or revolver or automatic."

She tried those word combinations. "Revolver" and "found" produced two hits.

"My God, it's in the Warren Commission Report," she said. The excerpt read—

A thirty-eight caliber Iver-Johnson revolver, Serial # 38–1286–334, was found lying in the grass under the trees on the east side of the Grassy Knoll. The pistol was loaded with six cartridges. None had been discharged. The revolver was examined for fingerprints, as were the cartridges, by the Dallas Police Department, then by specialists of the Federal

Bureau of Investigation. The weapon and the cartridges were absolutely clean of all fingerprints. What is more, the barrel was clean of all residue, demonstrating that the pistol had not been fired since it was last cleaned.

The serial number was traced. The pistol had been manufactured in 1934 and sold to a wholesaler in Illinois. The wholesaler had sold it to a retailer in Chicago, who in turn had sold it to a named customer. The name proved untraceable and was either a false name or the name of someone with no criminal or other record.

In view of these circumstances, the Iver-Johnson pistol did not seem a promising lead. That it was found clean of fingerprints is a suspicious circumstance. That its owner-ship could not be traced since 1934 made it seem extremely unlikely anything could be learned from it.

The second excerpt was from a news story in the *Dallas Morning News*—

A revolver found on the Grassy Knoll had not been fired and bore no fingerprints.

"A dozen men could have carried pistols away from Dealey Plaza," said Columbo. "In brown bags, lunch boxes . . . The rifle's somethin' else."

"When people are in shock," said Professor Trabue, "they see things that didn't happen and overlook things that did."

Columbo nodded. "Ten or twelve years ago, a man walked into a strip club on Sunset Boulevard and shot a man. He walked right up behind him, shot him in the back of the head, and turned around and walked out. Thirty or forty witnesses saw him. An' ya know what? We got as many descriptions as we got witnesses. He was tall, short, thin, fat, blond, dark, white, black, dressed in a suit, jeans, a sweater, a golf shirt, carrying a revolver, an automatic, a sawed-off shotgun . . . One witness swore the man was shot by a woman. We never cracked the case. Never did."

Karen Bergman sighed. "What next, Lieutenant?"

Columbo ran his hand over his forehead, then through his hair, and he turned down the corners of his mouth and shook his head. "Well . . . Let's look for a name. Sclafani. S-C-L-A-F-A-N-I. Never mind a first name. Just Sclafani."

"In the Grassy Knoll file?"

"Probably not. In whatever ya think."

"Let's look at the file of information collected in 1993," she said.

She changed to that file, typed in the name, and shortly the computer reported it found thirty-eight occurrences.

"Thirty-eight! Hey, that's *interestin'!*"

"We can reduce the number by adding a first name."

"Start with Giuseppe," said Columbo.

The first item found was an article from *The New York Times Sunday Magazine,* dated 1977. It was about the fall of major crime figures, some dead, some in prison, some in retirement. The part on the screen read—

Giuseppe (Joe) Sclafani, 70 years old, lives in semiretirement in a penthouse atop a casino hotel in Las Vegas, apparently content. No longer a menacing Mafia don, feared boss of the Brooklyn waterfront, he seems to have found a degree of respectability. Or perhaps he doesn't dare move back into the rackets, since he is under constant surveillance by more than one state or federal agency.

The article had been pulled from the vast electronic files of the newspaper by the NEXIS computerized research service, as had two other articles mentioning Giuseppe Sclafani as semiretired but still suspected of racketeering; and they had been entered in this private electronic library kept by Paul Drury.

Using the name Philip Sclafani, Karen Bergman found other articles. Philip was identified as the operating manager of the Piping Rock Hotel. Of him, the *San Francisco Chronicle* said—

The tall, handsome, graying bachelor has lived his life in the shadow of his commandeering father. Philip Sclafani never married. Although he is reputed to have used "muscle" for his father when he was a young man in New York, he has no criminal record that would preclude his gaining a Nevada gaming license. He keeps a "squeaky clean" appearance to the extent that he is said to have refused to allow some of his father's old friends to stay in the Piping Rock.

"This is all data Paul added to the data base in 1993," said Karen Bergman. "Let's see what he put in there in past years."

A little more searching showed that a few Sclafani items had been added to the data base in 1992 and none before that. In 1991, 1990, and other past years, a search based on the name produced nothing.

They went through the 1992 materials, then the rest of the 1993 materials, printing some of the excerpts.

"It's all very interesting," said Professor Trabue when they were finished, "but I'm afraid it doesn't prove anything."

"I beg your pardon, sir, but I think it proves somethin' very important," said Columbo.

"And what is that, Lieutenant?"

"It proves that Mr. Drury was very interested in the Sclafanis," said Columbo. "What's more, it was a new interest. Now, just whatta ya suppose that interest was about?"

SEVENTEEN

Locked out of the office of Paul Drury Productions,
with no particular project going, Alicia drank coffee and
ate Danish on her lanai, wearing her black bikini. She
made several telephone calls. Even though she planned to
marry Tim as soon as the investigation of Paul's death was
finished, she felt she had to keep up her contacts with
people in the television industry. She was sure of Tim but
not so sure she was willing to give up every other possibility
in life.

She had only one obligation for this Thursday, June
10. She had to be at the Topanga Beach Club for lunch,
in case Phil wanted to call her from Las Vegas. She
had asked Charles Bell to meet her there. The unhappy
fact was, she was running short of cash, and Charles
would sign the check. Paul Drury Productions owed her
a paycheck, but God knew when she would see that.
She was considering establishing a small home-equity
credit line on the house, to cover her bills until she
married.

She needed to make a couple of stops on her way to the
club, so she left the lanai about ten-thirty and went in the
house to dress. She pulled on a favorite outfit: a pair of tight

lime-green pants and a white golf shirt. Before leaving her bedroom she gathered up a bundle of soiled clothes to drop at the dry cleaner's. That was one of her errands on her way to the club.

Her car was something else from her marriage with Paul Drury: a big Oldsmobile station wagon he had once used to haul camera equipment and lights to locations. At the time of their divorce he had suggested it was something of a classic car and might increase in value over the coming years. She had accepted it.

She usually left it parked on the driveway, as she had done last night, and it sat there this morning, looking a little sullen in the heat of the sun. It would take its air conditioner ten minutes to cool it off. She walked to the rear. The dirty clothes belonged on the rear floor, not on the passenger-side seat. As she pushed the key into the lock on the rear door, her thought was that it might be well to drive with all the windows open for a few blocks, to let air cool the car some before she turned on the air conditioner.

As she turned the key she was startled by a yellow flash, then terrorized by the shock and pressure of a powerful explosion. As she fell to the driveway, Alicia saw steel and glass flying away from the Oldsmobile.

Columbo's cigar was almost short enough to throw away as he ducked under the police line held up for him by a uniformed officer and walked up the driveway toward the ruined Oldsmobile.

"Lieutenant Columbo! Doug Immelman." A young man waved to Columbo.

"Hi, Doug. I understand the lady survived."

Doug Immelman was a detective, LAPD. "Luckiest woman on the face of the earth," he said. "She opened the rear door to put some dry cleaning in the car. If she'd been at the driver's-side door, she'd have been killed for sure. She's in the house. She skinned her knees falling down, but otherwise she's okay, except for shock. The paramedics wanted to take her in for a checkup, but she insists she's okay."

Columbo stared at the station wagon, pressing down the right corner of his mouth with his right index finger. The driver's-side door was completely gone. Hunks of steel lying in the blocked street were probably parts of it. The windshield and front windows were blasted out. Strips of sheet steel had been peeled back on the front left fender and from the left rear door. Inside, the front seat had been shredded and blown up against the right-side door. The dashboard had been heaved up and hung out the hole where the windshield had been. Columbo pinched his nose and shook his head.

"Lieutenant, this is Sergeant Sharkey, the explosives man."

"Yeah. We've met. Hey, Sharkey! Good to see ya again," said Columbo, thrusting out his hand for a handshake. He frowned. "Some mess, huh?"

"Hey, Columbo. Yeah. Some mess. Not near what it might've been," said Sharkey grimly.

"What ya figure?"

"Plastique. A lot of it. Right inside the door. The way it looks, it was triggered by the courtesy lights coming on when the door was opened. And I figure there was about a one-second delay in the circuit. When she opened the front door, there was supposed to be just enough time for her to pull the door open and expose herself to the full force of the blast. Lucky for her, opening the rear door turned on the courtesy lights inside the car. When the explosion went off, she was behind the car with the rear door unlocked and just open. The explosion swung the rear door at her and knocked her down, just in time so she was missed by flying debris. One lucky lady."

"Professional job?" asked Columbo.

"I'd call it that. The guy knew what he was doin'. Ninety-nine chances out of a hundred the lady would have opened the driver's-side door and KABOOM!"

Columbo spoke to Doug Immelman. "Okay, Doug. You got any ideas?"

"No, sir. Not yet. We're working on it."

"Don't spend too much time on it. I *know* who did it. Do me a favor, Doug. Radio headquarters and ask them to have a coupla men pick up Charles Bell at the Topanga Beach Club. He may not be there, but he will be by noon. Suspicion of murder."

3

Alicia Drury sat in her living room, smoking a cigarette. Her pants were slightly torn at the knees, and her shirt was smeared with gray dirt, but otherwise she showed no sign of having just escaped an abrupt death.

"How ya feelin', ma'am?" Columbo asked.

She shook her head.

"He'll try it again, I guess," said Columbo.

"Who'll try it again?"

He looked around, spotted a big glass ashtray, and crushed the butt of his cigar in it. "Mrs. Drury, you know who did it, and I know who did it, and we know he'll try it again. He'll keep tryin' till he succeeds. You got any real, serious question about that?"

"Lieutenant Columbo, you have long since ceased to be funny. It will close a file for you and win you a commendation if you can make out a case that *I* killed Paul. Well . . . Even if I did, you couldn't prove it."

Columbo turned down the corners of his mouth and lifted his brows. "Because you were too clever," he said. "You figure? You figure you were that smart?"

"What good would it have done me to kill Paul? I guess you know about his will."

"Yes, ma'am. But I also know who tried to kill you this morning—who *will* kill you sooner or later, one way or another, if we don't some way stop him. Would you like a look at his picture?"

She looked away from Columbo, toward the window, and she took a last drag on her cigarette and crushed it in the same ashtray with his cigar.

"Look at this photograph, ma'am," he said. He hadn't sat down, and he pulled the picture from his raincoat pocket and handed it to her. "I bet you've seen it before."

What he'd handed her was the enhanced photograph of the two men standing on the Grassy Knoll.

"Charles Bell told me you'd found a cache of Paul's materials. If you eventually release them to us, maybe we can still do the fall show."

"No, ma'am," said Columbo. "That's why Mr. Drury was murdered, to prevent that. Whoever killed Mr. Drury to prevent it will kill *you* to prevent it—and Mr. Edmonds, and even Mr. Bell."

She tapped the enhanced picture with a fingernail. "Paul didn't know who these two men were. That's why he wanted to put this photograph on television screens all over America: to see if anyone could identify these two men."

"No, ma'am," said Columbo. "He knew who one of them was. I guess you're right that he didn't know who the other one was. But you and I know."

"You're playing games," she said sullenly.

He handed her a Xerox of the Diana Williams sketch of the taller man in the picture. "There's more than one way to enhance a photograph," he said. "That was done by an artist who's worked with me before. That's what the man in the picture looks like today. Somethin' close to that."

"A complete guess," she said.

"It's not a guess, Mrs. Drury. The woman who drew that is a very skilled artist. She never saw the man, just the enhanced photo. Amazin' likeness, don't you think?"

"It could be any one of ten thousand men."

Columbo stood before her. He began to walk back and forth, not pacing the floor, just taking two or three steps one way, then two or three back.

"It could be, I s'pose," he said. "It could be a coincidence that that drawin' looks so much like Phil Sclafani. And it could be a coincidence that Mr. Drury had been workin' the last six months or so to get into his computer files as much information as he could about the Sclafani Family. That puts two odd coincidences together. It could be a coincidence, too, that you owed the Sclafanis a lot of money. It could be a coincidence that you were so anxious to pay off your gambling debt that you became a prostitute to make the money to pay them. Oh, yeah, it could also be a coincidence that this morning you were the intended victim of what has all the marks of a gang hit. We got a lot of odd coincidences strung together here."

She shook another cigarette from her pack, and her hands trembled as she lit it. "These coincidences don't prove what you're trying to prove," she said.

"Right. But I got other evidence."

"Are you saying you're going to arrest me for murder?" Alicia Drury whispered.

"Well, I want a woman detective to do that. I'm waitin' for Mrs. Zimmer."

"But you *are* going to arrest me? I want to make a telephone call."

"You go right ahead. Do anything but try to leave. If you do that, I'll have to arrest you myself."

While Alicia Drury was on the telephone, Martha Zimmer arrived.

Alicia returned to the living room. "So . . . Am I under arrest *now*?"

"Sit down, Mrs. Drury. Let's go over some other stuff. You see, you made some mistakes. You were very clever, but you made some mistakes. Lessee . . . You remember the day when you and Mr. Edmonds and Mr. Bell sat at that table and I played you the tape off Mr. McCrory's telephone recorder? Remember that?"

"I remember."

"Do you remember what you said when you heard that tape?"

Alicia shook her head.

"Well, I do. You said, 'McCrory's tape.' But, Mrs. Drury, no one had told you that was a tape from Mr. McCrory's answering machine. He didn't tell you. I asked him not to. There was only one way you could have known the voice you heard on that tape was from Mr. McCrory's answering machine. You put it there, Mrs. Drury. *You* telephoned Mr. McCrory's office at eleven forty-seven, when Mr. Drury had already been dead more than half an hour. It made your alibi."

"This is speculation!"

"It didn't make you an alibi anyway. What you played into the telephone for Mr. McCrory's answerin' machine was a tape from your own answerin' machine . . . Or maybe from Mr. Edmonds's answering machine. A sound engineer caught onto that one pretty easy."

"Even if this is true—"

Martha Zimmer watched Columbo with curiosity as he stood and gesticulated as he spoke to Alicia Drury. He fumbled for a cigar, found one and found matches, but thought better of it apparently and didn't light the cigar.

"Mr. Drury died a little before or after eleven, as the medical examiner can testify to. You tried to manufacture an alibi for yourself for eleven forty-seven, by making a conspicuous appearance in a restaurant a little after eleven-thirty and being there when you played your tape into Mr. McCrory's answerin' machine at eleven forty-seven. You were confident that would work, so you didn't build much of an alibi for eleven o'clock or a little before or after. Mr. Edmonds told me you went out to Blocker Beach so you could have privacy in his car and . . . well . . . do whatever you wanted to do in privacy. But I drove out to that beach at eleven one night to see what it's like out there at that time of night. Privacy is the last thing you're gonna find at Blocker Beach at eleven at night, either on the beach or in a car."

"You can't prove *anything.*"

"We can add some more things. Mr. Drury was killed by someone who had one of those plastic cards that let you into his house. It's true you turned over *a* card when you were divorced, but nothin' says you couldn't have had another card. Mr. Drury was killed by someone who knew where he kept things in his house, like the crowbar. He was killed by someone who knew where he hid his laptop computer in his car. He was shot by someone your height. And besides that, you've lied to me a lot."

"What lies? Name one."

"You told me you owed the Sclafanis somethin' like sixty thousand dollars and that you sold yourself to men in Las Vegas to get the money to pay them off. Ma'am . . . That's something only a very desperate woman would do. You also told me you own this house free and clear, from your divorce settlement. And that's true; the city attorney ran the records for me. You could easily have borrowed sixty thousand on the house, rather than do somethin' so hateful to you as sell yourself in prostitution. The truth, Mrs. Drury, is that you owed the Sclafanis a whole lot more than that. A *whole* lot more than that. Phil Sclafani gave you almost unlimited credit, because he figured *Mr.* Drury would pay your gambling debts—or, better than that, he could get a hook into Mr. Drury and use him. Instead, Mr. Drury divorced you, leaving you into the Piping Rock for— For how much, Mrs. Drury?"

"I don't owe the Sclafanis a cent!"

"That's right. You did them a big service, and they wrote

off the debt. A *big* service. Now they're trying to kill you to cover their tracks. Where you think you'll be safer from them, Mrs. Drury: here, waitin' for the next attempt, or in jail?"

Alicia began to sob. "You don't have it right . . . You don't have it right."

"Detective Zimmer, place Mrs. Drury under arrest for the murder of Mr. Paul Drury. Read her her rights."

Before she read from the Miranda card, Martha stepped behind Alicia Drury and handcuffed her hands behind her back. "I'm sorry," she said softly. "We don't have any option. It's required procedure."

EIGHTEEN

Alicia Drury remained calm. She cried for half a minute only, then just sat looking defeated and desperate. Her cheeks glistened with the tears she could not wipe away because her hands were locked behind her. Martha stepped over to her and gently wiped her cheeks with a Kleenex.

Martha carried a tape recorder in her car, and she went out and got it.

"You don't have to talk, Mrs. Drury," said Columbo. "But if you cooperate, it could help you a lot. You're the witness that brings it all together. That's why they tried to kill you. Do you want to make a statement?"

"I might as well," said Alicia bitterly. "If I don't . . . You're right. The Sclafanis will try again."

"And again and again, until they get ya, ma'am. You'll be a lot better off where you're gonna be. A lot safer."

Martha switched on the recorder, and with the tape running she again read Alicia Drury her rights. She asked her to confirm, on the tape, that she was speaking voluntarily. Alicia confirmed that she was.

"Okay, how much did you really owe the Piping Rock Hotel?" Columbo asked.

"Over two hundred thousand dollars. They gave me that much credit because they thought they could get it out of Paul. He could've paid it. He *could've*. But one of the reasons he divorced me was that he'd found out I was a compulsive gambler. After the divorce, a collector came to see Paul at the office. Paul flatly refused to pay a nickel of my gambling losses. He almost fired me that day."

"Did he know how much you owed?"

"He had no idea. If it had been five hundred dollars, he wouldn't have paid. You see— Paul could walk into a casino, play blackjack or roulette for an hour, win a few hundred, lose a few hundred, have a good time doing it, and walk away from the game. I couldn't. I was sure I'd be a big winner, sooner or later. I wasn't like the other gamblers. Oh, no. Not me. I knew the games. I knew the odds. I knew *how* to play. I was going to break the bank. I *knew* I could. Maybe I would've, too."

"So you couldn't pay, and Sclafani put the pressure on you," said Columbo.

Alicia Drury nodded. "He told me I was going to pay, one way or another. He wanted more and more—always more. Eventually I was paying him half my salary—which left me with barely enough to live on, not enough, for example, to patch the stucco on this house. The next thing he did was, he made me pose for a bunch of pornographic pictures— which he wanted so he could blackmail me. Then he told me I would have to turn tricks. There was real profit for him in that. He set me up with heavy gamblers. The idea was to keep them at Piping Rock. I'd tell some sucker, 'No, I don't think we should go to Caesars. I really like this place. I know the tables are honest here.' I kept them in the house and encouraged them to play—and lose. Then of course I had to do what they expected—what they'd paid for."

"You discouraged Mr. Drury from doing a show on the odds in Las Vegas casinos."

"Sclafani credited me with five thousand dollars for that."

"Okay. Do you want to tell us about Mr. Drury?"

"Why? You have it all figured out."

"Where's the pistol?"

"Gone. You'll never find it."

Columbo went to the window, pulled back a sheer curtain, and looked at the men continuing their investigation of the explosion. "Do you confess to the murder of Mr. Paul Drury?" he asked.

"I might as well."

"Is that yes or no?" asked Martha.

"That's yes," said Alicia Drury quietly.

"Mr. Edmonds . . . ?" Columbo asked.

She shook her head. "He had nothing to do with it."

"Won't do, Mrs. Drury. He lied about the beach, so as to make an alibi for you for the time when Mr. Drury was killed. He was with you half an hour after the murder, in Cocina Roberto. You want me to believe he dropped you off at the house, left you there for half an hour while you killed Mr. Drury and ransacked his desk, then picked you up to take you to dinner?"

"The man's in love with me," she whispered. "That's who I called a few minutes ago. I warned him. Frankly, I hope he some way escapes."

Columbo shook his head and showed her an ironic smile. "It's not likely, ma'am. So, how about Charles Bell . . . ?"

She nodded. "He's in on it."

"In fact," said Columbo, "he's the second man in the computer-enhanced photo, right?"

"Right."

"What were they doing on the Grassy Knoll on November 22, 1963?"

"They were there to assassinate President Kennedy."

Two uniformed officers brought Charles Bell into Alicia Drury's living room. His face was flushed and gleaming with sweat, and he struggled against the two policemen, compelling them to guide him along with both his arms in their grip. He wore his Topanga Beach Club uniform: the lemon-yellow slacks and pale-blue polo shirt. His hands were locked behind his back.

"This one doesn't like being under arrest," said one of the officers. "He's not ready to settle down yet."

"You'll regret this, Columbo!" Bell shouted.

"No, sir," said Columbo. "Mrs. Drury has confessed. Whatta ya wanta bet Mr. Edmonds does? Besides, I've got some other evidence, I'm sure you know."

"Did you know he was going to try to kill me?" Alicia demanded of Bell.

"Who was going to try to kill you?" Bell muttered.

"Don't play games, Charles. What makes you think you aren't next? Or right after Tim?"

"Why don't you sit down, Mr. Bell?" said Columbo. "We've got a few little details I'd like to get cleared up. I guess I've told ya I have this thing—maybe you'd call it an obsession—with getting loose strings all tied up. You don't have to give us a statement, but I'd appreciate it if you would answer a question or two."

Bell glowered at Alicia. "You shot off your mouth," he said sullenly.

"Phil tried to kill me this morning."

"If you think so. If he did, he'll get you yet. There's no place you can hide from him."

"Nobody's gonna have to hide from the Sclafanis," said Columbo. "I've got one confession that'll convict them of murder. Maybe I'll have two. Maybe three. One will be enough to have both Sclafanis arrested and held without bail."

"Well, I'm not confessing to anything," said Bell.

"You don't have to," said Alicia. "I did, and I didn't leave you out. Neither will Tim. And neither will Phil Sclafani. You talked about the *omertà*. What you don't know about the *omertà* is that it only applies to other Sicilians. Even if Phil follows the code, it doesn't help *you*."

"I imagine Lieutenant Columbo would know about that," said Bell scornfully.

"I wouldn't know about *omertà*, sir. I'm not Sicilian. My family came from Perugia."

Bell flexed his shoulders. "Okay," he said. He coughed and for a moment weaved as though he were going to faint. He struggled against his handcuffs. "Okay," he whispered hoarsely. "Everything's gone to hell. Bring my hands around front, and I'll give you a statement."

"Yeah. We can do that. Do that for both of them," said Columbo.

With his hands in front, Bell rubbed his eyes, and for a

moment it looked as though he might cry. Then he drew a deep breath, stared for a moment at his manacles, and said, "Okay. Okay . . ."

"We'd like to record this on tape, Mr. Bell."

"What's the difference? The whole damned thing has got out of control."

Martha asked the questions and got the answers that established that Bell had heard his rights. She sat staring at the reels turning on the tape recorder, as though she wanted to be sure the machine was running right and capturing everything said.

"All right, sir. The enhanced photograph shows two men on the Grassy Knoll on November 22, 1963. One of those men was Philip Sclafani. And the other one was you. Right?"

"Yes."

"All right. So what were you doin' there?"

Bell sighed loudly. "We killed Paul Drury to keep this from coming out. But I guess it's coming out anyway. Okay. Phil and I were there to attempt to assassinate President Kennedy."

The first car of the motorcade was the pilot car, a Dallas police car running about a quarter of a mile ahead of the main section of the motorcade. The Dallas police officers inside scanned the crowd and buildings, looking for any sign of trouble. That car was followed by six motorcycles, charged with the duty of "trimming the curbs"—that is, keeping the crowds back. Next came the command car, an unmarked white Dallas police car driven by the chief of police. Also in that car were the county sheriff and two agents of the Secret Service. They, too, scanned the crowds.

Columbo: The Grassy Knoll

About three car lengths behind the command car came the presidential limousine, a black 1961 Lincoln convertible, given to the White House by the Ford Motor Company to replace the old Cadillac used by Presidents Truman and Eisenhower. The flag and the presidential standard whipped from small masts on the front fenders. Sunlight flashed from its highly polished surfaces. The car was equipped with a clear plastic bubble top, which was for protection against the weather only, since it was not bullet resistant. In today's fine weather it had been left off. The limousine was also equipped with running boards and steel grips, so Secret Service agents could stand outside the car to either side of the President. This President had given strict orders that agents were not to ride there and block people's view of him and the First Lady.

Four motorcycles followed, two on each side. Their purpose was to keep the crowd from swelling into the street after the limousine passed.

The Secret Service car followed. It was a 1955 Cadillac convertible. The eight agents in that car were heavily armed.

Next came the Vice President's limousine, another Lincoln convertible, this one obtained locally. The follow-up car, corresponding to the Secret Service car, was another Dallas police car. Several more cars, filled with local dignitaries and members of Congress, made up the rest of the motorcade, which ended with another police car and more motorcycles.

The crowds were thick and enthusiastic as the motorcade moved along Main Street. The motorcade moved slowly.

Then the lead car turned right onto Houston Street. The crowd was much thinner there, and the motorcade picked up speed. The open park here was called Dealey Plaza. The motorcade would make a sharp left turn onto Elm Street, which sloped gently toward the underpasses, along the west side of the Plaza. On Elm Street it would continue to accelerate, until it passed under the Triple Underpass. With that the parade would be over.

The building directly ahead, at the intersection of Houston and Elm streets, was called the Texas School Book Depository.

"That's very interestin'. I guess that's kind of obvious when you look at the enhanced picture. Sclafani had a rifle. What about you, Mr. Bell? Did you have a weapon?"

Bell shook his head. "No."

"You didn't drop an Iver-Johnson revolver?"

"No, but I know who did."

Columbo sat down at last, leaning forward with his hands on his knees, his raincoat hanging like a drape between his legs.

"Why don't you just start at the beginnin' and tell us the story, sir? Probably that's the easiest way."

Bell nodded despondently. "I've been trying to protect my father's name as well as to avoid being arrested on a charge of conspiracy to assassinate the President of the United States. My father . . . My father's name was Austin Bell. He was a businessman in Texas. He made a lot of money, in oil and other things. He hated Franklin D. Roosevelt. He hated Harry S Truman. And he hated John F. Kennedy. He hated the way they used the power of government to interfere in the way a businessman ran his business so as to make as much money as he could."

"Yes, sir. I read your father's biography."

"You read—!"

"Yes, sir. Mr. Drury's copy."

"He hated Kennedy in particular," Bell went on. "He fervently believed Kennedy was— He had a lot of names for him: 'pinko,' 'Com-symp,' 'bleeding heart,' 'nigger lover,' and . . . traitor. He called him a traitor. He used the word 'treason'."

"Your father was an idiot," said Alicia.

Bell ignored her. "There was talk about repealing the oil depletion allowance, and that drove my father into a rage."

"Sir," said Columbo. "Had your father been an investor in the Riviera Hotel in Havana?"

Bell nodded. "With Meyer Lansky. The Castro government confiscated it. My father put more than a million dollars into training the Cubans to go in and overthrow Castro."

"The Bay of Pigs," said Alicia. She sat slipping her handcuffs back and forth on her wrists, as though she couldn't quite believe she couldn't pull them off. "Kennedy didn't—"

"Kennedy didn't send in air cover that he'd promised," said Bell. "To my father that confirmed everything he thought about Kennedy: that the President was a Communist sympathizer and a traitor. You have to understand, he read all the right-wing newspapers and magazines. He read nothing but. He was absolutely sure Kennedy was selling out the country."

"So he hired the Sclafanis," said Alicia.

"When he found out Kennedy was coming to Dallas, he went to Meyer Lansky. Lansky wouldn't have anything to do with his crazy idea. But my father had other contacts. He contacted Sam Giancana. Giancana didn't want anything to do with the idea either, but he referred my father to

Giuseppe Sclafani. The Sclafani Family had lost millions when Castro took over their hotel, the same way Lansky had lost the Riviera. Giuseppe Sclafani had expected to recover his hotel when the Cuban 'freedom fighters,' as we called them, invaded and overthrew Castro. But . . . Bay of Pigs. He hated Kennedy almost as much as my father did."

Bell ran his hands down across his eyes and cheeks. "I've kept this secret for thirty years," he said.

"Yeah, I figured you were carrying around a deep secret," said Columbo. "When you've been in this business as long as I have, you get a nose for stuff like that. Carryin' a big secret around for years some way puts a mark on a man. Anyway . . . anybody got a match?"

Alicia watched Columbo light a cigar, and she asked, "Can somebody give me a cigarette? My own are on the kitchen table. Uh . . . they do let you smoke in jail, don't they?"

Bell stared at her as if she had suddenly demonstrated she was insane.

"Go ahead, Mr. Bell," said Columbo.

"My father and Giuseppe Sclafani met in Las Vegas. The Sclafani Family wasn't established there yet, and they thought it was a place where neither one of them would be known. I wasn't with them. Neither was Philip Sclafani. The two fathers struck a deal. My father agreed to pay four million dollars for the assassination of John F. Kennedy, one million just for trying, and three million more if Kennedy was actually killed. There was a kind of pledge between them, too. Phil was the hit man. I was to be present to be sure he did what he was supposed to.

"It was Phil who decided the Grassy Knoll was the place

where he'd fire his shot. He was absolutely convinced he could walk away afterward, that the crowd would be terrified and wouldn't touch him. Just in case there was any trouble, three Sclafani soldiers were around. They had pistols. If they had to, they'd kill anybody who interfered. But their instructions were to fire in the air and into the ground. The crowd would be terrified. Phil was sure nobody would move against him."

"What about cops?" asked Columbo.

"He said his boys could scare and confuse them for a minute or two."

"Go on."

"The picture. What I was doing there was handing him the keys to a Ford. He'd seen it and knew where it was. It was in the parking lot behind the Grassy Knoll. I'd parked it there two hours before. The parking lot was for employees of the railroad, but I gave the man five dollars. I told him I wanted to park so I could see the President go by and then get on to my job. Anyway, I gave Phil the keys to the Ford. A million dollars' cash was in the trunk. My father had told me to make sure he went out on the knoll and had his rifle with him before I gave him the keys. I gave them to him just before the presidential limousine came down Elm Street. Then I got fifty feet or so away from him. I was to watch him do it."

"Didn't anybody see that Sclafani had a rifle?" asked Martha.

Bell shook his head. "He'd detached the stock. The barrel and the action were wrapped in red and white cloth and looked something like a golf umbrella. One of the Sclafani soldiers handed him the stock just before I walked up to him. By that time, the motorcycles were in front of us, and everybody was staring at the limousine that was coming along the street."

"What kind of a rifle was that, sir?" Columbo asked.

"It was a Weatherby, a big-game hunting rifle, .460 magnum. The magazine held just two shots. It was an elephant gun! No matter where a slug from that rifle hit a man, it would have torn him apart."

"So what happened?"

"I walked away, up toward the trees on the knoll. I couldn't see the President so well from there, but I could watch Phil Sclafani. And he was ready. He wasn't going to lift the rifle to his shoulder till the last moment, because someone might have noticed him doing that. But he was ready. And then— Then all hell broke loose. I . . . Jesus!"

Everyone in the motorcade relaxed a little. Dallas was what the Secret Service called a "hot" city—that is, one with potential for trouble. But they had driven through crowds estimated at a quarter of a million; and, though they had seen a few hostile placards, the people had cheered and waved, and on the whole Dallas had given President Kennedy a warm welcome.

Driving the presidential limousine was Secret Service Agent William Greer. He was experienced at driving the President of the United States in motorcades and knew what he was doing. Beside him in the front seat was Agent-in-Charge Roy Kellerman.

Sitting in the two collapsible jump seats between the front and back seats were the Governor of Texas, John Connally, and his wife, Nellie Connally. The President had come to Texas, in part, to twist the governor's arm about a rift in the

Texas Democratic Party, and the governor's smile as he waved to the people along the route was a bit forced.

President John F. Kennedy sat to the right in the rear seat. He was forty-six years old and a handsome, winning man, as even his detractors acknowledged. His presidency had captured the imagination of the American people, and even editorialists and pundits who judged his administration harshly were all but unanimous in judging that he would be reelected by a landslide vote in 1964. He was comfortable with politics, with the presidency too, and the smile he showed the crowd was broad and relaxed.

Sitting to his left was the elegant Jacqueline Kennedy. She was an asset to her husband's presidency, probably the most popular First Lady the nation had ever known—not excluding Eleanor Roosevelt. She had been nervous about Dallas, as everyone in the presidential party had been. For the moment she was extremely uncomfortable from the heat and was glad the motorcade would soon pick up speed and rush on to the air-conditioned Trade Mart, where the President was to speak at a luncheon.

For a long time there had been no conversation in the car. No one could speak over the roar of the crowds. Now Nellie Connally turned and said, "Mr. President, you can't say Dallas doesn't love you."

Bell flushed and hesitated. For a moment he covered his face with his hands, then for another moment stared at his handcuffs. "We heard shots. I don't know how many. The motorcycles were backfiring, and you couldn't tell how many. People started screaming. I've never heard so much horror. It was just . . ."

"Where were you at this point?" asked Columbo.

"I was under the trees along the curving driveway that leads to the pergola. A man ahead of me raised a pistol, braced it against a tree, and fired. I was behind him and saw his shot miss the presidential car and knock a chip off a curbstone on the south side of Elm Street. He took aim again, but by then the limousine had stopped, and the President was down. The man shoved the pistol—it was a target pistol with a long barrel—down inside his jacket and trotted up the slope toward me. I was afraid he would kill me, because he must have seen me staring at him. But he ran on past."

"What was Sclafani doing?" Columbo asked, leaning forward.

"The limousine was stopped out there on the street," Bell went on, ignoring the question. "I mean, it was almost stopped, just barely moving. I could just barely see the President. He was *down!* I could see blood. People were screaming, and I ran down the slope to get a better look. The President was . . . blood! All blood! Mrs. Kennedy was trying to crawl out across the back of the car, and an agent was grabbing at her. Well . . . You've seen the Zapruder film. I guess we've all seen it."

Agent Greer now executed a rehearsed maneuver. It had been called a number of things, but the most often used name for it was Getting the Hell Out of Here. The Lincoln was a powerful car, and when he shoved down the accelerator it lurched forward, pushing the people in the rear seats backward.

Agent Clinton Hill, who was assigned to Mrs. Kennedy and had been in the follow-up Cadillac, had sprinted forward and reached the presidential limousine in time to grab one of its exterior handles and get his foot on one of the rear steps where Secret Service agents often rode. He shoved Mrs. Kennedy off the rear of the car and into the seats, then himself crawled forward.

In the vice-presidential convertible, Agent Rufus Young-blood shoved Vice President Lyndon Johnson to the floor and then vaulted over the front seat and threw himself down on him, shielding him with his own body.

On Dealey Plaza hundreds of people had dropped to the ground, some of them shielding loved ones by lying on top of them.

Abraham Zapruder remained erect, exposing his 8mm movie film.

The presidential limousine, followed by the vice-presidential limousine, passed the command car and roared into the cool dark tunnel of the underpasses.

Dealey Plaza fell silent, and people began to stand up.

The Secret Service, men shouting from one car to another, had already transferred its chief protection to President Lyndon Johnson.

"What was Sclafani doing?"

"Nothing. I looked back up the slope at him. He was standing there with his mouth open."

"Are you saying Phil Sclafani never fired a shot?" asked Columbo.

"At what? The President was already shot. He was already down, hardly visible."

"The second picture shows Sclafani escaping."

Bell nodded. "I spotted him going over the picket fence, headed for the parking lot. When I saw the enhanced pictures, I knew exactly what was happening. Phil was going toward the fence. The Sclafani soldiers were following him."

"So the only reason Phil Sclafani didn't shoot President Kennedy," said Martha, "was that he was already shot."

Bell nodded. "I've read since about other riflemen who were supposed to have been around, maybe on the underpass bridge. I've read that other shots were fired from the Grassy Knoll. I can tell you one thing for sure. President Kennedy was fatally wounded before Phil Sclafani could get off a shot. Maybe Phil would have, if he'd had the chance. But he didn't have the chance."

"What about the Iver-Johnson revolver?" Martha asked. "You said you knew about that."

"It belonged to one of Sclafani's hoodlums. He figured it wasn't a good idea to be caught carrying a gun. Phil had to carry the Weatherby rifle away. It had his fingerprints on it. But the Iver-Johnson was clean—as was any weapon those boys were carrying."

"So the Sclafanis got their million?" asked Alicia.

"The Sclafanis got *four* million," said Bell. "My father and Giuseppe Sclafani were holed up in a suite in the Rice Hotel in Houston, together with half a dozen right-wing loonies. They had three television sets going, one for ABC, one for CBS, and one for NBC. They were eating oysters and drinking bourbon, if you can imagine. It's ironic that my father drank bourbon with his oysters. A man he detested did that. Harry Hopkins. Anyway, when the flash came that Kennedy had been shot, they were all delirious— or so I was told. When the word finally came that Kennedy was dead, my father took Giuseppe Sclafani into a bedroom of the suite and gave him a suitcase containing three million dollars. It was two days before he finally got it through his head that *Lee Harvey Oswald* had killed Kennedy. Or probably had. Anyway, it was damned clear that Phil Sclafani hadn't done it. Then my father wanted his three million back. No chance. The Sclafanis used the four million to build the Piping Rock. My father could hardly go to the law and complain he'd paid someone four million dollars to kill the President of the United States and felt cheated because someone else had done it."

"So all these years—" said Columbo.

"All these years," Bell interrupted. "There's no statute of limitations on the crime of conspiring to assassinate the President. But after thirty years it looked safe. Then Paul Drury used this computer-enhancement business to make something out of those two pictures. I saw them in his office. I went to Phil and told him. We agreed. We hadn't killed anybody yet, but we had to kill somebody now."

"And you used Mrs. Drury for your trigger woman," said Columbo.

"Phil couldn't have done it. He's under constant surveillance by the FBI. I didn't have the stomach for it, I didn't think. But Alicia— Well, she owed the Sclafanis a hundred twenty-four thousand dollars. I agreed to pay half that, and Phil agreed to forgive the rest of it. She was perfect. She had the magnetic card. We worked out an alibi for her. Tim came in because he's a dummy. He doesn't even know she reduced her debt some sixty thousand by turning tricks. Neither Phil nor I wanted him in on the deal, but he's not the one who broke."

"Who broke is Phil," said Alicia. "If he hadn't tried to kill me, the case might have been damned hard to make."

"No, ma'am," said Columbo. "We had the case made."

Alicia wiped tears from her eyes with the fingers of her

right hand. "How long you suppose it will be before I see the street again, Columbo?"

He turned down the corners of his mouth in a hard grimace. "Not for me to say, ma'am, and I sure don't know. I wouldn't buy any baseball tickets for *this* century if I were you."